A Hodder Children's Books two-in-one special edition

Jill Has Two Ponies
Jill and the Runaway

JILL HAS TWO PONIES

The Jill Pony Series

Jill Has Two Ponies

Ruby Ferguson

*Hodder
Children's
Books*

a division of Hodder Headline plc

This special two-in-one edition published 1995
by Hodder Children's Books

ISBN 0 340 63474 X

Jill Has Two Ponies

Copyright © 1952, 1993 Hodder and Stoughton Ltd.

First published in a single volume in Great Britain in 1952
by Hodder and Stoughton Ltd.

Revised single volume edition published 1993 by Knight Books

The right of Ruby Ferguson to be identified as the Author of
the Work has been asserted by her in accordance with the
Copyright, Designs and Patents Act 1988.

10 9 8 7 6 5 4 3 2 1

A Catalogue record for this book is available from the British Library

Printed and bound in Great Britain by
Cox & Wyman Ltd, Reading, Berkshire

Hodder Children's Books
a Division of Hodder Headline plc
338 Euston Road
London NW1 3BH

Contents

1 I meet Rapide

'Here is Rapide,' said Mrs Penberthy, briskly leading out a bay pony. 'Look, he has taken to your little girl at once!'

From my point of view there were several things wrong with these remarks. In the first place, Rapide is a silly name for a pony unless it is going to be in a circus; in the second place, I think it is insulting to refer to a person of fourteen as though she were six; and in the third place, Rapide far from taking to me at once had given me a very dirty look out of his rather disagreeable eyes. The fact was, I didn't like Mrs Penberthy, I didn't like Rapide, and I didn't know what I was going to do about it. I was worried, because Mummy would be so upset if she knew, after going to all that trouble to get me a show-jumper.

Those of you who have read my previous book, *A Stable for Jill*, will remember that by devious ways I had amassed the sum of twelve hundred pounds to buy myself a second pony, and that Mummy had met some people on the boat coming from America who had just the very pony for me that they wanted to sell because their daughter had grown out of him. I was naturally excited about this pony because he was said to have done terribly well for the Penberthy girl, and for nights before we went to Little Grazings, which was the peculiar name of the Penberthys' house,

I dreamed about a pony beautiful to look at and wonderful in action.

So in the end Mummy fixed a Saturday with Mrs Penberthy and we went down by train, which took about an hour and a half. Mummy read a book in the train as calmly as if we were going to do some mere shopping – I don't know how grown-ups can *be* like that – and I fidgeted about and pulled at my gloves and felt like rushing madly up and down the corridor to work off some of my pent-up emotion, and Mummy kept giving me a look which said as plainly as anything, need you let everybody in the carriage think you are completely crazy?

I then began to feel sorry for the rest of the people in our carriage because they were obviously not on their way to buy show-jumpers but were just having to make this journey for some horribly mere purposes. I hope you will not mind me using the word 'mere' again so soon, but it is such a grey sort of word that I think it expresses all the dreary things that grown-up people do all the time, like seeing lawyers and having treatments and meeting people for lunch that they used to know about forty years ago.

There was a woman opposite me who was probably going to meet somebody for lunch, and the man next to me looked as if he was to have a treatment, and the younger man next to Mummy was obviously going to see a lawyer because he kept turning over a lot of typewritten papers and gnawing his thumb nail. I thought I was getting quite detective-ish, and then just for fun I started picturing those people mounted on ponies and it was so funny I gave a snort – like you do when you try not to giggle – and Mummy gave me more of a look than ever, so I went very quiet and stared out of the window giving myself marks for fields that had horses in them and taking off marks for empty fields or just cows.

So from this you will have an idea what I felt like all the way to the Penberthys', and how worked up I was when we got there and Mrs Penberthy opened the loose box and the pony was actually before my eyes.

Now you had better go back to the beginning of this book and read the first bit again. I looked at Rapide and Rapide looked at me, and we just didn't register at all. I felt like you do when you miss the vaulting horse at gym and land on the mat sitting down and the form giggles and you have got a crush on the gym teacher and want her to think you are marvellous.

I couldn't say a word, of course, because it seemed so rude and ungrateful, and Mrs Penberthy had been so nice – until she made the silly remark I have recorded – and had given us coffee.

So I thought I would put it all into my face like they do on the films. I put it all into my face and looked at Mummy hard, hoping she would understand, but I can't be very good at expressions, as she told me afterwards that how I looked was as if I had been struck dumb with joy.

When she had looked at me she looked at Mrs Penberthy who was hanging on to Rapide's halter as if she thought he would go up in the air, and said, 'I can see that Jill is quite overcome with excitement, Mrs Penberthy. He does look an awfully nice pony and so well groomed. But what we are interested in is his jumping. Do you think we could see him in action?'

'Oh, of course,' said Mrs Penberthy. 'I'm sure you'll be delighted with him. Joan has been riding him in the under-sixteens for two seasons and has taken so many prizes and cups we hardly know where to put them. She wouldn't think of parting with Rapide except that now she is seventeen she's out of the pony classes. We are going to get her a hunter for Christmas. But she adores Rapide and I'm sure she'll be heart-broken when he goes.'

I felt like saying, far be it from me to break the heart of even Joan Penberthy, but Mrs Penberthy went on, 'How old are you, Jill?'

'Fourteen,' I said.

'Ah, a lovely age for riding,' she went on. 'You still have two years in the children's classes. I'm sure Joan wishes she was fourteen again.'

I thought Joan must be a very funny person if she did, as it was the dream of my life to be seventeen and have a hunter, but I didn't say anything because as you go through life you find some people have the weirdest ideas and think them quite right and Joan might be one of those.

All this time Rapide was looking at me with the greatest disdain as if I wasn't a bit what he had expected, and I was trying not to look at him at all only I was sort of fascinated like they say rabbits are by snakes. I wish I knew if this is true.

'We'll have to wait till Joan comes in,' said Mrs Penberthy. 'She's gone down to the post office on her bike.'

She pushed Rapide back into the loose box as if she was putting a lawn-mower away, and Mummy stood smiling as much as to say, 'How marvellous everything is', and I just stood. I think Mrs Penberthy thought I was a bit dim, and I was surprised that Mummy didn't notice I hadn't much to say because I usually talk like mad all the time, only

of course she had got the impression I was dumb
with bliss.

I noticed that the Penberthys had a lovely big yard
and four loose boxes. It was just the sort of place I
should have liked for myself.

'Oh, here she is at last!' cried Mrs Penberthy and
Joan came round the corner of the house pushing
her bike. She was a very large, meek-looking girl
with spots and sticking-out teeth – I have noticed
that people with sticking-out teeth are often good
at jumping – and she was dressed in trousers and
a fawn pullover and a shirt with rolled up sleeves
and a green tie, and she had very short straight
hair fastened out of her eyes with a grip. I took a
dislike to her.

'Come and speak to Mrs Crewe and Jill, dear,' said
her mother. 'They've come about Rapide.'

Joan came and shook hands and said, 'Hello' and
then pulled a khaki handkerchief out of her trouser
pocket and started twiddling it about as if she didn't
know what to do next. I knew just how she felt, as
I would have felt the same.

'Don't stand there, dear,' said Mrs Penberthy. 'Get
Rapide saddled and show Jill what he can do.'

I must say Joan was very good with Rapide, and
when he was saddled he looked very nice, only I
couldn't make myself take to him however hard I
tried, and he just glanced at me in the most con-
temptuous way as much as to say, 'Who on earth
do you think you are?'

'I'm miles too big for him,' said Joan, and when
she was mounted her feet could have practically met
round his girths, if you know what I mean, but she
had a nice seat in spite of being so large and bulgy,
and we went into a paddock next to the yard and

Joan walked, trotted, cantered, and finally galloped Rapide for us to see.

Rapide was obviously a very efficient pony with no nonsense about him. In the paddock were six professional-looking jumps and I was very envious and wished I had them at home.

'Could we see him jump,' I managed to say huskily, and Mrs Penberthy nearly leapt out of her skin at hearing me come out of my trance, so to speak.

'Of course, dear,' she said delightedly. 'Joan, put him round the jumps. Now you're going to see something,' she added, only I wasn't listening because I think people who call you dear the first time they meet you are the very depths.

So Joan on Rapide went round the jumps, a clear round. The jumps were three foot, three foot six, and four foot six.

Mrs Penberthy beamed and said, 'There!' Mummy didn't say anything but she looked very impressed, and I just thought that Rapide had the weirdest action I ever saw in a pony.

He got over the jumps all right, but he did it in such a funny way. First he dashed at the jump, then checked completely for all the world as though he was going to refuse, then he made his mind up, popped up his forelegs, bucked up his middle, popped up his hindlegs, and he was over. He looked exactly like a rocking-horse, and quite frankly I thought he looked awful and like a very cheap, ungraceful rocking-horse. At the very idea of myself popping over the jumps at Chatton Show on Rapide I went cold in my middle. But of course I was bound to admit that he did it. He got over, and to people like Mrs Penberthy and Mummy who didn't really know anything about equitation, and to Joan who seemed to be a person who didn't care what she looked like anyway, he was probably marvellous. And as Mrs Penberthy said, he had won cartloads of prizes and cups, though I hope I will never have such a mere mind as to make that my main object in riding.

'He does look good,' said Mummy. 'Now do you think Jill might try him?'

Here was the moment I dreaded. Of course I had come in my jodhpurs all ready for the fray, so Joan got down and I got up, conscious that Rapide was tightening every muscle with loathing at contact with my hated form. (I expect this was all imagination, but anyway I did imagine it and it didn't make me very happy.)

I rode him round the paddock and at least he responded to my aids. He had been well schooled.

'Now try the jumps, Jill,' cried Mummy, and I went cold all over as I could tell from her voice that she meant, 'Just show these people how good you are.' I have found from talking to my friends that I am not alone in having a mother who does this sort of thing to one. If you are a person whose mother thinks you are the world's wonder because you have got a first in the Musical Chairs for under-fourteens, and gives you a sort of boiled look of pride from the rails that makes your blood run cold, then you will know what I mean. Because the great thing about riding is that you must never, never think you're marvellous, because there is always much more for you to learn, and anyway your riding is only a little bit of all the good horsemanship throughout the world, which should make you humble.

If you have read my previous books you will have heard about a girl called Susan Pyke who thought she was terrific on a pony, and of some of the things that happened to her, and you will doubtless be hearing of her again before I have finished writing this book because she is always cropping up in my life.

However, I couldn't say anything but OK to Mummy, and shutting my eyes and setting my teeth I gathered up the reins, gripped Rapide with my heels to show him that I knew what I was doing, and set him at the first of Joan Penberthy's jumps. He refused it. Three times.

He must have done that round of jumps dozens of times. He could have done it blindfolded. But to make a long story short, with me up, the jumps he didn't refuse he walked right through. It was too awful for words. I sat there thinking of all the terrible fates that I could bring myself to wish for Rapide, like pulling a miserable old rag-and-bones man's cart, or being sold to Susan Pyke who had been ordered out of the ring several times for using the whip too much.

I couldn't sit there for ever, so I rode slowly up to where Mummy and the two Penberthys were waiting and for a minute there was a deathly hush. Mummy was obviously mortified – for which I felt sorry but I couldn't help it – and Mrs Penberthy and Joan just as obviously thought I had never tried to jump before.

'You'll soon get into it,' said Joan kindly. 'I expect you'll be having some lessons soon.'

Mummy looked at me in reproachful silence beyond words, and Mrs Penberthy said briskly, 'Well, Jill has seen what the pony *can* do and I wouldn't be surprised if she's as good as Joan by the time the Pony Shows come round.'

She said it as if she would be very surprised indeed, and at that moment I made up my mind that I was going to buy Rapide if only to let him see that he couldn't beat me. I suppose it was silly, but if you have read my previous books you will know that most of the things I do are silly but often turn out all right.

Mummy suddenly gulped and found her tongue, and said, 'Well – wh – wh – what about it, Jill?'

'I'm going to have him,' I said.

Mummy went red with relief and Mrs Penberthy and Joan started beaming and telling me that Rapide would never let me down and I'd make a rider yet, and they could have got far more than twelve hundred pounds for him if they'd sent him to Tattersalls but all they cared about was knowing the home he was going to, and far from looking broken-hearted Joan began to whistle 'Thank U Very Much' and we all went in the house and Mummy wrote out the cheque.

Mrs Penberthy said, 'Won't you stay and have lunch?' but you can always tell by the way people say this whether they really want you to or not, and Mrs Penberthy obviously didn't want us to but was only being polite. So Mummy said, 'Oh, no, but it is very kind of you to ask us,' and after we had made arrangements for Rapide to be sent in a horse box to Chatton station we all shook hands, and the Penberthys went out of my life for ever.

2 Oh, why did I buy him?

When Mummy and I got to the station we found we had twenty minutes to wait for our train, and as we were both practically starving we went into the refreshment room and had some pink imitation meat sandwiches and very chipped cups of tea. The sandwiches were not very interesting and the tea tasted stewed, so I left most of my 'refreshments'. Mummy looked at the remains on my plate and frowned, and I could see that she was wondering about my apparent lack of appetite.

'What on earth was the matter with you, Jill?' Mummy asked.

'Nothing,' I mumbled.

'I suppose you were just trying to be different from Joan. It was very silly of you. I don't understand you at all.'

'How true!' I thought concerning the last remark.

'But I could see you were thrilled with the pony,' went on Mummy. 'He's a very good pony, isn't he?'

'Oh, yes,' I said. 'I'm not very taken with the name.'

'You could change that.'

'Ponies don't like having their names changed,' I said, being awkward. 'He can be Rapide if he wants. I don't really care.'

'You're making yourself over-excited,' said Mummy. 'You always get irritable when you're over-excited.'

We got into the train and opposite me was a man reading a new copy of *Horse and Hound* which is a paper you have to order, and I simply can't afford it.

I tried to read the back part which was all I could see, but Mummy nudged me and gave me a look.

Just then another man came into our carriage from the corridor and said, 'What on earth are you reading?'

'Oh, just something I picked up off the seat. It's not my line at all,' said the depraved and unappreciating man who was holding that marvellous paper.

'Well, we're nearly at our station,' said the first man, and soon the train stopped and they started collecting their things.

But my man still hung on to the paper for which I yearned and which was not his line at all. I gripped my thumbs till it hurt and simply willed him to put it down and leave it, but he didn't.

'Have you got everything?' said the other man.

'Oh, yes, I think so. There seems to be an awful lot.'

Oh please, please put it down! I thought.

Besides *Horse and Hound* he had the handles of two cases in the same hand. He began to get out of the carriage. He got right out and turned round to shut the door but he couldn't because he was carrying so much.

Put it down! I prayed. Oh please, please, put it down!

At the very last minute he suddenly looked at *Horse and Hound* as if he didn't know it was there, and contemptuously flung it back on the carriage seat. In about one second I grabbed it and clutched it to my heart.

'Really, Jill!' said Mummy.

But I didn't care. I buried myself in *Horse and Hound* till we got to Chatton and then folded it up and took it home to read again in bed.

When we got home we found a lovely fire and our tea laid and the kettle simmering on the hob, which had been done for us before she left by our daily help, Mrs Crosby, or N.R.T.B. as I call her meaning No Relation To Bing which is what she says directly she meets anybody new.

'I'll make some toast,' said Mummy. 'Meanwhile you'd better go and tell Black Boy he's going to have a brother.'

I rushed out to my little paddock, half of which is an orchard. The minute my pony saw me he came cantering to me, his beautiful eyes alight with joy, and I hurled my arms around his neck and hugged him. I loved him so much, and after all that had happened that day I felt as if I wanted to howl one terrific great howl, but I choked it down. I even felt a bit annoyed with Mummy for not understanding what I meant when I made faces at Rapide, so at that moment I decided that I cared more for Black Boy than for anybody in the world, and I wished I had a colossal amount of money – about two thousand pounds – so that he and I could ride away all by ourselves and live on an island and do exactly what we liked for ever.

I then came all over practical again, and forgetting my own tea I put Black Boy into his stable for the night for we were having early frosts already – and did his food in the outhouse and fed him.

Then I heard Mummy calling.

'Jill, are you never coming? What are you doing? The toast is going cold.'

I walked into the cottage and said, 'I've been giving Black Boy his feed and putting him up for the night.'

'Really, dear, if you're going to take so long over one pony, what will you do with two?'

I felt like saying I could as soon see myself winning the open jumping at Olympia as taking any time over Rapide, but I prudently didn't.

'I'm surprised,' said Mummy, 'that you haven't mentioned one thing, where you're going to put Rapide. There obviously isn't room in the stable.'

'Oh, I'm going to board him at the riding school,' I said.

'At Mrs Darcy's? But, Jill, I'd planned to build you two loose boxes for a Christmas present.'

'You needn't bother,' I said. 'Thanks all the same, Mummy, but it's silly to spend such a lot of money when he can perfectly well live at the riding school. Lots of children keep their ponies there. And Mrs Darcy won't charge me anything because she can use Rapide for the school.'

Mummy looked at me anxiously. She had been thinking all day that I was going mad, but I took no notice and heated up my toast in the oven and put loads of jam on it, and then sat with my feet up on the fender eating it.

We never mentioned Rapide again that evening, nor the next day which was Sunday. Mummy looked at me in a puzzled way once or twice, but she had something to take her mind off me as she had just begun a new book – I told you in my previous books that Mummy wrote stories about rather whimsical children such as, I think, never were on land or sea – and when she begins a new book she is usually not quite with us, or as Mrs Crosby (N.R.T.B.)

says, 'away with the birds'. So she didn't ask me any awkward questions.

On Sunday morning Mrs Crosby came to cook our hot lunch while Mummy and I went to church, and in the afternoon I saddled Black Boy and went off by myself for a lovely long ride.

It was a beautiful September day, crisp and sunny, and the leaves were beginning to turn yellow and gleamed in the sun like little gold coins. The sky was very blue and the fields and hills were lovely colours. I rode right across Neshbury Common and through what we call the Top Woods where there are grassy or pine-needle rides all the way, and then we crossed the main road and went along the bridle path round the old golf course and back down Milden Hill which is long and has a grass border which Black Boy loves. I think all roads ought to have grass borders for horses and when I get into Parliament I am going to see about it. I sometimes have visions of getting into Parliament and as long as I can combine it with being a champion show-jumper and matron of a big jolly orphanage at the same time, I don't see why I shouldn't.

We were out on this ride for about three hours and both Black Boy and I were dead tired when we got home, with that lovely fresh air tiredness that knows it is soon going to wallow in warmth and food. Though I was aching all over when I got in, I rubbed my pony down, fed him and put him up for the night. He looked beautifully contented and happy when I kissed him good night (I expect you think that is a soppy thing to do but I don't care) and he gave me a soulful look and his jaws just went round and round blissfully on his oats in a rather American manner. He looked sweet. I wouldn't even let myself think of Rapide.

I tiptoed into the cottage by the back door. The kitchen fire was nearly out and from the sitting-room came the weary, dreary rattle of Mummy's typewriter. She had been at it ever since lunch.

I crept upstairs, filled the bath, and got in. It was lovely. Then I suddenly had the feeling I had been rather a beast to Mummy. I expect you have all had that feeling at times but with me it always comes at the most inconvenient moments like now when I didn't want to get out of that nice hot bath. But conscience shoved me out all right. I got dressed and went downstairs. Rattle, rattle, rattle, went Mummy's typewriter, earning our bread and butter and other things. The fire was out, but I boiled the kettle on the hot-plate and made some tea and cut some bread and butter so thinly that you could have read *Horse and Hound* through it, and rummaged about and found the strawberry jam which Mrs Crosby hides because it is supposed by her to be too good to be eaten all at once by me, and I put all these things on a tray with the nicest cups and saucers and took it into the sitting-room. It was past six o'clock.

Mummy looked at me with the air of one slowly floating down to earth.

'Oh, Jill, you are a dear to think of tea. Somehow when I'm working the time flies and I never think of meals at all. I don't know what I'd do if you didn't look after me.'

'And I don't know what I'd do if you didn't work so hard for us both,' I said. By now my feeling of beastliness had fled. We ate our tea, and I said, 'Do tell me what the new book is going to be about, Mummy.'

'Well, it's going to be called *Angeline, the Fairy Child*,' she said enthusiastically, 'and it's about — '

She went on telling me what it was about between bites of bread and butter and strawberry jam, and I wished I could be more literary and appreciate Mummy's up-in-the-clouds stories as some children must have done or they wouldn't have bought them.

'I'm not too keen on the name Angeline,' I said. 'It's a bit corny, Mummy.'

'I think it's a lovely name,' said Mummy, and we argued happily for a bit. But we never mentioned Rapide.

Next morning as soon as I got into the form room my friend Ann Derry rushed up to me.

'Did you buy it?' she cried excitedly. 'The pony, I mean.'

'Yes, I did,' I said, putting down my bag and remembering that I had left my history notebook on the top of the corn-bin in the outhouse.

'What's he like? Do tell me!'

'He's all right,' I said. It was just as if something was clamping me down when I tried to talk about Rapide.

'Well, if you don't want to tell me you needn't,' said Ann rather huffily.

'I've told you,' I said. 'He's all right. He's quite a good pony and he can jump. There isn't anything else to say, is there?'

She just stared at me, because of course I am usually a person who has a great deal to say about everything. I thought gloomily that ever since Rapide had come into my life all my nearest and dearest had begun to think I was crazy. Perhaps I would be crazy before I had finished with Rapide.

By break-time it was all over the form that I had bought a show-jumper. Everybody was interested because most of them rode, and I had been meeting them in the show ring for the last two summers.

'So you've bought a new pony, for jumping?' said Susan Pyke as we ate our biscuits. 'I *shall* have to pull my socks up!'

I could have pointed out that I had beaten her in most events only that very summer but I felt too low to bother.

'What's he like? What's he called?' everybody was shouting at me. I'm sure they thought I had some sinister reason for being dumb about Rapide because it would never occur to them that anybody could be so mad as to buy a pony she didn't like.

I felt miserable by the time I went home that afternoon, and after tea I couldn't bear it any longer so I went over to see Martin Lowe who is the grandest person and taught me to ride, though he has to sit in a wheel-chair all the time because he lost the use of his legs in an accident.

I always liked going to the Lowes'. I liked their house which was big and old-fashioned and coun-trified and I liked all the whips and photographs of horses and the trophies which were hung up on the walls, and the piles of *Horse and Hound* in places where most houses have dreary magazines about knitting and fashions, and the wonderful stables at the back, and the way their groom hissed – all grooms hiss but the Lowes' groom was the world's champion hisser – and the huge paddock, and the sort of meals the Lowes had, and their cook who could make peppermint creams, and the general horsiness of everything. The only thing I didn't like was the way Mrs Lowe always treated me as if I were six, only Martin said she did that to him too.

Martin was writing in the dining-room with the window open as I rode up on Black Boy, and he shouted, 'Come in! You haven't been to see us for ages. I expect you're dying to tell me about the new pony. You did buy him, I suppose?'

I dismounted in a nonchalant sort of way – at least I hoped it looked like that – and tethered my pony. Then I went into the house.

'How's things?' said Martin.

'All right,' I said.

'*Now* what's the matter?'

'Nothing,' I said.

He picked up his pen and just went on writing, as much as to say, 'If that's all you're going to tell me, why did you come?'

I knew I was being silly and rude, so in a minute out it all came.

'Oh, Martin,' I said, 'he's awful. And he loathes me with a deadly loathing.'

(I got that bit out of an old-fashioned novel. I do think that people in the olden days used to say things in a much more exciting way than we do now.)

Martin put his pen down and asked calmly, 'What on earth did you buy him for?'

I poured out the story of the dismal visit to the Penberthys', and not wanting to disappoint Mummy who liked Mrs Penberthy so much, and about Rapide having turned against me from the very start and how he jumped a clear round for Joan Penberthy and wouldn't do a thing for me.

'So I bought him,' I said, 'just to show him that I wouldn't be beaten.'

'Well, that's one reason for buying a pony,' said Martin.

'I know it's crazy,' I said. 'Oh, do please understand.'

'But it isn't at all crazy,' he said. 'Friends of mine have done it before and it has all turned out extremely well. It's a perfectly good reason for buying a horse and shows you have the right spirit. Good luck to you.'

'Oh, Martin, I'm so relieved I could pass out!' I said. 'Promise me you'll never let Mummy know how I feel about Rapide. She thinks he's wonderful.'

'I shan't let a single hair of the cat out of the bag,' he said. 'You say this pony is actually a good pony and can jump?'

'Oh, yes, he's been well schooled. I saw him do six jumps that were the kind you get in the under-sixteens. He's won masses of prizes for Joan Penberthy. But he's got the weirdest action. He canters up to the jump, then checks and stops dead. Then he pops up his forelegs, sort of bucks up his middle, pops up his hindlegs and he's over. I can't think how he does it. I did so hope I'd get a soaring kind of jumper.'

'You don't think he's a mean-spirited pony?'

'No-oo,' I said slowly. 'It was just the way he looked at *me*, as much as to say, Who is this lower-than-worms creature? And I felt such a fool when he wouldn't try to jump for me. Mummy thought I was letting her down and the Penberthys thought I'd never tried to jump before. That was when I decided to buy Rapide. Rapide! Isn't it a silly name? He looks more like the Rocking-Horse Fly.'

'Well, I shall look on with interest to see what you make of him,' said Martin. 'After all, you can always sell him again.'

This thought, which hadn't occurred to me, cheered me up so much that I felt quite happy, and we went out to look at the horses and ate some peppermint creams in the kitchen.

3 Rapide is here

Wednesday dawned and it was the Day of Doom on which Rapide was going to arrive. We had arranged for Wednesday as it was my half-term and I could go and fetch him from the station. He was due to arrive at Chatton at quarter past two, so after lunch I changed into my riding things and picked up a halter. I wondered for a minute whether I should ride Black Boy and lead Rapide, but I decided to walk. It was silly of me but I didn't want Rapide to give my nice pony any of his black looks.

I got down to the station and went into the office. The clerk took me to a siding. Rapide had not only arrived but somebody had kindly taken him out of the horse box and tethered him to some railings, and there he stood giving little shivers and casting dirty looks at everybody and everything in sight.

'Now that's what I call a nice pony,' said the clerk.

I just said 'Hmph', or something like that.

'What colour would you call him?' asked the clerk.

'He's a bay,' I said.

'I never could understand these horse colours,' said the clerk. 'I mean, you always call a white horse a grey, don't you?'

'Oh, yes,' I said. 'And bay means a reddish brown, and then there's chestnut which is dark brown and roan which is light brown, but you sometimes hear people talk about light chestnut and dark chestnut and light bay and dark bay and light roan and dark roan, which is a bit vague and unhorsemanlike, I think. And then of course there's piebald which is black and white and skewbald which is any other colour and white.'

'You don't say!' said the clerk, unconscious that I was prattling on to put off the evil moment when I should have to tell Rapide I was here.

'Have you come for the pony?' said a porter coming up. 'Would he like a drink after his journey?'

He fetched a bucket of water and Rapide condescended to bury his nose in it and drink, making disgusting noises. I was ashamed of him, but the clerk and porter went on saying what a nice pony he was, in spite of the way he kept looking at them as if they were earwigs.

He had on an old, knotted halter which doubtless Joan Penberthy had thought good enough for him to travel in, so I took it off and threw it away and put on my nice white one. His skin shivered everywhere I touched it, and when his enormous eye was close to me it looked more disdainful and nasty than ever.

'Come on, you!' I said.

'I've seen you riding in the shows,' said the porter. 'You're good, aren't you?'

'Oh, not very,' I said. 'Heaps of people are better than me. I've improved though since I had lessons at the riding school.'

'Which one is that?' he asked.

'Mrs Darcy's at Ring Hill.'

'They say she's going out of fashion,' he said. 'All the kids nowadays are going to this new place, Lime Farm.'

'Then they're silly,' I said. 'Mrs Darcy is much the best teacher in this county.'

I had got Rapide moving by now. He came along not exactly willingly but sort of unprotestingly, like a French aristo being dragged through the streets of Paris by the mob.

'Well, I expect you'll be winning the open jumping now, ha-ha!' said the porter, which I didn't think was very funny.

I got Rapide home and Mummy was standing at the cottage gate to greet us, looking very excited, as we had talked so much about me having a new pony.

'He doesn't look any the worse for his journey, does he?' she said. 'He is a lovely colour.'

She held a carrot she had saved – and scrubbed – for this moment. Rapide sniffed at it, then turned his head away and looked bored stiff.

'Good gracious!' said Mummy. 'Doesn't he like carrot?'

'I suppose what he really likes is a dessert apple carefully peeled with a silver knife,' I said sarkily.

'What are you going to do with him now?'

'I'm going to put him in the orchard to have a rest after his journey – Black Boy's in the stable – and after tea I'll take him up to Mrs Darcy's.'

I shoved Rapide into the orchard. He took a long lazy look round and decided it wasn't bad, then began to crop grass.

Mummy came out and began to feed her hens. I can't say I am very taken with the hen as an animal, it has such a soulless expression on its face, but Mummy has such a beautiful nature that she actually likes hens for themselves alone and gives them names like Bonnie and Blossom, and *thanks* them for laying eggs. One year Mummy bought three cockerels to fatten up for the table. We called them Winken, Blinken and Nod. On Christmas Eve she got a man to come round and kill one of them for our Christmas dinner and we all went into the yard to choose which should be killed. They all three looked very fat and eatable and quite unconscious that the day of doom had arrived for them, which was rather sad.

Mummy said, 'Well, it can't be Winken because yesterday he took a bit of corn out of my fingers and it was so trusting of him. And it can't be Blinken because I love the way he puts his head on one side. It reminds me of a dog I had when I was small. And it can't be Nod because he looks so comical when he scratches I'm sure he has a sense of humour.'

The man said, 'Well, make up your mind, madam,' and Mummy said, 'No, not one of them shall be killed, they're all personal friends.'

So the man went away and I'm sure he thought we were far from sane, and Mummy and I cheerfully ate sausages and bread sauce for Christmas dinner. This just shows you what Mummy thinks of even such mere things as hens, and the only one we ever ate was one called Mrs Hitler who pecked at the others and had a mean and unworthy nature.

I went to the little outhouse which I sometimes called the saddle room and sometimes the forage room when I wanted to sound grand, and fetched a few oats for Rapide. He deigned to eat them, not in a nice affectionate pony-ish way at all, but looking at me as if I was trying to poison him.

After tea I saddled Black Boy, and leading Rapide I set off for Mrs Darcy's riding school and stables at Ring Hill. I always felt grateful to Mrs Darcy because she was so decent to me when I first got a pony and was such a bad rider, and she also let me work in her stable for a while, where I got a good deal of my present experience. Some people were terrified of her because she was so efficient and everything she said seemed to end in an exclamation mark, and if you did anything ham-handed or quite silly she came down on you like a ton of bricks. But she was awfully nice really and since I had been having regular lessons from her my riding had improved no end, and I had also learned a good deal about that most noble of all creatures, The Horse.

When I turned in at the white gate from which a bridle path ran round the paddock to the yard, Joey, Mrs Darcy's stable-man, caught sight of me and I saw him run to find her.

She came to meet me and cried, 'Well, well! The new jumper! And a very nice pony too!'

Oh dear, I thought, everybody but me thinks Rapide is a nice pony. Are they all crazy or am I?

I slipped down off Black Boy, and said, 'He came today. Do you think he's all right?'

'Well, he has lovely hocks,' said Mrs Darcy. 'His rump is higher than his withers.'

'I know,' I said humbly, 'but I think it makes him look like a worn-down steeplechaser, or even a kangaroo. And don't you think his neck is rather unyielding?'

'Why, what's the matter, Jill?' she said. 'You're talking about your new pony in a very disparaging way. I thought you'd have been wild with enthusiasm.'

Then of course I had to pour it all out again. I felt rather a fool, telling an expert like Mrs Darcy that I didn't like Rapide and he didn't like me and I had only bought him from sheer cussedness and to save Mummy from being disappointed.

'But the point is, can he jump?' said Mrs Darcy. 'Surely you wouldn't buy a so-called jumper if he couldn't?'

'Oh, yes, he can jump,' I said, 'but you should see him! He looks awful. He jumps from a standstill, all buckled up.'

'My dear idiot,' said Mrs Darcy, 'you're much too conceited about how you look on a pony. That's what you're thinking of, isn't it? Well, I've seen some of the best show-jumpers with the most awful conformation, and there are all types of jumpers and ways of jumping. Now just get along home and leave that pony to me, and mind you're up here tomorrow to groom him because goodness knows he needs it after the train journey and nobody here has the time!'

She laughed gaily and took hold of Rapide's halter, and like magic his whole nature seemed to change and he walked humbly along by her side with the meekest look on his face. I felt terribly humiliated and began to think that after all I didn't know anything about horses.

When I got home Mummy said, 'Well? Did Rapide settle down nicely with Mrs Darcy?'

I felt like saying, 'And how!' but Mummy has stopped me using American slang so I just said a feeble, 'Yes, thank you,' and went upstairs to change.

4 Some people will do anything!

In the middle of the night I woke up suddenly, and it was just like in detective stories where the great detective suddenly sees the vital clue revealed to him as though by a flash of lightning across the midnight sky. He is then overjoyed, but what was revealed to me didn't overjoy me at all, just the opposite. It was something that the porter had said at the station about Mrs Darcy, 'They say she's going out of fashion. All the kids nowadays are going to this new place, Lime Farm.'

As I thought this over I went hot and cold, and I knew I couldn't go to sleep any more so I put my dressing gown on and sat up in bed, nursing my knees and feeling miserable. I daren't put the light on in case Mummy saw the reflection and came in.

I must have been pretty blind, but now a lot of things were clear to me. Angela, Mrs Darcy's head girl who used to ride her horses in the Hunter Trials and Grade C Jumping, Stackwood who drove the horse box and looked after the ponies at shows, and other dependable people had gone off to other jobs and now Mrs Darcy was doing all the skilled jobs herself with only the help of Joey – who loved horses but wasn't very bright so nobody would employ him – and a girl of fifteen called Wendy Mead who helped at weekends and odd times in return for riding lessons. And when I thought about it still more – and it hurts like anything thinking in the middle of the night because you get so hungry – I realised that it was months since Mrs Darcy got any new pupils. And yet lots of new children were learning to ride, and they were all going to Lime Farm!

Lime Farm belonged to some people called Captain and Mrs Drafter and it was a very dashing sort of place with gallons of new green and white paint splashed about, and all the horses there had dark green blankets bound with yellow, and E.D. in the corner. E.D. were the initials of Captain Drafter. I don't know what the E stood for but I expect it was something revolting like Ebenezer or Eustace. Captain Drafter was very tall and thin and had a bluish face with a nose like a setter and hard little eyes like unripe gooseberries. He rode a jet black hunter that was supposed to be worth thousands of pounds, and when he was hunting he took a flea-bitten grey as his second horse that was also frightfully valuable and nipped other people's less wonderful horses, and the Master had had to speak to him more than once, which I think is the lowest form of disgrace.

Mrs Drafter rode side-saddle, which I think was just to show that she could do it, and used her whip an awful lot. Ours is a very friendly Hunt and the Master encourages children to follow on their ponies, and even on bikes and on foot if they haven't ponies, which doesn't shut anybody out just because they are poor and honest, but Mrs Drafter looked round and said, 'What a rabble'. I looked Rabble up in the dictionary and it said, a disorderly crowd or mob, which was quite untrue and makes one think of the French Revolution and not a lot of nice children who were keen on riding, so I always hated Mrs Drafter ever after.

All the pupils at Lime Farm Riding School were taught to ride in a very dashing way, which pleased the sort of parents who had loads of money but didn't know much about the noble art of equitation, and Susan Pyke was the star pupil. And it was sad but true that all the new children were going to Lime Farm, and not to Mrs Darcy's where they would have learned to ride well and have good manners and care for their ponies.

By the time all these Frightful Facts had come to me I was very cold and practically starving. I tried to go to sleep again but I couldn't. It was no use, I had to go downstairs and find something to eat, so I didn't even put my slippers on as they are apt to go slippety-slop, and I sneaked down the stairs on my bare feet so as not to waken Mummy. I didn't even put the light on in the kitchen because the switch makes such a click – isn't it funny how switches click like mad in the night and don't make a sound in the daytime? – and I groped my way to the cupboard where the tin of biscuits is kept, and opened the door and felt my way up to the second shelf. I had just got hold of the edge of the biscuit tin when my dressing gown sleeve caught something and over it went! The next minute there was a hideous crash, then thud, thud, thud, and the sound of something rolling over the kitchen floor. I put on the light. What I had knocked down was a big pudding basin, right on to the jars of newly made blackberry jelly which Mummy had left to set on the ledge under the cupboard. Four of them had gone over like ninepins, and all across the kitchen floor was a trail of purple jelly which made me wonder how so much could ever have been crammed into only four jars.

Of course by then Mummy was in my midst, so

to speak, and she was furious and told me I might at least have had the sense to put the light on before rummaging in the cupboards, and she didn't seem a bit impressed when I told her I had only been trying not to wake her up, so what with that row and worrying about Mrs Darcy, to say nothing of a sleepless night and Rapide on my hands, I got up next morning feeling really low.

By the time I had fed Black Boy and done all my early morning jobs and had some cocoa and sausages I felt a bit better – because food is very good for sorrow – so I thought I would bike up to Mrs Darcy's before school and have a look at Rapide.

As I jumped off my bike in the stable yard the sight of two empty loose boxes looking too horribly clean and bare for words reminded me that Mrs Darcy had been selling ponies instead of buying them. I decided that being a detective was very depressing.

'Hello, Jill!' she called out, coming towards me with her shirt sleeves rolled up and her arms full of tack she had been cleaning. 'Have you come to see how Rapide is? Well, he's still alive, you'll be glad to hear. Wendy had him out for half an hour before breakfast and she says she thinks he has it in him but is rather unresponsive. She hasn't jumped him, of course.'

Rapide was in the middle of his breakfast. He took his nose out long enough to look at me as if I were a spider he had found in his oats.

I said, 'Good boy!' rather half-heartedly and stroked his nose. He shied, side-stepped into Mrs Darcy, rebounded towards me and fairly snorted his disgust.

'I'll tell you what,' she said, 'I think there's something funny abut those Penberthys of yours. This pony has been ill-treated or I know nothing about horses.'

'Oh, no!' I said. 'It couldn't – I mean, he couldn't – they couldn't. They were terribly nice and truly horsy people, and it was only me that seemed all wrong that day, and Joan Penberthy did six clear jumps on him, and he's won her stacks of cups and things.'

'Fish!' said Mrs Darcy, which was her way of saying, Rot. 'I've got a strong idea that your Joan Penberthy's idea of schooling a pony is to whip him round the jumps until he takes them in sheer terror of being whipped. Is that what they did to you, eh, Rapide?'

'I can't believe it,' I gasped.

'My dear Jill, when you've been in the horse world as long as I have you'll know that there are people who will do *anything*, and then pass themselves off as nice, horsy people – as you call it. Well, you've bought Rapide, and I expect now you'll want to sell him again.'

'Would that be a good thing?' I asked.

'Well, you certainly won't want to bother with him. I'll get rid of him for you, if you like, and then you can find something easier and more to your liking.'

'Who would you sell him to?' I asked.

'I'd probably send him to auction. I don't do that to my own ponies but I haven't any feelings about Rapide. I daresay he'd make a good pony for a tradesman.'

'But what will Mummy say?'

'Oh, I'll put that right,' said Mrs Darcy kindly. 'I'll tell her I don't think Rapide is suitable for you and that I'll help you to find something better. She won't mind.'

'Oh, thank you very much, Mrs Darcy,' I said. 'It is kind of you.' I then looked at my watch and said, 'Oh, help, it's quarter to nine. I'll have to pedal like mad to get to school.'

A great weight had rolled off my mind. I was never going to see Rapide again, it was too good to be true.

At break I grabbed hold of Ann Derry and dragged her to a rather sordid part of the school garden where they kept the grass clippings and things that had lost their handles, and there were bits of old bonfire lying about and it was smelly too, but nice and private.

'Listen,' I said, 'it's terribly important. I've been awake for hours in the night. We've got to start a campaign.'

'What's that?' she said densely.

'Like a crusade,' I said, 'only more tough. I mean, the Crusades went on for years and never got anywhere, but Wellington had campaigns and they overthrew Napoleon.'

'Gosh, are you trying to be top in history, or something?' she said.

'No,' I said. 'It's about Mrs Darcy and the riding school.'

And I told her all about everything I had thought of in the silent watches of the night.

'Yes, it's true,' said Ann. 'There are some new people in our road and they have a Rolls-Royce and a beastly girl called Patience, and her mother came to tea and asked Mummy if I went to Lime Farm Riding School and Mummy said no, to Mrs Darcy's, and Patience's mother said, "Oh, but they tell me that Lime Farm is *the* place. Patience has started there already." And then Mummy asked me if I was satisfied with Mrs Darcy's or would I like to change and go to Lime Farm too.'

'Gosh! What did you say?'

'I said that the very fact that Susan Pyke had changed to Lime Farm was enough to put me off it, and Mummy doesn't like the Pykes either so she didn't say any more.'

'Well we've got to do something about it,' I said. 'But the point is, what?'

'We'd better start a club,' said Ann, 'and get some of the good people like the Heaths and Diana Bush to join. We could call it the B.L.F. Club, Bar Lime Farm, you know.'

Ann was always very good at thinking of names for things.

'I think it sounds a bit rude,' I said. 'It isn't much good starting off by being rude, or our mothers might bar the Club. What about calling it the B.M.D. – Boost Mrs Darcy.'

'Oh gosh, yes!' said Ann. 'I think that's terrific.'

'OK,' I said. 'That's enough for now, and the bell's just going. But in Geography you can think like mad about things the B.M.D. can do, and I'll think too. And I'll see you after school.'

After school we hadn't really thought of anything, but we told Diana Bush and the Heaths and they said they would join, so we decided to have a meeting the next day in the lunch hour.

Ann and I biked home together and all of a sudden she said, 'By the way, how's Rapide? Have you had a chance to try him yet?'

'Oh, I'm selling him,' I said. 'Mrs Darcy's going to send him to auction.'

'What for?' said Ann, nearly falling off her bike but saving herself by a daring dirt-track swerve while an old lady on the pavement said 'Tch-tch-tch.'

So I told her what Mrs Darcy had said and all the awful revelations about the Penberthys being fiends in human shape and about it being too much trouble to try and do anything with Rapide, and how I was going to get a really good pony, and was frightfully relieved at the thought that I should never see Rapide any more.

'Well, of all the soulless things I ever heard,' said Ann, 'I call that the absolute worst.'

'How do you mean?' I said haughtily.

'I mean, you go and drag a poor ill-treated pony away from its horrible owners and take it to a nice place like Mrs Darcy's and give it the idea that it's going to live there for ever and ever, and just when joy is waking in its downtrodden heart and it thinks that it might even have a shot at being a jolly decent pony in return for people being kind to it, you go and shove it into a beastly auction and it will be bought by a cold-blooded baker with brutal eyes and he'll make it pull about forty times more than it can, and one day it'll fall down on a hill and die. And you talk about loving horses!'

'Oh, don't be silly, Ann,' I said. 'Rapide will probably be bought by a terribly nice greengrocer and he'll be able to turn his head round and eat the dessert apples off the cart.'

But talking about dessert apples gave me a nasty cold feeling down my spine as I remembered how Mummy had offered Rapide a carrot and he had turned his head away. Could it be because nobody had ever kindly offered him anything before in his life, but hit his nose instead? I went colder and colder until I was cold all over. When we got to Ann's road

I just said, 'Flog-oh' – which we had got from a radio programme and were saying a lot just then – and hared off home. Mummy was out so I made a cup of cocoa and sat on the kitchen floor and drank it. And I thought and thought and the more I thought the more awful I felt. I wished Ann hadn't said that about Rapide thinking he had got to a good home at last and then having all his hopes dashed to the ground. And of course I didn't really believe about the cold-blooded baker – because bakers can't help being nice when they have such lovely shops full of luscious things to eat – but I had to remember the poor pony I bought in my other book called *A Stable for Jill* from a disgusting man called J. Biggs who sold firewood and was a beast of the first water. And I suppose if there was one J. Biggs there might be others. Perhaps that very J. Biggs was looking for another pony by now and might buy Rapide?

By the time Mummy came in I felt quite weird with thinking so much.

5 That pony again

After supper I said I was going to Mrs Darcy's. Mummy said, 'Now look here, Jill, I oughtn't to have to speak to you about all this running off to the riding school. It's a weekday and your lessons ought to come first. You never seem to be thinking of anything but those ponies.'

'But it's important,' I said, 'and I've done my homework. I did it before you came in. Please, Mummy! I'll only be ten minutes.'

So she said I could go but I must be back before dark. I biked along like mad. I seemed to have spent most of the day rushing about.

Everything at the stables was closed up for the night, so I went and knocked on the house door. Mrs Darcy opened it. She and Zoe were having their supper. Zoe was Mrs Darcy's niece who stayed with her, and we were rather frightened of her as she had been second in the under-sixteen jumping at the Royal International Horse Show.

'Have you sold Rapide yet?' I blurted out.

'Yes,' said Mrs Darcy, and my heart sank. 'At least I've sent him over to Bidworth. There's a horse sale there tomorrow, mostly working horses. You ought to get a good price for Rapide.'

'Could we get him back?' I said. 'I've decided I don't want to sell him.'

'But you said you did,' said Zoe.

'Well, would you?' I said. 'You may think I don't know my own mind, but such utterly soulless people buy horses, and just when Rapide thought he was getting a good home – '

'I see just what you mean,' said Zoe, and I felt grateful to her, and wasn't frightened of her any more. 'I couldn't sell a pony I'd had anything to do with unless I knew the home it was going to.'

Mrs Darcy smiled all over her face.

'Are you prepared to take a lot of trouble with Rapide?' she said, looking at me. 'Or will you be sorry in a day or two that you went all soft about him?'

'If he's worth taking trouble with, I'll take it,' I said.

'I think he is and so does Zoe.'

'Oh, please get him back,' I said, feeling awful at the thought of what poor Rapide must be feeling like now, all among strangers and perhaps tied up to a ring in a dirty wall in a large, empty hall, which is the kind of place where they sell horses.

'I'll ring up at once,' said Mrs Darcy, 'and tell them to withdraw Rapide, and Joey can go over in the morning and fetch him back.'

I hovered about while she telephoned, standing first on one leg and then on the other, and at last Mrs Darcy came and said it was all settled, I had got Rapide again. I said 'thank you' about nine times, and Mrs Darcy started telling Zoe about Chatton Show where I had won a few events, and I looked at the photos of hunters on the wall and wondered what Mrs Darcy would think if she knew about the B.M.D.

Next day at school I said to Ann, 'I do think you're a wash-out. You've made me take Rapide back, and now if he gets me twenty-four faults it'll be your fault.'

She just said, 'I thought your Better Self would Triumph,' which I recognised as being out of a book which our domestic science teacher read to us while we did darning.

In the lunch hour it rained, so we got the members of the Club together and went and sat by the radiator in the gym.

I started off the meeting by saying, 'Some of you ought to have thought of something by now.'

Actually I felt a bit guilty as, with all that Rapide business, I hadn't had time to think of a thing myself.

'Daddy was telling us last night,' said Val Heath, 'about when he was abroad somewhere – I don't exactly remember where – but they were boosting something up – only I forget what it was but it doesn't matter because it was *something* – and they started off with about an hour of fireworks and people came from miles around to see what it was, and then they sent up rockets and then flares and whatever it was they were trying to boost was written in green and red letters all over the sky. It must have been wonderful.'

'Well, that would cost a million pounds,' I said witheringly. 'Doesn't anybody know anything cheap?'

'If it's carrying banners and marching,' said Jackie Heath, 'I'm jolly well not going to.'

'I take a dim view of that too,' said Diana Bush. 'I asked my mother about it last night and she says the only thing we can do is to display such good horsemanship and good manners that everybody will see how much better taught we are than the Lime Farm crowd.'

'But that'll take such a long time,' said Ann. 'I mean, we can't wait until next summer's events to boost Mrs Darcy. She may not have any riding school left by then – except us.'

'There's the Hunter Trials,' said Diana.

'That's mostly for grown-ups, and two events for under-sixteens.'

'I think in a way Diana's right,' I said, 'and we've simply got to do well at the Hunter Trials. But we must do something else too. There are a lot of new girls in the school and they're sure to get keen on riding soon with hearing us talk about nothing else, and we've got to make sure that they'll go to Mrs Darcy and not to those Drafter people.'

'I know!' shouted Ann. 'Let's write a letter to all the new girls and tell them all about it and ask them to go to Mrs Darcy's and not Lime Farm. Like an advertisement.'

'Oh, yes,' said Val Heath, 'and I could paint a skull at the top. I can paint the most marvellous skulls.'

'I think that's silly,' said Diana. 'We ought to put at the top, "In the cause of Good Riding", or something sensible like that.'

'I've got it!' I fairly yelled. 'Not a letter, just an advertisement. "For good riding's sake go to Mrs Darcy's." And we could do it on postcards.'

'Oughtn't we to say something about how awful the riding is at Lime Farm?' said Jackie.

'They could send you to prison if you did,' said Diana. 'It's called libel, or something.'

'There are about twenty new girls,' I said, 'and there are five of us, so that means doing four postcards each and we can put them in their desks.'

'I'll get the postcards,' said Ann. 'Daddy has masses of them in his study, I'll bring some tomorrow.'

We were all excited about doing the postcards, and next day Ann brought them to school and we all took four home to do. I whizzed through my homework and then lettered the postcards in pencil and went over the outlines in Indian ink and then round the capital letters in red paint. They looked terrific and I laid them out on the kitchen table to dry. FOR GOOD RIDING'S SAKE GO TO MRS DARCY'S done four times over made me feel as if something was really happening. Mummy was thinking about something else, as she often is, and didn't even notice what I was doing. She just wandered by and murmured, 'Making Christmas cards, dear?'

Next morning at break we collected our buns and met on the netball court. Everybody had done their postcards. Ann had done each of her four in a different colour, red, blue, green and purple, and Val Heath had painted a little skull on hers but she said it was just her signature and didn't mean anything, and Diana had forgotten the word 'sake' so her cards said, FOR GOOD RIDING'S GO TO MRS DARCY'S which made sense, so we didn't bother to have them done again.

We soon found out who the new girls were and which forms they were in and where they sat, so in the dinner hour we nipped round the form rooms and did the deed, and that was that.

As we came out of school in the afternoon Ann said, 'I wonder if Mrs Darcy has got Rapide back? I expect she has by now. Couldn't we go and have a look at him? I'm dying to see him.'

I didn't feel at all enthusiastic, in fact all day I had been trying to forget Rapide, so I muttered something about going straight home.

'I think you're a horrid meanie if you don't let me go with you,' said Ann.

'And us too!' shouted Diana, Val, and Jackie who

had overheard all Ann's tactless remarks. 'We took you to see our new ponies.'

I tried to mumble something about Mummy wondering where I was, but it didn't work because they all pointed out that we'd be passing the cottage in any case and they'd gladly wait while I went in and explained. So we set off, and on the way I told them that Rapide was really a cross between a Gorgon and a rocking-horse and had been wished on me by an evil fairy and that all who gazed on him were doomed to frightful mishaps.

'What a scream!' said Diana. 'What sort of mishaps?'

'For you,' I said, 'it will be losing your stirrup irons. Every time you go out you'll never for a minute be able to keep your feet in your stirrup irons. Jackie's pony will run out of every competition and Val's will bite the judge, not just once but every time.'

'What's going to happen to me,' said Ann, 'if I gaze on Rapide.'

'I'll tell you,' I said. 'Your mother will send you to Lime Farm to learn to ride, and Captain Drafter will take you out on a leading rein with the tiny tots.'

They all said I was crackers.

We stopped at the cottage and I went in. Mummy was in the sitting-room, typing. I went and hovered over her a bit, then I said, 'You do type well, but it wastes your time to have to do all that copying. I could soon learn to type and do it for you.'

'That's an idea,' she said, 'but I'm busy now so don't bother me, there's a good girl.'

'I'm rather in the mood for learning to type now, this minute,' I said.

'And I'm rather in the mood to get on with this

by myself,' said Mummy. 'Thanks very much all the same. Now do push off.'

'Don't you want me to make the tea?' I said.

'It's too early for tea,' said my callous mother with a complete lack of intuition. 'Let's wait till about half-past five.'

'Isn't there anything you want me to do?' I said. 'I mean, I'm quite free at the moment.'

'You've already made me type the same line twice,' said Mummy. 'And what are those girls doing outside? Good gracious!'

My friends' faces were pressed against the windowpane, looking in in a very sinister way.

'All is lost!' I said dramatically, but it was wasted because Mummy just said vaguely, 'Yes, you can go out and play with them if that's what you're worrying about. Don't be late back.'

'Play!' I said bitterly.

I couldn't do a thing about it, so I went out and said, 'It's all very inconvenient,' and got on my bike in what is called in some books High Dudgeon. (I once looked this up in the dictionary and there isn't any Low Dudgeon, it's always High.)

'But your mother said you could come,' said Val, who was a bit dim. 'We heard her through the window.'

When we got up to Mrs Darcy's all was perfect peace. Zoe was cantering a pony round the paddock.

'Where will Rapide be?' said Ann.

'Probably sitting by the fire reading a book,' I said with terrific sarcasm.

'I don't think that's a bit funny,' said Diana. 'He's more likely to be lying at the point of death in his stall because his ghastly experiences at the sale have broken his heart.'

'Well, Ann shouldn't say such obvious things,' I said crossly. '"Where will Rapide be?" Where are ponies usually kept at a stable?'

I pushed open the gate and we all streamed in, then I let it clang to again and we walked up the paddock. Zoe recognised us and came cantering up.

'Hello,' she said. 'I thought you'd want to see him. He looks all right, doesn't he?'

She patted her mount's neck. I nearly fell over backwards.

It was Rapide.

When I became conscious again, which was about two minutes later, I heard Ann say, 'I think he's sweet!'

'Oh, Zoe, let me try him,' said Diana.

'And then us,' said Val.

'I think he's had enough for today,' said Zoe. 'He's had a long journey back from town, but when he arrived back here he looked round him in a most satisfied way. I rubbed him down and gave him a feed and he ate oats out of my hand. So after he'd had a rest I saddled him and we've had half an hour round the paddock and we've both enjoyed it, haven't we, Rapide?'

Rapide looked at Zoe as much as to say, 'I think you're all right, but defend me from these others.'

'I can't see anything the matter with him,' said Jackie. 'When we were coming along and I saw you in the paddock, Zoe, I thought, what a jolly nice pony. I thought he lifted his feet beautifully. Didn't I say to you, Val, doesn't that pony Zoe's on lift his feet beautifully?'

'Did you?' said Val. 'I don't remember. But I don't think he's a bit like a Gorgon or a rocking-horse either.'

'Is that what Jill told you he was like?' said Zoe. 'She's crackers.'

'It's only me that he doesn't like,' I said.

'Come on, Jill,' said Zoe. 'Get up on him now while he's in the mood.'

'Not likely,' I said. 'Not in front of all you people, and you said he'd had enough.'

'Well, give him a kind word,' said Zoe, 'for pity's sake.'

'Hello, Rapide,' I said, cautiously touching his nose. 'So you're back?'

He stepped back hastily into Ann, who sat down looking very surprised. Then he tossed his head about and rolled his eyes at Zoe as much as to say, Take me out of this.

'No go,' said Zoe. 'He's had enough. Come on, let's put him in his stall.'

So rather reluctantly – at least I was reluctant and the others seemed to enjoy it – we went and put Rapide into his stall, and while Zoe unsaddled him Jackie gave him a good hug and he blew at her in a most friendly way.

'Look, he simply adores me,' said Jackie. 'Don't you, darling?'

'I wonder why he doesn't like Jill?' said Ann. 'Perhaps she reminds him of the Penberthy girl.'

'Well, of all the insults!' I said. 'Joan Penberthy was a complete hag.'

'There may be something in what Ann says,' said Zoe. 'It is possible that Rapide associates you with the place he hated. After all, you rode him down there didn't you? You'll have to be awfully kind to him, to make up. I don't think you've been particularly nice to him yet.'

I went rather red, and then somehow we all got

away, but I remembered what Zoe had said, and next morning I went up there early by myself, and I fed Rapide and made as much fuss of him as he'd let me. All of a sudden I felt terribly sorry for him, and when you feel really and truly sorry for a person or a horse they seem to know it and a thing called a Bond of Sympathy is Forged. I don't say that the Bond of Sympathy between me and Rapide was very hot all at once, but it began to be there. And that was Something.

6 The day of the meet

Next morning at school we all got it in the neck. As soon as we got back to our form room after prayers Miss Fox, our form teacher, said, 'Who is responsible for this unappetising and illiterate concoction?' – she talks like that – and she held up one of the handwritten slips that we had put in the new girls' desks. It wasn't even one of the better ones either, it was one of the bad ones that Diana had done which said, FOR GOOD RIDING'S GO TO MRS DARCY'S.

We all looked at each other, and then Ann, Diana, Val, Jackie, and I got up simultaneously and said, 'Me.'

Of course Miss Fox being the English teacher and mad on grammar we couldn't have said anything worse if we'd tried.

I needn't go into details because all my readers who have been in a similar situation will be able to imagine them, but the result was that we all had to stay in that afternoon after school and write out one hundred times a frightfully untrue statement which made our blood boil, namely, THERE ARE MORE IMPORTANT THINGS IN LIFE THAN HORSES.

After I had written this out about twenty-two times I found that I was tapping it out with my feet. (You try it, it's rather fun.) I think Miss Fox must have had what they call a sense of rhythm without knowing it.

Then I found it was even more fun to do it like a five finger exercise.

Anyway, when we eventually got out of prison aching from head to foot, Ann said modestly, 'It was you tapping on the desk, Jill, that gave me an idea and I've written a poem.'

It was such a nice poem that I've put it down here so that you can all see it. I think it ought to be in all poetry books.

LIFE by ANN DERRY

There are more important things in life than horses,
At least that's what Miss Fox would have us know,
She never went for rides on autumn mornings,
Or felt the thrill of riding's lovely glow.

There are more important things in life than horses,
But if your pony loves you, you don't care.
They can keep the things they seem to think
    important
And when they dish them out I shan't be there.

There are more important things in life than horses,
There are more important things in life than food,
But somehow when I'm eating or I'm riding
There's nothing else in life seems half so good.

You may think the last verse is a bit hoggish, but if you're an honest person you'll have to admit that it's true. I copied this poem out and sent it to my pen-friend in America. My pen-friend in America is the daughter of some people that Mummy stayed with at Philadelphia, and she is awfully nice, though Mummy says my duty is not to give her a misleading idea of English life. I don't know why Mummy should think I would. I just tell Louise my adventures and she tells me hers, and hers are much more exciting – she was once chased by a bison in a national park – while mine, as you will have gathered from my books, are dull in comparison.

I am sorry to say that after the episode of being kept in to write lines for putting notices on behalf of the Boost Mrs Darcy Club in the new girls' desks, the Club seemed to lapse a bit. The reason was that we were all being rather restrained at home and at school in case any tactless behaviour of ours suggested to our parents that it might be a good idea to stop us from attending the crack meet of the season which was being held at the end of November. I don't want to raise your hopes by pretending that we were expecting to attend the meet as part of the field because we were far from being members of the Hunt, and children were not allowed to follow at the crack meet in any case, but I and my friend Ann are great believers in being on the spot, because you never know. I once read a book in which a girl of fourteen dressed in her riding clothes went to watch a crack meet, and the Master happened to have a spare horse he wanted ridden, and he said, 'Here, girl, you look as though you could ride, what about hunting Hector for me?' And the girl never turned a hair but vaulted lightly upon Hector's seventeen-hands-high saddle and led the field (you know those hunting stories where everybody goes round by the bridge except the heroine who clears the awful ditch with feet to spare) and finally got the brush.

When I was twelve I might have believed this sort of thing, and though now I believe it couldn't possibly happen – still, as I said before, you never know.

The night before the meet I went to stay at Ann's house so that we could have the fun of grooming the ponies together the next morning. I don't know about fun, as it was the blackest, coldest morning I ever remember, and as we groomed Black Boy and George – who was the new pony Ann got when her old pony Seraphine was handed down to her little sister – our teeth played the castanets in a very Spanish way. It was only six o'clock and we started singing *Oh What a Beautiful Morning* to cheer ourselves up, and Mrs Derry, who is the world's most fussiest mother, put her head out of the bedroom window and called, 'Oh, girls, it's much too cold for you, do go back to bed,' which shows you the depths unhorsy people can fall to.

It was rather nice to get our frozen hands into hot water and soapflakes when we washed the tails, but we funked bandaging and plaiting, it was too jolly cold, anyway we weren't actually hunting. Then we fed the ponies and I carried back the bucket to the Derrys' spotless kitchen, and of course I tripped in avoiding a sort of mat thing that was just inside the door (it was so spotless and pure that I couldn't realise it was for such a squalid purpose as wiping the feet on) and went headlong into the kitchen with the bucket going in one direction and the very dirty and soapy contents in the other. I expect you, dear reader, are the sort of person who would have remembered to empty the bucket outside, but I regret I am not like that. Ann came in with the saddles and things and I cleaned up the floor to a certain extent, while she put the kettle on with one hand to make tea and with the other hand began to shake up the metal polish for cleaning our tack. At first the polish wouldn't come, and then it arrived in a gush all over the table, and at that point the Derrys' housekeeper came in and told us that girls of our age with no more sense than we had ought to be in a Home, and take those great ugly saddles out of her kitchen. We daren't say we had come in just for warmth, so we crawled out again into the cheerless dawn and got on with the job of doing the saddles and the leathers and all the metal bits.

Eventually we were ready. We had done our best to look very nice indeed so that if any casual observer happened to say, 'How neat you two girls look,' we should be able to reply that we represented Mrs Darcy's equitation establishment. We didn't really suppose that anybody would, but again you never know. Our jodhs and coats were speckless and we had new shirts and very well-tied ties and brushed hats and neat hair and what the books call irreproachable gloves and boots. We didn't expect to stay like that for long, but had hopes.

It turned out to be quite a pleasant day for November and we rode off slowly to the *Grinning Mouse* which was where the meet was to be. We saw other people on the way, and presently there was an important sort of clatter and we were overtaken by Susan Pyke and her father mounted on magnificent thoroughbreds. Susan was a member of the Hunt now – her father had given her horse to her for a birthday present – and she never let anybody forget it. She looked terrific in her black and white, and the gloss on her boots made you blink, but as usual she was riding a horse too big for her, it was her weakness.

'Hello,' she said in a friendly let's-encourage-the-tiny-tots way, 'going to watch the meet? You'd better hurry. You'll never get there if you jog along like that, you know.'

'Thank you,' said Ann. 'We're not fond of arriving in a lather.'

'Nice little ponies!' said Susan, looking at Black Boy's ears, and my blood boiled as she knew perfectly well that my pony had whacked hers hollow in loads of events when we were both in the under-fourteen classes.

She then used her crop in a very dashing way to go forward and catch up her father, and gave an inelegant lurch and lost one stirrup-iron. Ann and I couldn't help giggling.

The meet as I told you was a crack one, and there were a number of distinguished visitors including Lord and Lady Prance whose pictures you often see in *Harpers and Queen*, if you are the sort of person who goes to the dentist's frequently. The scene outside the *Grinning Mouse* was most exciting and the horses and riders looked wonderful. We hovered on the outskirts with a lot of other people of our age, and when the Master came by we all said good morning and he lifted his cap and smiled at us very gallantly, only nothing book-like happened. I mean, he didn't stop and say how smart we looked and where did we learn to ride, or ask us if we'd like to hunt on a spare horse he happened to have handy. This was disappointing, but so like Life.

When the Hunt moved off we went along the lane to a place where we could see them draw the first covert. Then the hounds streamed away into the distance with the riders after them, the musical cries and thunder of hoofs died on the still November air, and that was that.

We hadn't done, of course. We followed at a respectful distance, and I must say without seeming to boast that both Black Boy and George jumped marvellously and we even overtook some of the laggards and had to hang back so as not to look as if we were in the field.

There was a check in the middle of an open sixty-acre field and we had a splendid view of the Hunt eating its lunches, so we ate ours and then they were off again – hounds having started another fox out of what we call Mucky Pup Spinney – and this time they streamed away from sight and we followed rather laboriously but lost them and took a wrong turning down a long lane that ended at a farm.

The farmer's wife came out and said, 'Be off with you!' which we thought very unfriendly of her as we hadn't done any harm, so we rode down the long lane again and got back to where we started.

By now presumably the Hunt was miles away and our ponies were blowing.

'What now?' said Ann. 'Are we going in search?'

'There doesn't seem to be anybody to ask,' I said.

Just at that minute a rustic swain appeared with a load of turnips, and when we asked him if he had seen anything of the Hunt he said he had seen them going full cry towards Ritchwell Forest ages ago and they would be miles away by now.

It was disappointing, and as we didn't quite know where we were ourselves we asked him, and found we were miles from home. It was nearly three o'clock, so when he obligingly pointed out a short cut we thanked him and galloped down a long steep field, only to find that we had to toil up an even longer, steeper field at the other side which our tired ponies didn't enjoy one bit. We decided that we should have asked for the nearest road and stuck to it, but one hates to do obvious sensible things like that on a hunting day.

Eventually we found ourselves on a common full of rabbit holes, in fact there were so many that we dismounted and led the ponies.

'Listen, can you hear anything?' said Ann.

'What sort of thing?' I said.

'A dog whining,' she said.

'Yes, I can!' I cried. 'It's quite near, but there's no dog.'

'Gosh!' shrieked Ann. 'It's in a rabbit hole. I bet it's a hound. Come on, let's search.'

We crawled about on the ground for a bit, and anybody who had seen us would have thought we were raving, but there was no one to see us, and as twilight fell we at last located the very hole from which the faint whimperings came.

'He's down there,' I said. 'Poor old thing. If he'd only stop scratching and not use his strength up. I say, what a good thing we came along.'

'We're not much good without a spade,' said Ann. 'You wait there and I'll go and find the nearest farm and borrow one.'

To make a long story short she was gone half an hour, but at last she came back with a fork.

'You might have brought a man,' I said. 'This ground'll be frightful to dig. And the dog's gone quiet, I expect he's suffocated.'

'There wasn't a man,' said Ann. 'There was only a woman and she wasn't at all pleasant either.'

For the next twenty minutes we nearly broke our backs wielding the fork. It was almost dark and our gloves which we kept on to save our hands were in ribbons. At long last we got through to the burrow, and Ann lay flat and shoved her arm down it, struggled a bit and cried out, 'I've got him.'

Between us we managed to drag out a young

hound, absolutely plastered with earth and quite exhausted.

'That's what you get,' I told him, 'for leaving the hunt and going off after rabbits.'

We were nearly as exhausted as the hound and a mass of blisters and aching bones, so we sat down and had a rather cold, damp rest and then, quite forgetting to return the fork to the farm, we trudged wearily off, leading the ponies, and the hound on a sort of halter and lead made out of the lucky piece of string I always carry in my pocket for emergencies. This was an emergency all right.

Soon we struck a main road and found a signpost and made for home, riding, and taking it in turns to hold Ranter's string. We had to call him something.

It was a slow ride and we were starving, besides wondering what sort of welcome we were going to get from our loving parents who had told us on no account to be out after five. It was already past six.

'I feel this is the beginning of something wonderful,' said Ann.

'Such as?' I asked sarkily.

'Well, you know this might easily prove to be the Master's favourite hound. Or it might be Lord and Lady Prance's favourite hound. Anyway, we shall be invited to Moss Hall and given a banquet, and gold tie-pins with foxes' heads.'

'And we'll tell Lord and Lady Prance about Mrs Darcy's,' I said, 'and they will send their five daughters there, and Mrs Darcy will be made for life.'

'Good show!' said Ann.

We decided that we would take the hound straight home to our cottage, and next morning we would get up at six and make ourselves look very tidy and we'd sponge and press our clothes and groom the ponies and set off with the hound to Moss Hall where the Master, Colonel Swift, lived. The prospect made us nearly forget how hungry we were and how late it was.

'We didn't see much of the hunt,' said Ann. 'I wonder what happened?'

(A few days later we learned that they had lost three foxes, and that they wouldn't draw again because all the distinguished visitors wanted to get home before dark, and altogether it wasn't a very good run, so we hadn't missed much. At least the one thing we did miss which we might have enjoyed was the sight of Susan Pyke sitting in the middle of a mud splash where her too-large horse had deposited her, and picking bits of thorn hedge out of her hair. A few days later she told everybody at school that she thought hunting was silly and she only did it to please her father. Ann and I nobly forbore to tell her that the hedge she had brought down with her was one that our ponies had jumped easily; she wouldn't have believed us anyway.)

Meanwhile we were riding home in the misty darkness, and it was quite dangerous as cars kept passing and sometimes the drivers yelled things at us, which was horribly rude and they might have discovered our unfortunate circumstances first.

Then it began to rain. We were soaked to the skin in addition to being filthy and starving. The only thing that kept us going was the thought of the book-like things that would be happening to us when we took the hound home tomorrow.

It was eight o'clock when we crawled into Chatton and our parents had roused the village to organise a search party for us. You can imagine how popular we were. My mother behaved quite well considering all things, but Mrs Derry wept all over Ann, which was very shaming.

I said, 'When you hear all you'll know we weren't to blame,' in a very heroine-ish sort of way.

I then explained how we had saved the life of the Master's favourite hound and nearly worn ourselves out in the process.

'And tomorrow,' I said, 'we're going to take him to Moss Hall, but he'll have to stay at the cottage tonight.'

'But where is the hound?' said Mrs Derry. 'I don't see any hound.'

Will you believe me, neither did we! There just wasn't any sign of the hound, beyond my lucky string, broken at the end where it had been round his neck. Just *when* he had got away I don't know. I had had him at the main crossroads and Ann had had him when we were nearly at Chatton, so whether he had escaped in the general hullabaloo of our arrival one couldn't tell.

Ann was quite ready to go off and find him, in fact so was I, because cold and hungry as we were we couldn't bear not to have the prospect of returning him and getting the enormous feed and the gold tie-pins at Moss Hall, but our heartless parents wouldn't hear of it.

So we were dragged off to our respective homes and fed and soaked in baths, and we spent rather a miserable night, alternately sleeping like the dead and wondering what had happened to Ranter.

What had happened to Ranter was eventually revealed. He wasn't the Master's favourite hound. He wasn't Lord and Lady Prance's favourite hound. He wasn't in the hunt at all. He was recovering from hard-pad and was boarded out at the farm where Ann had borrowed the fork from the woman she thought wasn't pleasant, and when he escaped from us he made his way home and they never even knew anything had happened to him.

But worse was to follow. The woman at the farm complained to the Master that a girl from the Hunt (which Ann certainly was not) had called and borrowed a fork and hadn't even had the good manners to take it back but had left it out on the common where it had been picked up dirty and rusted. Every woman in the Hunt took this to heart (including Susan Pyke) and began to say, who could it have been, and poor Ann nearly pined away with her guilty secret. It was as bad as being sent out of the field for unsportsmanlike behaviour.

I wondered what I could do about it, and then to my surprise one Saturday morning I saw the Master himself, going into the corn merchant's in Chatton main street. Without thinking I shot in after him, and because I didn't know how on earth I was going to speak to him I just got in his way as much as possible in the hope that he would speak to me.

After he had fallen over me about five times in a very patient way I couldn't bear it any longer and squeaked, 'Oh, I am sorry!'

'You seem to be rather all over the shop, young woman,' he said, not unpleasantly, and I was so overcome that I stepped backwards into a sack of Spratt's Ovals and brought the whole lot down. As I staggered about, I managed to capsize a pile of cat powders and nearly finished up in a meal bin.

'I say, what *is* this?' said Colonel Swift.

I shoved my hair back with the front of my arm (my hands were full of cat powders) and said all in one breath, 'Oh, I must tell you, it was me – I – that forgot the fork, not anybody from the Hunt.'

'I beg your pardon?' he said.

I went on like a river in spate, 'I sent Ann to the farm for the fork and I'd never have forgotten it but it was dark by the time we'd dug the hound out, and there's been such an awful fuss and it wasn't anything to do with the Hunt, it was me, and then the hound got away so we hadn't anything to show, and I'm so glad I saw you because I simply had to explain, because of Ann.'

'I don't exactly follow you,' said the Master, 'but I'm getting a glimmer. Is this something to do with the day of the meet? You're not telling me you followed hounds, or did you?'

'In a sense, yes,' I said, 'but actually no, because chil – I mean, juniors weren't allowed, but we kept catching up with the laggards and had to hold back so as not to be really in the field.'

'Excuse me,' interrupted a woman rather coldly, 'but could I possibly get served with some duck rings as I have to catch a bus?'

I thought for a minute the Master was going to wave me aside and insist on being served, as it was really his turn, but to my amazement and delight he stepped aside and said, 'If this is anything to do with the meet I want to hear about it. Now, young woman, take a deep breath and try and tell me what you're talking about.'

So I poured it all out. It sounded a frightful jumble and my breath was coming in what the books call thick pants (I'd always wondered what that was, and now I knew), but I managed to tell him everything that had happened on that dismal day.

'So all the trouble arose from having given up a lot

of time to tracing and digging out a hound trapped in a rabbit hole,' he said thoughtfully. 'No one ever told me that.'

'Nobody knew,' I said. 'The ghastly hound got away and went back home and we hadn't any evidence.'

'Let me see, what's your name?'

'Jill Crewe,' I gasped, and with terrific presence of mind added, 'and I represent Mrs Darcy's equitation establishment.'

'And a very good place to represent too,' said the Master to my delight. 'I've noticed that the boys and girls turned out by the excellent Mrs Darcy are neat and sportsmanlike, and they can ride.'

Will you believe me, this interview was so much like a fairytale already that I flung caution to the winds and the next minute I was telling this distinguished and magnificent man all about the Boost Mrs Darcy club.

He smiled and said, 'Young woman, you needn't worry. I'll tell you something for your encouragement, worth always wins in the end. Don't envy other people, never show bad feeling or resentment, just stick at your job of riding in the very best way you possibly can. Good riding and good manners are never showy but they will stand the test of time, while showy riding and false manners fade out and disappear. You can tell your school friends what I say.'

'Oh, I will!' I gasped. 'Gosh, I think you're wonderful!'

He smiled in the nicest, most understanding way, and I was so overcome that I stood on one leg and wiggled the other about, and over went the Spratt's Ovals again. Then he burst out laughing and so did

I, and when the shopman not unnaturally looked a bit peeved, Colonel Swift just said, 'We seem to be knocking your dog biscuits about. Just send the whole sack up to my house, will you?'

Then, believe me or believe me not, this highly distinguished man and I left the shop together and I would have given anything for the whole school to have seen me at that moment.

He then shook hands with me – me! – and said finally, 'Tell your friend Miss Derry not to give the matter another thought. Neither she nor you have a stain on your characters as horsewomen and I'm extremely grateful to you for your public-spirited action in digging out the hound. Good luck with your riding!'

'Oh, thank you!' I gasped.

I stood there muttering 'thank you' long after he was gone, and then I pelted off to tell Ann and Mummy, and I wouldn't have changed places with the Queen of England.

7 Just ducks

You may or may not remember that while I was in the corn merchant's a woman came in to buy rings for ducks. I hardly noticed her at the time but she turned out to be Diana Bush's aunt who had a farm at Corbridge a few miles away, and I little knew that I was one whom Fate had destined to put those rings on those ducks.

When I told my friends at school about the amazing interview I had had with the Master of Foxhounds at first they could hardly believe me, but as the meaning of his noble words dawned upon them they realised that this was the best boost the Boost Mrs Darcy Club had ever had.

The next Saturday Diana asked me to ride over to Corbridge with her to see her aunt's farm.

'It will be a good ride for Rapide,' she added.

Yes, I was riding Rapide at last. I had put in a good deal of work on him and he was responding quite well, and though I couldn't make myself feel very fond of him I had to admit that he hadn't let me down.

I would much rather have ridden Black Boy that Saturday, but Diana had said Rapide – it was amazing how all my friends seemed to be such supporters of my peculiar pony – so Rapide it had to be.

Saturday was a glorious day, still and golden, and though the trees were bare their branches made a lovely lacework against the blue sky. It was the sort of day you would like to get in the summer, but don't.

Rapide looked almost happy and when Diana presented him with an apple she had brought for him he flapped his eyelashes at her as much as to say, 'Come, things are looking up.' We rode happily along the grass verge of the road towards Corbridge, and Diana told me that her aunt, Miss Bush, was a bit weird but very kind-hearted, which I think is a good way of describing most aunts. She ran this farm on lines of her own which were so odd that she couldn't get any experienced people with fixed ideas to work for her, but that didn't worry her. She was a whale for work and went at it herself from five in the morning to eleven or so at night, and was always full of beans and saying things like, 'Cheers, chaps!' and 'Up, boys, and at 'em.' She usually had some friend with farmy ideas staying with her, and they would work together as long as the friend could stick it. When she had had enough another friend would turn up, and so it went on.

'Mummy said I was to be sure and ask if there was anything I could do to help,' said Diana, 'so don't let me forget. If I forget, cough at me or wiggle your nose or something. I suppose you wouldn't mind helping a bit?'

'Oh, I'd like to,' I said. 'Only I haven't much patience with hens.'

'I've always wanted to lead a bull,' said Diana. 'Preferably at a Show, but anywhere would do for practice.'

'All right, you can,' I said, as Rapide, enjoying himself, broke into a canter and carried me ahead.

'That was nice, Rapide,' I said, patting him encouragingly, 'so don't look as if you thought you'd done wrong.'

At last we came in sight of Miss Bush's farmhouse. It was just like ones you see in pictures, made of mellow red brick with twisty chimneys, with a porch over the door where roses had climbed in summer. Diana said that her aunt had made it that way, and had even twisted the once-straight chimneys, but I don't know whether that was strictly true. There was a cobbled yard and just a few small farm buildings, because Diana said the whole place was only about twenty acres, which I suppose is quite enough if you want to do farming in an odd way on lines of your own.

Miss Bush saw us from afar and came rushing out to greet us, and at once I recognised her as the woman who had asked for duck rings at the corn merchant's.

When I am going to meet anybody new I always make up my mind beforehand what they are going to look like, and as I am always wrong I don't think I can have much of what they call intuition. I had pictured Diana's aunt as tall and thin with a long nose and the peering kind of spectacled eyes that you would find in anybody who sat up at nights with sick cows by the light of a dim lantern. Instead she was short and thick, the same thickness all the way down, and she had a round red face and a thick tweed coat and skirt that was so thick it hadn't any shape in it at all, and wellington boots and a red beret on the back of her head.

She waved to us as though welcoming an ocean liner and shouted out, 'Cheers, chaps! Come and eat! Jolly nice ponies, what!'

We liked the idea of eating and we were soon sitting round a table putting away sausages and chips and baked apples with brown sugar in the middle, along with Miss Bush – who said everything was either ripping or topping – and a friend who was staying with her called Mrs Dulbottle.

Diana and I were trying to hide our giggles over this weird name when Miss Bush said, 'Now where's that daughter of yours? I don't intend the good old chap to work herself to death and miss her meals.'

She then strode heartily to the back door and gave a yell of 'Mercy! Mercy!'

Diana and I nearly jumped out of our skins, thinking Miss Bush had been attacked, but suddenly there appeared a very lanky girl of about sixteen with a bucket in her hand, and it turned out that she was helping Miss Bush on the farm while she convalesced after some disease or other, and she was Mrs Dulbottle's daughter and her name was therefore the unfortunate one of Mercy Dulbottle.

Diana and I were so sorry for Mercy, who seemed a bit dim – and who could wonder with a name like that? – that we didn't wince at being introduced as 'two ripping girls, one of them's my niece'.

After dinner Miss Bush jumped up, nearly knocking off her red beret which she had worn all the time, and cried, 'Come, come, my hearties, there's work to be done!'

This meant washing-up, which we quickly did, and then we all went round the farm. This didn't take long as there wasn't much to see, ten dairy cows in a sort of cowish place where they were kept, two pigs asleep in a dark corner, and a lot of hens that got under our feet.

Miss Bush kept telling us how happy she was and

how this farm was the dream of her life come true, and I thought it was jolly nice that somebody's dream had come true and hoped that mine would – I mean, about being a champion show-jumper, etc.

We admired everything terrifically, and Diana said, fancy having a farm and no place for horses, where-upon her aunt explained that there had been two stalls but she had turned them into a garage for her car, and this struck us as such a soulless thing to do that we were smitten dumb, which was a good thing considering what we might have said.

Then we drifted back to the house, and Miss Bush said, 'And why aren't you two chaps at school this afternoon?'

We pointed out that it was Saturday, and she just said, 'Oh,' as if she didn't bother about such mere things as the days of the week.

Suddenly I remembered that Diana hadn't said any-thing about what her mother told her about asking if she could do anything to help, so I coughed several times and wiggled my nose.

Diana said, 'What's the matter with you? – Oh, I see! Auntie, is there anything we could do to help while we're here?'

'Oh, I say, chaps, that's simply topping of you,' said Miss Bush in her own peculiar language. 'I wonder now – by Jove, I have it! The ducks!'

She then explained that she had two dozen young ducks on Corbridge Marshes which needed ringing, and she simply hadn't had the time to get over there and do them, but seeing we had the horses didn't we think it would be rather fun?

I didn't really see Rapide capering about on marshes in search of ducks, but Diana was thrilled at the idea, and as Mercy said she would like to come too, on her bicycle, we all set off. Mercy had the rings in a box in her trouser pocket and very pretty they were too, made of mauve plastic.

When we first got to the marshes we couldn't see any ducks at all, but presently one came shooting out of some reeds and we all dashed after it. We soon caught it up and it looked scared to death, as well it might. By the time Diana and I were off our ponies, Mercy – who preferred to dash out on foot – had caught the duck and we all assisted at putting the ring on its foot. Actually it took all three of us to perform this simple task, one to hold the duck, one to hold its foot, and one to push the ring over its knuckle – or whatever ducks call their joints.

When the ring was on it looked very pretty, and the duck looked quite self-conscious and vain, so we let it go and it whizzed out of sight.

It took us two hours to round up and ring eleven ducks. Then unfortunately we started catching the same ducks over again.

'We were mugs,' said Diana, 'not to put the ones we had ringed into that hut over there until we'd got the lot. This is the third time I've caught that green one with a squint. Let's start from now, putting them in the hut.'

So we started catching all we could, ringed or unringed, and Diana and I on our ponies carried them squawking madly to the hut and fastened them in.

At last there were only four ducks left to catch, and as dusk was falling it seemed an impossible task.

'There just aren't any more ducks on this marsh,' I said. 'They must have flown off to Africa.'

'Look!' yelled Diana. 'There are three together, in the reeds!'

We swooped down on the unfortunate cluster of

ducks like Red Indians on the warpath. Our ponies seemed to be enjoying this game tremendously, even Rapide.

'Gosh!' I cried. 'Will you look at this?'

I held up the duck I had caught. It was wearing a mauve plastic ring.

'Mine has one on too,' said Diana. 'That's funny. We shut them all in the hut.'

What do you think? Mercy, who I told you was a bit dim, hadn't shut the door of the hut properly, and when we went back to see there wasn't a single duck left in there at all.

It was now nearly dark and we knew it was no good spending the next two or three hours rounding up ducks which were already ringed in the hope of catching four that weren't.

'We'd better get back to the farm,' said Diana. 'Anyway, we've done our best. I wish we could have finished it and got those other four. You'll have to come down and have a go by yourself, Mercy.'

'Oh dear, it's all my fault!' said Mercy miserably, sounding as if she was going to cry.

'Oh, buck up,' I said, 'and don't be so dank.'

I know it was rather cheeky of me to talk like this to somebody sixteen, but strangely enough Mercy did buck up – as I could not have done with a name like that – and told us a lot of funny stories which were very funny indeed, though I couldn't remember one of them afterwards. Isn't it funny how you never can remember funny stories when you try to tell them to anybody after?

Listening to the stories we weren't looking where we were going, which is silly on a marsh, and Rapide and Sylvia were soon up to their knees in a bog. They stuck there, and while Mercy stood and yelled, Diana and I had to flop off into the bog and drag our ponies out. By this time most of the bog was on us and we carried it home. It was rather smelly bog too, and Mercy kept saying, 'Oh dear, you do smell!' which made us sorry we had been kind to her.

When we got back to the farm we told Miss Bush the whole story and how sorry we were about the other four ducks that we couldn't catch. Mercy didn't let on about leaving the hut door open, which we thought she might have owned up to, seeing we were so late.

'How many did you ring?' said Miss Bush.

'Twenty.'

'Well, that's all there were, my hearties,' said Miss Bush with a beam.

'But we've got four rings over,' I gasped. 'You said there were two dozen.'

'Two dozen rings, I meant,' she said, pulling off her beret, wringing it about in her fingers, and putting it back crooked on her head. 'Not two dozen ducks, old chap. Only twenty.'

'Can you beat it?' said Diana, as we trotted home through the dark lanes with red rear lights at our stirrup leathers. 'And now I expect we shall get into a row for being late home. That's what comes of helping people.'

However, when we got to our cottage fortunately Mummy was out and had left the key on the hook in Black Boy's stable and a note on the kitchen table to say she had gone to the Women's Institute. So we rang up Diana's mother and fortunately she had gone to the Women's Institute too, so nobody ever knew what time we got back. We made dripping toast for tea – at least I made it while Diana obligingly rubbed down both ponies and gave them a feed

– and we sat over the fire and ate, and it was gorgeous.

'I was just thinking,' said Diana, 'if I had to marry somebody called Mr Dulbottle what I should call my daughter. I think something frightfully harmless like Mary, so you'd hardly notice it at all.'

'Or else something terrific like Veronica or Esmeralda that would bang people in the eye before they had time to catch on to the Dulbottle part of it,' I said. 'Anyway, not Mercy.'

'She was a blot, wasn't she? But it was a smashing ride and the ponies loved duck-hunting. Didn't Rapide do well?'

'He wasn't bad at all,' I admitted.

8 Our Christmas

Christmas came, and Mummy had kept her promise to give me two loose-boxes. The old stable was pulled down, and while this was being done we could eat nothing at the cottage but boiled eggs as the wind was our way, laden with lime, mortar, ancient dust, and bits of everything under the sun. However, the new place was simply superb with its own little harness room and fodder room, and the doors were painted green, and it was the most magnificent present anybody ever had.

With Black Boy's head looking out over one half-door and Rapide's over the other I was so impressed that I tried to draw a picture, and Ann helped me and put in all the finishing touches.

Then I invited all my friends to come for tea and the official opening, which was performed by Martin Lowe who taught me to ride. Mr and Mrs Lowe came too – you have read about them in my other books – and Mrs Darcy and Zoe and Wendy, and all my school friends and some of their parents. After the opening which was out of doors, of course, Mr Derry, Ann's father, gave us a talk on horsemanship and always considering our ponies before ourselves, then Mrs Darcy was asked to make a speech and she said, cheer up, it wouldn't be long until summer and the pony shows, and then we all went inside the cottage and had an enormous tea with iced Christmas cake and mince pies.

Mrs Darcy started telling everybody the story of Rapide and the Disgusting Penberthys, realising too late that this was all news to Mummy.

'Oh dear,' she said. 'Have I dropped a brick? I only wanted people to know that Jill has done a good job on this pony who had such a bad start in life.'

'Jill, you never told me this,' said Mummy. 'Is it really true that poor Rapide was badly treated? I remember how the day he came I offered him a carrot and he didn't seem to know what to do with it. How pathetic! To think that nobody had ever been kind to him before!'

'I think that people who can be unkind to ponies ought to be slowly tortured to death,' said Ann indignantly.

'No, that isn't the right way,' said her father. 'They must be taught to be more thoughtful and understanding. Cruelty to animals is more often thoughtlessness than deliberate beastliness, and it is up to you children to teach and educate other youngsters in kindness, and to give your whole-hearted support to all organisations that work for animals' welfare.'

'I haven't been as nice as I should to Rapide,' I confessed to Mummy after all our guests had gone, 'because I resented the fact that he didn't seem to like me, but that wasn't his fault and I ought to have been more patient. I don't think I shall ever love him as I do Black Boy, but I am getting fonder of him, and now he's got the idea that I'm not a blackhearted horse-butcher we may see some results. I used to think his action was very queer, but when Zoe rides him he doesn't look bad at all.'

'I thought he looked very well indeed, when you were riding him yesterday,' said Mummy, and knowing that she would not flatter or say anything that wasn't strictly true I was quite relieved.

After this superb Christmas present she had given me I felt that anything I gave Mummy would be an anticlimax. However, I had saved twenty pounds of my last summer's prize money on purpose to buy her something rather special, and I spent it on a very rich-looking white brocade cushion for her bedroom from a shop that appeared to be the kind of place that furnished palaces.

It was worth every penny of the twenty pounds when I saw this queenly cushion sitting on the blue chair in Mummy's room, and she was thrilled and kept walking round it and touching it and saying it was the crowning touch to her blue-and-white room, because though we live in a cottage our ideas are not entirely folk-weavish.

As for my other presents, by some strange trick of fate they nearly all turned out to be handkerchiefs. As I opened mysterious parcels in the cold light of that Christmas dawn and more and more handkerchiefs fell upon my bed I began to think I was under a spell, like people in fairytales. Of course I could understand getting handkerchiefs from rather soulless people like my Aunt Primrose and my cousin Cecilia (of whom you have read in my previous books) and handkerchiefs I got, six white linen ones of a rather dainty size with a white J. for Jill in the corner; but when it came to Ann Derry I just couldn't guess what she was thinking about! The six she sent me were jolly big ones and would come in for stable rubbers, but why shouldn't a horsy person *send* another horsy person stable rubbers and have done with it?

Mrs Lowe, Martin's mother, had also sent me handkerchiefs. Seven of different colours with the name of the day of the week in the corner, upon which day I suppose that particular handkerchief had to be used. I began to wonder if some awful Fate would befall the careless person who used the wrong handkerchief on the wrong day. In any case it would probably put you off pretty badly if you pulled out your handkerchief and found it said Monday when you knew perfectly well it was Saturday.

When I went into Mummy's room and told her about all these handkerchiefs she laughed like anything and said it was a judgment on me for all the hundreds I had lost in a long and energetic lifetime. Then we heard Mrs Crosby (No Relation to Bing) letting herself in downstairs and I went down to give her her present. Then she gave me what she had brought for me, which was a handkerchief, an enormous yellow cotton one with red horses' heads all over it. Apart from the fact that I have never seen a horse with a bright scarlet head and an expression like a dying parrot, the whole thing was very practical, and because it was so large I could see it coming in useful for all kinds of emergencies, even for joining a broken girth if I should ever be so unlucky as to suffer such a frightful disaster.

I might add that not all my presents were handkerchiefs. For instance, when I opened Diana Bush's parcel I found she had given me a tin of saddle soap, which is a jolly good present for any pony-owner, only it happened that my present to Diana was also a tin of saddle soap.

I found that with two ponies to look after now I had to work very hard, but it was worth it. I exercised them in turn, because I found they both hated being led while I rode the other one, and on Boxing Day morning it happened to be Rapide's turn.

It was a good morning for riding and Rapide was very cheerful, which in this case took the form of throwing his head and making faces. I soon discouraged that and we cantered along happily on the grass verge. Just as I was thoroughly enjoying myself I saw somebody leaning in a miserable sort of way against a field gate and chewing the stalk of a dead chestnut leaf.

It was Wendy Mead, the girl who helped Mrs Darcy with the riding school.

'Hello, Jill,' she said in the dim sort of way one does say hello when one is not enjoying one self and other people are.

I drew in Rapide, who looked around as much as to say, What on earth are we stopping for?

'What's the matter, Wendy?' I said.

'Oh, nothing,' she said. 'Only Mrs Darcy has had a telegram. She has to go and look after her brother's horses in London while her brother has an operation, so it means the riding school will be closed for about a fortnight. You see, there's only me and Joey and all we can do is look after the ponies. It'll be awfully dull.'

'What about Zoe?' I said.

'Oh, didn't you know? Zoe went home for Christmas and she isn't coming back. Her people want her.'

'I call that rugged,' I said, and rode on thoughtfully.

About half an hour later I met Diana Bush and her brother James coming back from a ride over Neshbury Common and I told them the news.

'Oh, but the riding school can't possibly be closed,' said Diana. 'People will hate to miss their lessons, especially those who are keen on entering for the Hunter Trials. And some of the beginners might even leave and go to Lime Farm if they can't get their usual lessons. I think it would be disastrous to close the riding school for a whole fortnight. We've nearly got a new pupil for Mrs Darcy too, haven't we, James? A boy who's come to live next door to us.'

'I think it would be disastrous too,' I said. 'You remember those notices we put in the new girls' desks and got kept in for? Well, they weren't all wasted because Rhoda Richardson – '

'Rhoda *who*?'

'That tall girl with big ears in Four A. She's much nicer than she looks. She said that if her mother would let her learn to ride after Christmas she'd go to Mrs Darcy's. Well, it's after Christmas, isn't it?'

'It's the Christmas holidays,' said James, 'when naturally everybody wants to have a lot of lessons. It's pretty awful if a riding school isn't open in the holidays.'

James spoke very knowledgeably as he was sixteen and had won Class C jumping at Chatton Show the previous summer, which I think was a terrific achievement.

'Listen,' I said in an inspired sort of way. 'What's to stop us running the school ourselves if Mrs Darcy will let us?'

'Us?' said Diana looking a bit stunned.

'We could, you know,' said James. 'The more experienced riders mainly want to practise the sort of jumps they'll get in the Hunter Trials and I know all about that sort of thing, so I could at least help them a bit, and you girls could manage the beginners blindfolded. It would be something to do and we'd get heaps of riding.'

'Oh, do you think Mrs Darcy would let us?' said Diana. 'I mean, we are pretty experienced and we know her ways of teaching – '

'Let's go round there and see,' I said, beginning to feel very excited.

When we confronted Mrs Darcy with the idea she started making difficulties, as people over the age of forty always seem to do as a matter of course, though perhaps I am libelling Mrs Darcy in suggesting she was over forty. I don't think she could have been really, as she was quite healthy and not at all bowed with age. However, underneath it all I could see she hated the idea of having to close the riding school for a fortnight and was ready to grasp at any straw.

'I don't suppose you could do any actual harm,' she said slowly. 'But you'll find it rather a bind.'

'Oh, no, we shan't,' we all said in a chorus, and Wendy Mead started brightening up and said she thought it was a brilliant idea.

'Well, provided your parents consent you can try it,' said Mrs Darcy, and we all said there wasn't a doubt about their consenting as they liked to see us doing something useful in the holidays.

So it was all arranged and we spent that evening writing postcards to all the pupils saying that lessons would continue as usual in Mrs Darcy's unavoidable absence, under the tuition of well-qualified teachers, with particular attention to those who wished to practise for the Hunter Trials.

On the first morning after Mrs Darcy had gone we all turned up at the stables before it was light, so as to give Wendy a hand and to look keen. I came to the conclusion that there is nothing gives you the needle so much as responsibility, but as the day wore on Diana and I got into the way of things and didn't do anything awful, and James was so busy building his jumps that we hardly saw him.

You would hardly believe that there were human beings so dim as to be practically incapable of keeping their heels down, or their knees up, or their hands down or their heads up, and yet I seemed to be coping with such people hour after hour. The beginners weren't so bad, they were at least humble, but it was the people who had had three lessons and thought they could ride who gave all the trouble. There was one girl called Jennifer Jackson who actually tried to canter with her toes down, her elbows out like teapot handles, and her chin sitting on the knot of her tie, and just as I was going to tell her how truly awful she looked she piped out, 'Mother says that now I can ride she's coming to watch me.'

I feared that if her mother should see what I saw she would collapse and die.

I said, 'Jennifer, do hold your head up. I've told you before.'

Jennifer gave a lurch which caused her unfortunate pony to stagger – he was her own pony – and said, 'There! That's what happens when I try to hold my head in that awkward position you taught me.'

'Of course that will happen,' I said, trying to sound calm and cool, 'if you don't keep your heels down.'

'If I keep my heels down,' said Jennifer rather crossly, 'my knees sort of come up.'

'So they should,' I pointed out. 'And do put your elbows to your sides, Jennifer.'

'Oh, I can't ride like that,' said Jennifer. 'I feel like a brown paper parcel.' And off she went again, looking *exactly* like a brown paper parcel that is coming untied.

I felt very hot indeed by teatime, much hotter than Diana who had had quite a good time with the Shetland pony crowd, aged six or seven.

'You've had the best of it,' I said.

'Don't you believe it!' she said going bright red. 'I had one little beast who yelled, "Hold the nasty pony's head like Nanny does while I get on!" It turned out that his big fat nanny practically smothered the pony with both arms and her apron while the horrible child climbed up him as if he was a stone wall. I was simply livid. I said, "Nobody's going to hold the pony's head, and it's you that's nasty, and either you learn to mount him decently or you needn't bother to come here any more."'

'Oh, I say, you'd better be careful,' I said in a fright. 'Supposing he doesn't come any more! We simply can't afford to lose any of Mrs Darcy's pupils, even if they are little beasts.'

'Yes, Di, you've got to be frightfully tactful when you're running a riding school,' said James coming up. 'I've found that out already. You should have heard me! I think I'm destined to be an ambassador or a royal courtier or something. I had people this afternoon who've got as much chance of completing the course at the Hunter Trials as I have of winning the open jumping at Wembley. But I just took a big swallow and said, "Quite good, quite good."'

'Then I think you're a galumphing great hypocrite!' said Diana to her brother. 'You're downright dishonest and that's one thing you can't be in a riding school, isn't it, Jill?'

'Well, I think you can sort of strike the happy

medium,' I said and Diana said, 'What's a medium anyway, and why should it be happy, and how do you strike it when you can't see it?'

9 Running the riding school

The next day we made a duty rota, so that we shouldn't all be working at the same time, and Wendy and I went on for the afternoon.

'Help!' said Wendy. 'Here come the Fisher twins – *and* their mother!'

I didn't know the Fisher twins, who turned out to be a boy called George and a girl called Georgina who were ten years old and brought their own ponies, which were beautifully groomed, not by them it turned out but by their father's groom. All their tack was new and beautiful and shining, the sort of tack I'd have all the time if I could afford it.

Mrs Fisher was small and fair and all smiles, but she had rather a warlike expression.

'I thought I'd come along with the children,' she said, 'as Mrs Darcy isn't here. I want to see that they're properly taught. It's so important that they shouldn't learn anything the wrong way at this stage.'

'I'm going to begin jumping today,' said Georgina, who looked much more like a boy than George, who looked much more like a girl than Georgina.

'Oh, but you can't,' said Wendy. 'You've only had four riding lessons.'

'But I don't agree with that attitude at all, not at all,' said Georgina's mother, looking sweet in a rather horrid way. 'I think it's so wrong to check a child and

Georgina doesn't know fear. Why, the first time I was ever on a horse I was only seven years old. My uncle picked me up and put me on his great black mare, and said "Away you go" – pointing to a hedge that must have been over five feet high. And of course, knowing no fear, I just clung on and over I went, like a bird. After that I could jump anything.'

During this improbable story I stood with my mouth slightly open, but when Mrs Fisher had finished Wendy had the presence of mind to say in a matter of fact way, 'Well, Georgina won't go over anything like a bird so long as she keeps on losing her stirrups. Look at your feet, Georgina! And do try to keep your heels down. Anyway, you're not nearly ready to jump.'

'Yes, Georgina, you really must keep your heels down, dear, and I think it's quite wrong of Miss Wendy to tell you to look at your feet. Mrs Darcy always says, keep your head up,' said Mrs Fisher.

'I didn't meant it like that,' said Wendy going scarlet.

'Now that's very nice, Georgina, very nice indeed!' said Mrs Fisher. 'Come along, dear. Sit well back.'

'You mean, sit well forward,' I said, quite unable to bear this.

Mrs Fisher glared at me, and said, 'Now dear, let Mother see a smart trot.'

I thought, who's supposed to be giving this lesson, anyway?

But Wendy firmly took Georgina's rein and said, 'Let's start from the beginning again. Georgina, your seat is awful and your hands are anywhere but where they ought to be. You look as if you were playing the piano.'

She then began to get Georgina organised and just

when she had got her into something like a decent position the horrible child said, 'If I can't jump I'm not going to ride. I'm going home.'

'Oh, no, darling, oh, you must be a good girl!' cried Mrs Fisher, dancing round in a flappish sort of way. 'Do it nicely, just for Mother.'

'I won't,' said Georgina, and began to slither off her pony, while Mrs Fisher grabbed her and tried to push her back. Wendy and I stood by helpless, looking at this awful exhibition and thinking what we would do to Georgina if we could have her alone and at our mercy for five minutes.

After a good deal of undignified heaving Mrs Fisher won the day, and when she had Georgina back in the saddle looking like a sack of potatoes with a scowl on its face, she turned to us panting and said, 'She's so highly strung, that's the trouble. You have to know how to deal with her. But highly strung people make the very best riders. I'm sure she's going to be wonderful. I do hope you'll keep on telling her that, Miss Wendy. Highly strung people need such a lot of encouragement.'

'If you want me to go on with the lesson,' said Wendy, keeping her temper remarkably well, 'we'd better go back to the beginning, and first of all I shall want Georgina to walk a circle.'

'I don't want to,' said Georgina with an even heavier scowl. 'It's babyish. I won't walk a circle.'

'Need she?' said Mrs Fisher. 'I mean, it's like being a beginner all over again, isn't it?'

'It may surprise you,' I said, chipping in, 'to know that even the best riders usually begin schooling by walking a circle. It's good for the pony.'

'Georgina darling,' said Mrs Fisher, 'do walk a circle, just to please Mother.'

'I will if I can jump afterwards,' said Georgina stubbornly.

I'm afraid I should have told her to take her Frightful Little Self straight home, but Wendy who had a great deal more patience said, 'All right then, I'll put a bar at eighteen inches and you can try it, if your mother wants you to. You'd better come with me now, and walk a circle.'

'Oh, all *right*,' said Georgina rather rudely, and starting off jerkily followed Wendy to the marked out circle in the level field that was the riding school.

I realised now with a sinking heart that I was left to cope with George, who all this time had been sitting on his pony fiddling with some Meccano parts.

'I must tell you about George,' said Mrs Fisher. 'I think he's rather special. I'm not saying that because he's my own child, but I do think he has the look of a first-rate rider, and I feel that with the right coaching he'll be able to compete with *anybody* when the gymkhanas begin next summer.'

'How many lessons has he had?' I asked.

'Six.'

'He's got quite a long way to go,' I said tactfully.

'Ah, but wait till you see him,' said Mrs Fisher proudly. 'He's going to win every single event next summer, aren't you, George?'

(I hope not! I thought.)

George put the Meccano parts in his pocket and sat up very straight on his pony. He certainly looked much better than his sister.

'Look at his hands,' said Mrs Fisher. 'Beautiful. So light and sensitive. You have to be born with hands like that.'

George's hands didn't look any different from

any other beginner's hammy ones, but I didn't say anything.

'He's much more advanced than his sister,' said Mrs Fisher. 'Come along, George, let's see some action.'

Action was hardly the word for what happened next. To my horror, for I had been in a kind of daze up to now, I saw that George carried a full-size hunting crop and this he brought down with a whack on his unfortunate pony's flank, and off they went at a pace I can only describe as an uncontrolled lope with George bouncing about in the saddle and using his beautiful, sensitive hands every now and then to push himself off the pony's neck.

'Isn't he spirited?' said Mrs Fisher.

'He's got a lot to learn,' I said firmly. 'For one thing, he isn't allowed to use a hunting crop, or even a stick while he's schooling. And for another you can see the daylight between his legs most of the time. And he mustn't stick his feet out like that! And he hasn't really got a bit of control over his pony – look at that!'

George's headlong career had brought him to the verge of colliding with his sister's pony, now walking in a passable manner round the circle under the direction of Wendy. He leaned back and dragged on the reins, the pony threw back his head in an outraged sort of way and dipped his haunches, and the next minute George was rolling about on the grass.

'If he did that at a gymkhana,' I could not resist saying, 'everybody would die with laughing.'

That really did make Mrs Fisher look a bit worried.

'I'm afraid he'll have to go a bit slower,' she said, 'but he'll find it very boring.'

At this point Wendy came to the rescue and said, 'Look, Mrs Fisher, I really think it unsettles the children to have you watching. Couldn't you come back for them later?'

I held my breath for fear Mrs Fisher would refuse, but after a moment she said, 'All right. I'll come back in half an hour. But do give them a really good lesson. I mean, if it's just riding round and round in a circle they can do that at home.'

I refrained from saying that if they would do that at home they'd probably begin to learn a little bit about the principles of riding, and off she went.

After that we got on a bit better. George wasn't a difficult boy at all when I got him alone, and though he had so many faults that I hardly knew where to begin he was keen to learn. Meanwhile Wendy put the bar down and gave Georgina a little elementary instruction about how to sit when jumping. Georgina needless to say took no notice at all, leaned well back, put down her toes, and when by a miracle she found herself on the other side of the jump and still on her pony's back she yelled, 'I've done it. I told you I could. Now put it up to a proper jump.'

'Let's do it,' I said to Wendy, 'just to take her down a peg.'

'Daren't,' said Wendy. 'She'll break her neck.'

'That wouldn't be a great loss to equitation,' I muttered.

However, with her usual great patience Wendy raised the bar to two feet, and George bounced over it gaily, nearly standing in his stirrups, and flopped back on his unfortunate pony's withers with a resounding slap.

Then Georgina tried, lost her stirrups, slithered

over her pony's tail and lay on the ground till Wendy went and picked her up.

'Are you hurt?' said Wendy coldly.

'No,' said Georgina.

'Then you should get up by yourself. And now perhaps you'll realise that you can't jump before you learn to ride.'

'I jumped,' said George. 'I was jolly good.'

'If you jumped like that in a competition,' I said, 'your pony would give you three refusals next time and you couldn't blame him. You looked frightful.'

'Did I?' said George with a faint gleam of intelligence.

'Look,' I said, 'I'll show you how to do it.'

I took Georgina's pony – not George's which showed signs of terror – and did the jump in a reasonably competent way.

'I'll do it like that,' said Georgina. 'Show me how.'

'Not now,' said Wendy firmly. 'Ponies aren't machines and can't go on for ever, especially after the knocking about you give them. If you two are sensible and want to be real riders you'll do just as we tell you in future. Get it out of your heads that you can ride already because you can't. You're terrible, both of you, whatever your mother says. Now do you want to ride properly so that you can enter for competitions and not disgrace yourselves, or don't you?'

'Yes,' muttered George. Georgina said nothing but looked a bit more interested.

'Right,' said Wendy. 'Come tomorrow at the same time, and come by yourselves if possible, and we'll have a proper lesson. Now let me see you mount your ponies and sit exactly as I tell you to.'

They both mounted, not too well, but Wendy got them into position, heads and knees up and heels and hands down.

'There!' she said. 'You look quite decent. Tomorrow you will walk, looking like that. Then in time you will learn to trot and canter, still looking like that. Eventually you will also learn to jump, still looking like that. You get the idea?'

'Yes,' said George.

'Georgina?'

'Yes,' said Georgina.

'You can tell your mother,' said Wendy, 'that you've had a good lesson this morning. I can see her coming. You can go and join her. Slowly!'

George and Georgina rode away at a snail's pace. They didn't look bad at all.

'Oh, Wendy, you are marvellous!' I said. 'I do think you're a good teacher.'

'Whew!' said Wendy, fanning herself with both hands, 'A bit more of that would have killed me.'

By now I had begun to admire Wendy.

'What do we do next?' I said.

'Let me see,' she said, 'I'd better exercise Blue Smoke for half an hour.' (Blue Smoke was Mrs Darcy's own gorgeous hunter.) 'There's a boy called Tom Vale waiting for a lesson, over there. Could you take him? He won't give you any trouble. He does everything you tell him and he's very slow.'

'Do you mean dim?' I said, my heart sinking into my boots.

'No, it's just that he doesn't want to ride and his people make him. He's ready to jump really, but he'll probably pretend he isn't.'

I felt rather sorry for Tom Vale as I saw him coming towards me, looking rather like a cockerel going to its doom, if you know what I mean. He had on jodhpurs and boots that were too big for him. His black velvet cap was also too big for him and his brown tweed coat was much too long. His tie was pulled so tight it creased his collar, and he was very round-shouldered.

I said, 'Hello, Tom, have you got your own pony?'

He said, no, he usually rode Mrs Darcy's Picture.

I said, 'Well, I thought you'd have got him out and saddled by now.'

He said, 'OK, I'll go and do it,' and shuffled off. I got the idea he was trying to put off the evil day.

After about ten minutes he came riding out on Picture.

I said, 'Does it take you ten minutes to saddle up?'

He said, 'Yes, usually.'

I thought, Help!

He sat quite well, but didn't attempt to do anything.

I said, 'What do you want to do today, Tom?' and he said he didn't know.

For this lack of keenness I could have bitten him, but I just said, 'Well, do a collected walk round the circle,' and he did it, correctly, but looking as if he was about to go to sleep.

I said, 'Now show me a trot.'

He started off on the wrong leg, and I brought him back and made him do it properly. He just did it, in a quite mechanical way. He then went right round the circle at a very nice collected trot and came back and stopped by my side. By now poor Picture looked as bored as her rider.

'Miss Wendy says you're ready for jumping,' I said.

'No, I'm not,' he said.

'Look here, Tom,' I said, 'you ride quite well. What's the matter with you?'

'Nothing,' he said.

'It can't be true,' I said, 'that you don't want to ride?'

'Well, I don't,' he said.

I just gasped.

'It's Father,' said Tom. 'He wants me to go in for jumping competitions so that he can watch me, and I'll never be able to. I'll just make a fool of myself.'

Then it all came out. Will you believe me, poor Tom had never seen boys of his own age jumping? His father had taken him to Hickstead to see first-rate show-jumping and had calmly said, 'There! That's what you've got to do.'

Tom was naturally a scared sort of boy and had been very crushed at home, and he had panicked. He was only eleven and he had got the idea that he was going to have to compete with men.

I said, 'Wait a minute,' and I went and consulted Wendy.

I said, 'I know what's the matter with Tom. Tell me, quick, is there a boy of eleven who can jump? Somebody we could get hold of quickly?'

'There's Tony Adams,' she said. 'He's only ten – '

'All the better,' I interrupted. 'Could you phone him and ask him to come round here at once?'

'OK,' she said. 'What's the idea?'

To make a long story short, in about ten minutes Tony Adams came round. I recognised him. I had seen him jumping in children's classes the previous summer and he was quite good.

'Hello, Tony,' I said, 'would you mind getting up on Picture and going round the junior jumps?'

'Could we have them down to two foot six?' he said. 'Picture's only twelve hands.'

So Tony and I dashed round and lowered the wall and pulled the top off the hedge and put the bar to two foot six. Then Tom got down off Picture and Tony got up and away he went.

I could have found a few faults with his jumping, and he knocked a block out of the wall, but the point was he looked as if he was thoroughly enjoying himself and so did Picture. He did the three jumps three times each, and the third round he cleared them all beautifully and came back laughing, and patting Picture.

Tom was looking at Tony with his eyes popping and his mouth open.

'Thanks very much, Tony,' I said. 'How long have you been jumping?'

'Well, last summer was my first season in competitions,' he said. 'I got two seconds and a reserve.'

'What about it, Tom?' I said, with a grin. 'Would you like to try?' Tom gave a gulp and said, 'I'd like to do that, but it looks a bit high.'

'Of course,' I said. 'You'll start on the bar at eighteen inches. Come on, Tony, let's put it down for Tom.'

I could see Tom pulling himself together with a do-or-die look on his face, but he had the pluck to do just as I told him. There he sat looking rather pale, but his seat was right and so were his knees, feet and hands, and Picture took the jump like a floating feather.

When Tom realised that he had actually jumped, you should have seen him! He couldn't believe it.

'I like it!' he said, as though he had expected it to hurt him.

Tony and I started to shriek with laughing, and presently Tom joined in.

'Please can I do it again?' he said.

So he did it again; quite enthusiastically, in fact I had to tell him not to bounce.

'Can I come and have another lesson tomorrow?' he said. 'When are you coming again, Tony?'

I arranged to give them both a jumping lesson during the week, then I sent Tom to unsaddle Picture and give her a rub down.

'My Russian Rabbits!' said Wendy when she saw him doing this, looking so keen and excited. I told her what had happened.

'Well, that's a feather in your cap, Jill,' she said. 'That boy has been coming here for weeks and we couldn't do a thing to rouse his interest. Why on earth couldn't his father have taken him to see some children's jumping instead of plunging him straight into Hickstead and scaring him stiff? I shouldn't be surprised if Tom's a credit to the riding school in next year's events. I'd put his chances before George Fisher's anyway!'

10 The three fats

The next day it was the turn of Diana and James to take the teaching, but I couldn't resist going round in the afternoon to see how they had got on.

They had had a wonderful time. In the morning they had done a little competition with the Babies – which was what we called the under-tens, who were very docile and thought we were grown-ups – and in the afternoon they had collected all the people who wanted to do hacking and didn't want to do schooling, and taken them for a country ride.

'I must say, you've had a jolly easy day compared with mine yesterday,' I said.

'Oh, no, we haven't,' said Diana, because people loathe to be told they've had an easy day.

'I had to do a lot of very tricky teaching,' said James. 'All that lot were simply frightful in traffic, especially a girl called Meadows.'

Wendy gave a shriek of rage, as she was very keen on Phyl Meadows.

'She *was* frightful,' said Diana, sticking up for her brother. 'Her pony was nervous about the bit where the road is up in Charlton Lane, and she hadn't a clue how to steady him down and get him round it. James had to take the rein and lead him.'

'You must have put her off,' said Wendy loftily, 'because I would say that Phyl Meadows is actually the best all-round rider we've got.'

'Coo!' said Diana.

'Doesn't say much for the others,' said James.

'Gosh!' said Wendy. 'What makes you think that you can come up here and criticise the riding?'

'Oh, chuck it, everybody,' I said. 'Either we're trying to run this place or we're not. OK, James and Diana have had a very hard day. And tomorrow it's you and me, James.'

The first lesson for next morning was booked for ten o'clock. I overslept and was late for breakfast. Then I spilt porridge on my jodhpurs, and couldn't find the cleaner and knocked a lot of other bottles over, and Mrs Crosby said if I was her girl things would be different, that they would, and I said, 'What you said just now doesn't make sense'; and she said she was sick and tired of me mixing up the brown polish shoe brush with the black polish shoe brush and she sometimes wondered why she went on.

Just at that moment the telephone rang, and it was Wendy. She sounded rather excited and said, would I mind bringing Black Boy and Rapide with me, as there were three new pupils waiting for a lesson and no ponies for them.

'Help!' I said. 'They're not groomed. I got up late.'

'Well, bring them as they are,' said Wendy, 'and we'll have a go at them here. I'm terrified these three will go away again if they think there aren't going to be ponies for them.'

Fortunately, Black Boy and Rapide didn't look bad. I gave them a quick brush over, and off we went. When I got to Mrs Darcy's there was a scene of wild activity. The two ten o'clock pupils had arrived, and were mounted on the school's own ponies, Cocktail and Picture, while James walked them round the circle, and there before me, as though awaiting their doom and mine, were the three fattest girls you ever saw in your life. They were aged twelve, eleven and nine and they looked just like bouncing balls. They were nicely dressed in very new-looking jodhpurs and coats which looked strained to the uttermost. They said their names were April, May and June Cholly-Sawcutt, and their mother said they were to pay by the hour. Then they handed Wendy the money for their lessons.

I said, 'I don't think I've ever seen you before. Have you lived here long?' and they said, no, only about a fortnight.

Wendy said, how did they hear about the riding school, and April said that their father had asked their neighbour, Mr Vale, if there was any establishment where they wouldn't mind teaching three great lumps to ride because he hadn't the strength himself, and Mr Vale had told them to come to us and ask for Miss Jill, because if she could teach his son Tom to jump she could teach anything from a hippopotamus downwards.

My eyes nearly popped out, and Wendy said to the fat girls, 'Does your father ride, then?' And May said, 'Sort of.'

Wendy screwed her forehead up and said, 'I feel as if I'd heard your name before,' and June said, 'Once heard never forgotten,' and then they all giggled and ended up roaring with laughter.

Wendy said to me, 'I'd better give you a hand with these three,' and she told Joey to saddle Patsy, who was a very sturdy pony, almost a weight-carrier.

Then we started to teach the three to mount. After half an hour the sweat was pouring off us and we were nearly deafened by their yells of laughter, but we had got them up. Black Boy and Rapide kept turning their heads to give me reproachful looks for doing this awful thing to them, though they only had to carry the two younger Cholly-Sawcutts, May and June. Patsy, who looked to be sagging, had April. We spent the next half-hour teaching them to sit properly and then we led them round the circle, while James who had finished teaching stood watching and nearly strangling himself to keep from laughing.

Actually the three girls were quite keen to learn and did everything we told them, only they looked so funny and they were so noisy. I could just picture them in years to come, riding to hounds and yelling till the echoes rang and the whole field was practically unconscious from the din, and being told to shut up by some mythical future Master of Foxhounds, possibly me.

When the hour was up Wendy and I were tottering, and Wendy said she would go and make the elevenses and we would have a heartening drink of cocoa before my next lesson.

When she got back the three fat girls had gone.

'They liked it,' I said. 'They thanked me. They're coming twice a week, Tuesdays and Fridays, and they want to know if they can soon ride well enough to go on a Saturday afternoon hack. They'll be here on Friday at ten, and it's you and Diana to take them.'

Wendy was flapping her eyelashes with excitement. In her hand she held a copy of *Horse and Hound*, a back number, rather battered.

'Look,' she said. 'I can't believe it. I knew I'd heard the name before.'

There was a picture of a man in hunting kit. Underneath it said, 'Captain Cholly-Sawcutt of the British jumping team which has just returned from its triumphant Italian tour. His famous mare, Petronelle, has the distinction of never failing to win a place in any competition this season.'

'Do you think he's their father?' I said with a gasp.

'He'll have to be some relation with a name like that,' said James.

We could hardly wait for Friday, and at ten o'clock when the fat girls turned up for their second lesson we were all there, Wendy, Diana, James and I.

'Oh, yes, that's Daddy,' said April calmly.

'But I asked May if your father rode,' shrieked Wendy, 'and she said, sort of.'

'Well, he only sort of rides,' said May. 'He jumps mostly.'

'You might have told us,' I said, 'that your father was practically one of the most famous men in the world.'

'We never thought you'd be interested,' said June. 'Can I ride Rapide today?'

We all helped the fat girls to mount, almost reverently.

'Clear off, you two,' said Diana to James and me. 'Wendy and I are doing this.'

James and I went and sat on a hurdle, dithering with excitement. Across the mild January air came shrieks of laughter as April, May and June Cholly-Sawcutt yelled encouragement to each other.

'Do you think their father will want to come and see how they're getting on?' said James.

'Shouldn't wonder,' I said. 'We'll get his autograph. The girls at school will go mad.'

'Don't you see, idiot,' said James, 'that the riding school's made for life? "Under the patronage of Captain Cholly-Sawcutt of the British Show-Jumping Team" – Mrs Darcy can put it on her advertisements.'

'But are we?' I said, 'I mean, under his patronage?'

'Of course, you dope. He sends his daughters to be taught here. That's being under his patronage, isn't it?'

'I expect it is,' I said. 'But I don't think Mrs Darcy will put it on advertisements. She hates showing off. She says that good riding is its own advertisement.'

'Well, she can't help being pleased we've got her the Three Fats,' said James. 'I hope she comes back soon before they fall on their noses in the thorn hedge and we lose our reputation as teachers.'

'You'd better stop calling our star pupils the Three Fats,' I said. 'I wonder if there's the slightest chance of their father coming here? I'd die with excitement.'

We talked about the Cholly-Sawcutt girls for days, but though they came regularly for their lessons nothing else was said about their famous father and we didn't like to ask.

Meanwhile I was putting in quite a lot of work on Tom Vale. Tom and Tony had struck up a great friendship and wanted to have their lessons together, and of course nothing could have been better for Tom's riding. Nothing would hold him back. He had made up his mind to be as good as Tony in as short a time as possible, and the fact that Tony was a year younger than he was made him grit his teeth with determination. So Tom got on, and did easy jumps very nicely, and even clamoured for higher ones which I daren't let him try yet.

Then Rhoda Richardson turned up, the girl with big ears in whose desk we had put one of our doomed advertisements. She brought her own pony, at least it was her uncle's pony and he had lent it to Rhoda to learn to ride on. It was a strange-looking pony of a peculiar shade of yellow. It had a very large head, very thin legs, and a depressed expression which wasn't surprising since it had the unfortunate name of Treacle.

Rhoda's legs were too long for Treacle and she did look a bit comic, but as James said, she was a new pupil and we had got to treat her with respect.

He gave her her first lesson himself, and she tried very hard and turned out to be an awfully nice girl.

She asked when she would be able to ride well enough to go for a Sunday afternoon hack with the rest of us, and when she had left Diana said, 'Don't let her, James. She looks so frightful, she'll let us down.'

But James said coldly, 'I shall let her. She'd knock spots off you for keenness, and she's the most decent girl I've taught so far.'

He continued to stick up for Rhoda and Treacle, and I must say they both made a lot of progress and Diana had to shut up, completely squashed. Which proves that you shouldn't laugh at people and think them comic.

Mrs Darcy had hated to leave her hunter, Blue Smoke, and had weighed down Joey and Wendy with instructions about what she had to have and what she hadn't to have, and about what had to be done for her each day and at what time. Joey and Wendy carried out these instructions to the letter. They were always fussing over Blue Smoke, her oats and her blankets, her hay and straw; they spent hours grooming her and examining her feet, and if she had been a frail little baby they couldn't have measured out her food more carefully.

Every day when it was fine Blue Smoke had to have just the right amount of exercise, no more and no less, and only Wendy was allowed to mount her.

Blue Smoke's exercise nearly drove James, Diana and me frantic. To see that beautiful mare ambling round the paddock, for ambling is the only word to describe the pace allowed by Wendy, while passers-by leaned over the gate to watch, was nearly more than we could stand.

One morning while Wendy was dealing with a rather sticky pupil and Joey was leading out the hunter shiningly groomed and blanketed, James said, 'Let me exercise Blue Smoke, Wendy, while you go on with the lesson.'

'Oh, no, James,' said Wendy. 'Nobody's supposed to ride her but me.'

'But that's screwy,' said James. 'Honestly speaking, Wendy, who is the better rider, you or I?'

'Well, you are, of course' – began Wendy, realising what a lot of prizes and cups James had won in his long riding career and how he had finished with children's classes and would be in open classes next season.

'You admit that,' said James, 'and Mrs Darcy knows it, and you know that Mrs Darcy knows it. So it stands to reason that if you can ride Blue Smoke I can.'

'So what?' said Wendy.

'Oh, go on, Wendy, don't be so dim! Let me take her round, just once.'

I think Wendy wanted to avoid being thought stuffy by James, whom she rather admired, so she said, 'Well, only for five minutes, and do be careful.'

James ran off eagerly, and the next minute he was up on Blue Smoke. He looked marvellous and he knew it. He walked the gorgeous mare round the circle, then put her to a canter and did a perfect figure of eight. Wendy couldn't help admiring James's performance, while keeping one eye on the lesson she was giving.

James rode up and dismounted, patting Blue Smoke's neck.

'Oh, James!' I said. 'Could I get up? Just for one minute. I've never sat a hunter like Blue Smoke and I've always dreamed of it.'

'Why not?' he said. 'She's too tall for you, but I'll give you a leg up and adjust the leathers.'

When I found myself actually mounted on Blue Smoke it was the thrill of my life. I walked her very carefully, dithering with excitement and nervousness. By now Wendy had got her pupil down at the far jump and wasn't noticing James and me.

'Wouldn't you like to try a jump?' said James. 'The bar's at three foot and she can do five easily.'

'Gosh, no!' I said. 'I'm coming down.'

I slid down, not too cleverly, and said, 'Do you think she's had enough?'

'Enough!' said James. 'This mare isn't getting enough exercise to keep her ordinarily fit.'

Just at that moment Wendy called me to settle an argument between herself and her pupil. I went haring up the field where the jumps were.

'Ruth says that these jumps aren't as difficult as the ones we shall get in the Hunter Trials,' said Wendy.

'Of course they are!' I said. 'Mrs Darcy told me that if anything they were a bit stiffer.'

'I rode in some Hunter Trials last year,' said Ruth

– who was a girl who was always telling you about the marvellous things she had done at other places – 'where the jumps would have made these look like baby's first lesson. But that was in Leicestershire where they really ride.'

'I wouldn't bother with our Hunter Trials, if I were you,' I said sarkily. 'I mean, nobody over the age of three goes in for them, actually.'

'If you think these jumps are too easy, Ruth,' said Wendy, 'I suggest you let me see you do a clear round and then I can judge what you are capable of.'

Ruth piped down at once, because she knew perfectly well she couldn't do a clear round of our practice jumps.

Suddenly Wendy gave a shriek. I nearly jumped out of my skin and turned round to see if there had been an explosion or something.

All I saw was James on Blue Smoke, sailing over the five-foot hedge which very few of us have ever attempted. He looked magnificent. It was a perfect jump with inches to spare, and he made a perfect landing.

'James! Get down this minute!' yelled Wendy. 'Get down, you idiot. Oh!'

'All right,' said James, calmly, dismounting with a smile. 'Keep your hair on.' He patted Blue Smoke, and said, 'You'd like more of that, wouldn't you, old girl?'

Wendy rushed up and took Blue Smoke by the bridle.

'You'd no business to do that, James,' she said furiously.

'It hasn't done her a bit of harm. Don't be so stuffy, Wendy.'

Wendy said no more, but led Blue Smoke away and handed her over to Joey.

The rest of the morning things were a bit strained, as Wendy was huffy and James was sulking, but I didn't care. All I could think of was how it felt to ride a wonderful hunter of sixteen hands, worth twenty thousand pounds in actual money and about a million pounds in pride to her owner, and I started making mad plans to save twenty thousand pounds. At the rate of two hundred pounds a year – which would be about all I could manage – it would take me just a hundred years. (I wasn't very hot at arithmetic, but even I could do that sum.) I would be a hundred and fourteen years old when I got my hunter. It didn't seem worth the effort.

11 Trouble at Ring Hill

Mummy was very interested in what we were doing at the riding school. She used to say she could hardly wait for each evening to hear about our adventures and our pupils, ghastly and otherwise.

On this particular evening I didn't say anything about Blue Smoke as I felt a bit guilty, and I was afraid Mummy would rub it in as even the best of parents seem as though they can't help doing. I rubbed the ponies down, fed them and put them up for the night. Then I sat over the fire and read a book called *Tschiffely's Ride* which you ought to read if you haven't read it already, as it is about a man who rode two horses across Central America.

Then I had some cocoa and buns and went to bed. Mummy sat up to alter a chapter in her new children's book, which was even more whimsy than usual and still called *Angeline, the Fairy Child*. I mean, much as I admire Mummy's skill as a writer, can you *imagine* anybody called *Angeline, the Fairy Child*? But the publisher was clamouring for Angeline, and the American rights were already sold, so it just shows that it is true what Shakespeare or somebody said, that half the world doesn't know how the other half lives.

I had been asleep and woke to hear the telephone ringing. It felt like the middle of the night, but just then the grandfather clock downstairs struck eleven and I heard Mummy answering the phone.

I heard her say, 'But Jill's in bed and asleep by now, Wendy.'

Some frightful premonition chilled the blood in my veins, as it says in books. I tore downstairs in my pyjamas.

'Is it Wendy?' I said. 'Please let me speak to her.'

'I don't know what she's thinking about, ringing up at this time of night,' said Mummy, in a very parentish voice. 'And you must not rush about the house without your dressing gown, Jill.'

But I had already grabbed the phone and said in a gasping sort of voice, 'What's the matter, Wendy? This is Jill.'

'Oh, Jill!' said Wendy, as if she was crying. 'It's Blue Smoke. She's ill. What shall I do? *Do* come up here!'

I went cold all over.

'Mummy,' I said, 'Wendy wants me to go up there. Blue Smoke, Mrs Darcy's hunter, is ill.'

'But you can't go up there in the middle of the night! Tell Wendy to send for the vet.'

'You don't understand,' I said. 'It's my fault about Blue Smoke, at least partly. I must go. I simply must.'

Mummy stood there looking slightly stunned while I tore about looking for some clothes and a mac and shoes.

'Jill, you *can't*,' she kept saying.

'I've got to,' I said, bashing my way through the kitchen cupboards in search of my bicycle lamps and feeling certain that the batteries would be finished. I found the lamps and they weren't very good, but they did light.

'I think it's perfectly ridiculous,' said Mummy, being thoroughly grown-uppish and not at all understanding, which wasn't really surprising considering

I hadn't told her anything she could understand. 'Racing about the lanes in the middle of the night!'

'I'll be as quick as I possibly can,' I promised. 'I'll just help Wendy to get the vet.'

I rode off into the dark with my bike wobbling all over the place. It was the most frightful moment of my life. I had visions of Blue Smoke being dead when I got there. I couldn't think of anything that I or James had done that could upset her, but we must have done something. I felt ghastly.

I found Wendy sitting on the ground in Blue Smoke's stall, between two lighted hurricane lamps, with Blue Smoke's head on her knee. Wendy had been crying. The mare had her eyes shut, every now and then she quivered and gave a slight moan.

With pedalling furiously up the hill I had stopped being cold all over, but now I went cold all over again.

'Is she dying?' I gasped. 'Where is she hurt?'

'I don't know,' said Wendy, stuttering with cold and misery. 'I've felt her all over but I can't find anything wrong. Oh, why did I let James ride her! Now she'll die and I shall lose my job here and never get another.'

I quite saw Wendy's point, it was awful.

'I can't think of anything that James did to her to cause this,' I said. 'He rides so well. And,' I added miserably, 'I was on her myself for about two minutes. I can't think of anything I did.'

'It must be James's fault,' said Wendy. 'She was all right before.'

'Have you sent for the vet?' I said.

'Yes, of course I rang him, and he's out at some farm with some sordid cow. His wife said she'd send him here if he came back in time.'

'In time for what?' I said.

'In time for Blue Smoke still being alive, I suppose.'
Wendy began to cry very splashily.

I sat down in the straw and sadly stroked Blue
Smoke's cheek. She opened her eye and gave me a
dismal look of woe. I felt frightful. I was sure she
was very ill indeed and though I didn't see how it
could have been James's fault and mine I was sure
it must be. Mrs Darcy would never have anything
more to do with me, the future looked so black.

Joey came creeping in with some colic medicine,
just in case it was colic that was the matter with
Blue Smoke, but when she had had it she didn't seem
any better. Anyway, she didn't seem to have colic. I
thought of that hideous bit in 'How we brought the
good news from Aix to Ghent,' where it says, 'All
of a sudden the roan, rolled neck and crop over, lay
dead as a stone.' I couldn't help wondering if jumping
the five-foot hedge had done to Blue Smoke whatever
it was that riding from Aix to Ghent had done to
the roan.

We were all very miserable. I went into the house
and phoned Mummy to tell her that I was staying
the night with Wendy. I didn't tell her we were
spending the night sitting on the ground in Blue
Smoke's stall.

'I think you might have sent for James as well as
for me,' I grumbled.

'I did,' said Wendy. 'But his father answered the
phone and said James had gone to bed and he wasn't
going to give him any message at that time of the
night. I know James would have come if he'd known.
He'll be furious tomorrow when he knows.'

I couldn't even bear to think of tomorrow.

I suppose we must have fallen half asleep, because

suddenly a big torch was shining in our faces. The vet had arrived.

'Now what's the matter with Blue Smoke?' he said. 'Can't be much. She's usually fit as a fiddle.'

'I think she's dying,' said Wendy. 'We both think so.'

'Well, you girls clear out,' said the vet, cheerfully, 'and let me have a look. Go and make me a cup of tea. I've been sitting up with a cow for hours.'

We thought it was very heartless of the vet to want tea, but we went into the house and made him a cup. We didn't make any for ourselves, it would have choked us. Every time I caught Wendy's eye she gave a gulp, and every time Wendy caught my eye I gave a gulp. We did nothing but gulp at each other. Outside we could hear Joey shuffling up and down in the yard.

I set off down the yard with the vet's cup of tea and it slopped all over into the saucer.

'You dope, you're spilling it all,' said Wendy.

'Well, carry it yourself if you're so clever,' I said.

Then suddenly I saw the vet before me. The heartless man was grinning all over his face.

'She's just been playing you up,' he said. 'A touch of toothache, that's all, but you know these thoroughbreds are all nerves and at the least touch of pain they act as if they are dying.'

'Are you sure?' gasped Wendy. As for me, slosh! – down went the cup of tea all over the flags.

'Of course I'm sure. I'll show you where her gum's swollen. I've put a touch of something on it and she's OK already.'

We followed him into the stall. Blue Smoke was up on her feet and looking very sheepish. She nuzzled Wendy's arm and made a whiffling noise.

'Gosh!' said Wendy. 'She's asking for apples. You fraud, Blue Smoke!'

The vet lifted her lip and showed us the swollen gum.

'When's Mrs Darcy coming back?' he asked.

'Not till the end of the week.'

'Oh, that's all right,' he said. 'She won't take any harm for a week and then we can get the tooth examined. It may only be a bit of cold.'

'Could it possibly be with riding her?' I asked anxiously. 'She was jumped this morning.'

'Do her good,' said the vet cheerfully. 'She's not getting enough exercise by a long shot.'

So that was that. It was now one o'clock in the morning, an hour at which I had never been up before. It felt very peculiar. Joey fastened everything up and I went back with Wendy to her house. I don't know if I mentioned before that she lived at the farm next to the riding school.

We let ourselves in by the back door of the farm, which was never locked. The farmhouse was about six hundred years old.

Wendy said it felt like a good opportunity for seeing the ancestral ghost who – or which – was a headless yeoman riding a headless mare down the stairs, but he – or it – didn't appear and I wasn't sorry as I felt much too tired to cope with ancestral ghosts.

We both got into Wendy's four-poster bed and fell fast asleep. Mrs Mead woke us at seven next morning and it didn't feel a bit nice getting up. I went straight home to find Mummy far from pleased about everything, and I did see her point and agreed with all she said. I didn't want to be stopped from going to the riding school.

I changed and went up there about eleven. James was there, and wasn't a scrap impressed with the story of our sufferings which Wendy had poured out to him. He rather pooh-poohed the whole thing and said we were pretty dopey not to know when a horse was dying from some internal injury and when it merely had toothache. We rather hated James.

However, we couldn't keep it up for long, as he was full of an idea he had for a field ride which would be good practice for the Hunter Trials. He had fixed it for the Wednesday afternoon and had got permission from the farmers whose fields we wanted to cross – which you should always do if you are planning a field ride.

As only the experienced pupils were taking part in the ride we knew it would be fun and not much trouble.

I had been keeping my two ponies at the school because of the work they were doing with the new pupils, and the night before the ride Wendy said to my surprise, 'I say, Jill, could I ask a favour?'

'Of course,' I said. 'What is it?'

'Would you let me ride Rapide tomorrow?'

If she had asked me to let her ride an elephant I couldn't have been more surprised.

While I was still gasping in a fishlike way she went on, 'I've been schooling him quite a lot when you weren't here. I've had him over the practice jumps heaps of times and I like him. I'd love to ride him tomorrow, and I know you're going to ride Black Boy.'

'Gosh!' I said. 'You can ride him with pleasure but I don't know why you want to.'

'You'll know why tomorrow,' she said.

It was a mild sunny day next day for the ride and

not at all like January. Eleven of us turned out and we had grand fun. The ponies had the freedom of the fields which they loved, and we jumped low hedges and any sort of natural hazard such as you get in Hunter Trials.

When I saw Wendy going over everything on Rapide you could have knocked me for six. I had put in a bit of schooling on Rapide myself, but this was magic. The pony had quite lost his miserable, suspicious looks and was enjoying himself as much as the others. And his peculiar action in jumping wasn't nearly so marked as it had been. He certainly could jump.

Afterwards, when we were rubbing down, Wendy said, 'Had you thought of jumping Rapide in the Hunter Trials?'

I said I hadn't.

'I think you're crazy not to enter him,' said Wendy. 'He's got tremendous pluck and he's a born jumper. You really haven't given him a chance.'

'I don't know if he'd do for me what he's done for you,' I said, rather humbly.

'He would if you'd give him the chance. If I were you I'd put two months' hard practice in on Rapide and stop being so distrustful about him.'

I didn't say anything but I was quite impressed by what Wendy said, when I remembered what she had been able to do with Rapide. I had to admit that I hadn't done my best with him, and I had always ridden him for duty and Black Boy for pleasure. So I expressed my regrets to him that afternoon with a bit of petting and an extra handful of oats.

I was cleaning out the bucket in the harness room when I heard someone behind me. I jumped up and saw two men who looked vaguely like people's fathers.

'Am I addressing Miss Jill Crewe?' said one of them, who was tall and thin.

'That's me,' I said.

'Stand back a bit,' he said. 'You're something of a curiosity.'

I thought perhaps he was a bit screwy, so I stood back and wished I didn't look so dusty and unhorsemanlike, with most of my hair in my right eye.

'Behold!' he went on. 'The girl who taught my son to like riding!'

'Oh,' I said. 'Are you Tom Vale's father?'

'I certainly am,' he added. 'I've been singing your praises as a teacher far and wide.'

'I'm not really very good,' I said. 'Tom rode well before I had him but he just didn't take any interest until he saw other boys of his own age doing things. I think it was jolly unkind,' I added, carried away by my feeling, 'to show him what show-jumpers did at Hickstead and expect him to do the same. It would have put me off for life.'

When I had said this I realised how rude it sounded and wished I hadn't, but Mr Vale only smiled in a feeble sort of way and the other man said, 'Bravo, I couldn't agree more.'

'Anyway,' said Mr Vale, 'I've recommended your riding school to a lot of people and you'll be over-whelmed with pupils soon, I fancy.'

'But it isn't my riding school!' I yelled. 'You should see Wendy Mead, she's an absolutely magic teacher, and it's really Mrs Darcy's riding school only she's away, and she's the best teacher in the county, only people go to Lime Farm to Captain Drafter's because he teaches their horrid children to bounce about on ponies and their ghastly parents think it's smart – '

I gasped for breath, wondering what awful things I was going to say next, but the man who wasn't Mr Vale smiled nicely and said, 'Well, you won't have to suffer from Captain Drafter's establishment much longer. He got into trouble, owing money all round the district, and he's packing up and getting out. Honesty is the best policy, as they say.'

'Gosh, yes it is, isn't it?' I agreed warmly.

Just then harsh peals of laughter rang out behind me and the ground seemed to rock. Only one person on earth could have a laugh like that. It was April Cholly-Sawcutt.

'Miss Jill doesn't know it's Daddy!' she chortled. 'She doesn't know it's Daddy!'

My legs nearly gave way under me. Was I really talking to the great hero of the show ring, Captain Cholly-Sawcutt himself? I was!

My head spun round and round and I said, 'Oh!' Then I shouted, 'Please, please, please wait till I fetch Wendy! She must see you! We do want your autograph. And James too. And Diana.'

At the same time I was afraid to go away in case he should vanish, but just then Wendy came along and we both shook hands with the great man, feeling dizzy with excitement. It was quite the greatest moment of my career.

Wendy said, 'I'd give anything to see Petronelle.'

'Why not?' said Captain Cholly-Sawcutt very obligingly. 'Supposing I bring her round on Saturday afternoon? Some of your pupils might like to see her too.'

We couldn't believe our ears. The moment the

distinguished visitor had gone we rushed off to find Diana and James who were having tea at home.

At first they thought that we were having them on, because things like having Captain Cholly-Sawcutt on Petronelle coming to your riding school on a Saturday afternoon don't happen except in the sort of dreams you get after eating too many mince pies on Christmas Day, but when they found it was true they couldn't eat any more tea and Diana went quite white, and Mr and Mrs Bush took a dim view of the proceedings; so we cleared off and I went home at ninety miles an hour and told Mummy the whole thrilling story.

12 A great day for all

You'd be surprised to know how quickly the great news went round. Half our school stopped Diana and me in the street and said, 'Is it true that Captain Cholly-Sawcutt is going to be at Mrs Darcy's place on Saturday, with Petronelle? Could we come and see him?'

Yes, we said, it was true, but of course there would only be room for people belonging to the riding school. Practically everybody then rushed off to ask their mothers if they couldn't join the riding school before Saturday, and we had to make a rule about fees in advance.

Finally who should come along but Susan Pyke who had always looked down on us and had been the star pupil at Lime Farm Riding School.

'Hello, Jill,' she said in a frightfully friendly way. 'I hear you're having Captain Cholly-Sawcutt on Saturday. I've met him before, you know. I suppose it's all right if I come along?'

'I'm afraid it isn't,' I said. 'We only have room for Mrs Darcy's own pupils. But if you wait at the field gate,' I couldn't resist adding, 'you might see him go by.'

Susan crumpled up a bit, but said it really didn't matter as she'd be seeing a lot of Captain Cholly-Sawcutt in the future when she rode at Wembley, possibly next year, and I said, 'How lucky for you,'

and Ann Derry who happened to be with me said,
'You ought to pal up with April, May and June.
They'd be just right for you.'

'Are they up to my standard?' said Susan, and Ann
said, 'The question is, are you up to theirs?'

On Friday we collected all the pupils and gave
them instructions about being properly dressed and
having their ponies perfectly groomed. We started the
grooming on Saturday at seven o'clock in the morning, washed tails, polished hoofs, scrubbed and
cleaned and had everything looking magnificent by
lunch time. We couldn't eat for excitement.

By two o'clock all our pupils were assembled
and we held an inspection. They looked very nice
indeed after we had retied everybody's ties and
made them rerub their boots and put their hats
on straighter. Even George and Georgina Fisher
looked quite decent, and when Tom Vale stood up
straight he didn't look a bit round-shouldered and his
clothes seemed to fit better. Wendy and I brushed
each other's coats till we were quite exhausted.

'Gosh, look at all the people in the lane!' said
Diana.

I think half Chatton was lingering outside the
paddock, as if waiting for royalty, and there were
dozens of autograph books held in people's expectant
hands. Even Susan Pyke had swallowed her pride and
was sitting on the top rail of the gate with an open
book in one hand and a fountain pen in the other.

'I've booked in twenty-seven new pupils,' said
Wendy, who was quite tomato-coloured with excitement, 'and they're all taking a minimum of twelve
lessons, starting from next week.'

'He's coming!' shrieked James.

And up the drive through the paddock rode

Captain Cholly-Sawcutt himself, on Petronelle, that famous show-jumper.

I can't describe what a wonderful time we had. Picture it for yourself! He signed all our books and let us pat Petronelle, and then he told us about his experiences in the show-jumping world and gave us a short lecture on equitation which we all drank in eagerly, and then he finished up by jumping Petronelle round our jumps. It was like a fairytale. All the people in the lane had a good view too.

We were so taken up with watching that none of us noticed a taxi ploughing its way through the crowd. Something made me turn my head, and there coming up the paddock was Mrs Darcy, tottering slightly and looking quite overcome.

I raced to meet her. She looked at me in a dazed sort of way.

'Is it a fire?' she said. 'Or is somebody being arrested?'

'Look!' I gasped, pointing to the magic figures of a horse and rider flying over our five-foot rail fence.

She passed a hand over her face.

'I'm going mad,' she said. 'Do you know, Jill, I actually thought I saw Captain Cholly-Sawcutt on Petronelle jumping the five-foot in our field.'

'Yes, you did,' I said. 'It's him.' (Which is bad grammar.)

She ran both hands through her hair.

'I'm quite crazy,' she said. 'I must be. I thought I came home, and there was an enormous crowd at the gate, and Jill Crewe told me that Captain Cholly-Sawcutt on Petronelle was doing the jumps in our field. I must be in the last stages.'

'You're not mad,' I said. 'It's happening. I can

explain everything. Look, here's Wendy. We'll tell you all about it.'

'After this,' said Mrs Darcy, 'nothing that you could do, Jill – nothing! – could cause me the slightest surprise.'

Then she went and shook hands with the hero, whom she had met before in the show ring, and everybody talked at once, and we had a gorgeous time. After it was all over, and Captain Cholly-Sawcutt had praised the riding school and thanked us for the way we were teaching April, May and June to ride, which was a thing he couldn't have faced attempting himself, and had promised to come again some day, he went off and we calmed down a bit.

'And now,' said Mrs Darcy, 'somebody might tell me just what's been going on.'

We didn't know where to begin. For about a minute we stood with our mouths open and not a sound came, then all of a sudden we all began talking at once and then we couldn't stop. We told her about the Three Fats and how they turned out to be the daughters of the famous rider, and about Tom Vale, and about all the new pupils. We told her about Blue Smoke's toothache, and believe me, she laughed. When we had finished and were gasping for breath she looked rather awkward, and then said, 'I just don't know how to thank you.' Which was a tremendous lot, coming from Mrs Darcy.

We all fidgeted and said things like, 'That's quite OK, we loved it,' and then she said briskly, in her old way, 'Well, thank goodness you'll all be back at school next week.'

The thought was a bit blighting.

'We know,' said Diana. 'But after all it's only eleven weeks to the Hunter Trials.'

I don't remember much about what happened at school that term, except that we had a Careers Week. This was an invention of Miss Grange-Dudley, our headmistress, and was for everybody in the school of thirteen or over.

In the afternoons instead of the usual lessons we were to have talks on careers by people who had done them, and as well as the talks everybody had to have an interview with their mother and Miss Grange-Dudley in the head's room, which sounded to us simply awful.

'I'll bet you all the talks are about humdrum things like domestic science and nursing,' said Ann as we biked home together. 'There couldn't possibly be anything decent like air hostesses or breeding cocker spaniels.'

The fact was, Ann had definitely decided either to be an air hostess or run a kennel. Actually, nearly every girl in our form wanted to do something with dogs or horses except for a rather dim girl who wanted to run a teashop, and one who wanted to be a gym teacher, and one who wanted to be an explorer after reading a library book called *Two Girls and a Tandem in Tibet*.

Ann was quite right. The talks were all very dull except for one on Ballet by a woman who had been at school with Miss Grange-Dudley and had something to do with Sadler's Wells, and as she kept on saying you couldn't begin too young and preferably at about eight, it didn't seem to be much use.

There wasn't a single career talk that even mentioned dogs or horses, you'd think they didn't exist.

Ann went for her interview before me. She came out looking a bit hopeless.

'What was it like?' I said.

'Awful,' said Ann with a groan.

'Did you tell her you were going to be an air hostess? You said you would.'

'I couldn't get it in,' said Ann. 'First Miss Grange-Dudley made a speech, the same one she makes every speech day, and when she stopped for breath Mummy chipped in about wanting me to know about antiques so that I could run an antique shop, and when she'd done they both looked at me and said, Well, that's all settled, and the next minute I was outside and it was over.'

'You feeble thing!' I said. 'You ought to have interrupted.'

However when it came to my turn I found it wasn't so easy to interrupt. But just when I was getting desperate Mummy said in her nice way, 'When all is said and done, Jill is the one to decide. I should like her career to be entirely her own choice, and whatever it is I shall help her in every way.'

I gave her a huge smile and knew that everything was going to be all right.

'And what does Jill want to do?' said Miss Grange-Dudley in a sort of here-come-the-horses voice.

I had made up a speech about the three things I wanted to do all at the same time, being a champion show-jumper and an M.P. so that I could get some decent laws passed for horses and other animals, and all the rest, but when I came to the point all I could get out was, 'I want to run an orphanage.'

Miss Grange-Dudley was so surprised that she nearly fell off her chair.

'Well!' she said. 'That's very praiseworthy of you, Jill. It's the unexpected that always happens.'

'A jolly sort of orphanage,' I said.

'I've always thought,' said Miss Grange-Dudley,

'that you had it in you to become a writer like your mother.'

This was a new idea for me and I thought it was terrific. Yes, I *would* be a writer, but not like Mummy. I would write pony books! I could hardly wait to get home to start. It was wonderful to think I had found a career I could begin at once while I was waiting to be old enough to do my other three things.

On the way home I bought a writing block, and directly after tea I began my first book which I called *Jill's Gymkhana*. You have probably read it.

13 The hunter trials

I would like to be able to say that the day of the Hunter Trials dawned bright and fair, because that is what it would have been like in a proper book, but truth compels me to relate that it was raining. When I first opened my eyes I could hear the steady drip-drip, but I pretended I was dreaming it and jumped up and rushed to the window. Everything looked wet and misty.

However, rain or no rain it was Hunter Trials day at last and six o'clock, so I got into my old jodhs and mac and tore down to start on my ponies. It is a bit discouraging to groom and polish horses and wash their tails and comb and plait their manes on a wet day because you think perhaps it is all going to be wasted after all and they will eventually arrive at the scene of action looking like draggled rats. I tried not to think of it like that, but thought instead of all the other people I knew at this moment who were also grooming and washing and polishing and combing and plaiting.

Isn't it funny how well you can plait on days when it doesn't matter, and when it does matter the plaits come out looking like something you tried for the first time in your life?

I dashed about, oiling hoofs, washing tails, flourishing a stable rubber. When Black Boy finally looked like patent leather and Rapide like polished mahogany

I tied them carefully so that they couldn't spoil themselves and went into the kitchen to see about breakfast.

'There's nothing like hard work in a good cause,' said Mrs Crosby.

'It's a good cause all right,' I said. 'Hunter Trials. We've all been waiting for this for ages.'

'Never heard of it,' she said cheerfully. 'What do you do?'

'Oh, just jump over things,' I said.

'Well, don't you go bringing no more silver cups home for me to clean,' she said.

'Not much hope,' I said. 'It's mostly for grown-up people and big horses. Only two children's events and I don't stand an earthly in either of those. Mrs Crosby darling, could I have an awful lot of porridge this morning?'

'I'm doing you two eggs,' she said kindly.

'Angel!' I said. 'While you're doing it I'll clean my boots, and then there's the ponies' lunch to pack and mine.'

'Ponies' lunch!' she said.

'Oats,' I said. 'And please, Mrs Crosby, could you look for my fawn tie and I can't find the hat brush either.'

She said I'd lose my head if it was loose, and I couldn't think of a reply to this as I had my mouth full of porridge and was looking for something to make myself some sandwiches for my own lunch at the same time.

Mummy came in and said, 'Now don't get too excited. Isn't it time you went up to dress?'

'Oh, Mummy,' I said, 'you might look for my fawn tie. It isn't in the drawer.'

'There's something else that isn't in its proper

place,' said Mrs Crosby, coming in with my riding hat. 'In the glory hole under the stairs, it was. I'd better give it a brush. You'd lose your head if – '

'Yes, do brush it for me,' I said, 'that is, if you can find the hat brush, I can't.'

'It's a good thing you look after your ponies better than you look after yourself, Jill,' said Mummy, discovering my fawn tie in the knife drawer.

In the end I found the hat brush in the harness room. All the time I was dressing I was wishing it would stop raining, and when by the time I was ready I found it actually had stopped I couldn't believe that one of my wishes had come true. It still looked very damp everywhere but it wasn't raining.

'Rain before seven, fine before eleven,' said Mrs Crosby who was very good at little mottoes and things like that.

'You look very nice,' said Mummy. 'I do hope you don't have to ride in a mac.'

'I shan't in any case,' I said. 'Are you sure my jodhs are the same fawn as my tie?'

'Identical,' she said. 'Really, you horsy people are so fussy.'

She was coming later in the Lowes' car to watch, and bringing the lunches and the grooming tools.

By the time I got to the course the weather was brightening a little. Several of my friends were already there, and Diana was moaning because her pony, Sylvia, hated wet ground and never did much good except on dry.

'The course,' said James, 'is awful. Downhill and uphill.'

'Well, that's what you'd get in hunting,' said Ann,

'and Hunter Trials are supposed to reproduce natural hazards you'd find on a cross-country ride.'

'Thanks for the information,' said James rather huffily.

Everybody we knew seemed to be there, and they all looked much better mounted and more confident than we did, but this is something that one always feels at the beginning of competitions.

Ann and I rode round to look at the course and loosen up our ponies, as the first class was the children's class in which, with a lot of misgivings, I was riding Rapide. Of course I had put in a lot of practice on him, but it was the first competition for which I had entered him. Spurred on by Mrs Darcy, Wendy and everybody else, I couldn't do otherwise, but I didn't think much of my chances and was looking forward more to riding Black Boy with Ann in the partnership.

There were eight jumps for the children's class and two more were to be added for the open classes. Five of the jumps were gorse fences. Two were plain, one downhill and one uphill; two with water on the take-off side, and one that gave me the needle, with a ditch on the landing side. Ann said it didn't worry her, the one she hated was the uphill one. There was also a brook to be jumped twice, going out and coming in, and a natural in-and-out formed by a grassy lane with low hedges.

By the time the steward called us into the collecting ring and began to explain the course to us I for one was past caring. I was quite sure I was going to have three refusals at the first fence, or else no refusals but about twenty-eight faults.

I could see Mummy and the Lowes at the rails as the first competitor, a girl called Madge Madden, took off. We all held our breaths and watched, as one always does watch the first competitor.

Madge didn't have a very good time. She did an enormous jump at the first fence where it wasn't necessary and a feeble one at the first water jump where she got four faults. We lost sight of her at the in-and-out which was in a sort of a dip, and when she did reappear she got three refusals at the uphill fence and that was the end of her. I felt very sympathetic.

Diana was next.

'She's taking it too fast,' said James who was standing beside us. 'Sylvia doesn't like wet ground but she needn't rush her along like that. There! She's crashed that easy fence with her forelegs!'

Diana collected both herself and Sylvia after that and seemed to do quite decently, but when she came back to us she said she had got at least twelve faults.

'Didn't you clear the brook both ways?' asked James. 'I couldn't see you properly but I thought you did.'

'I did going out,' said Diana, 'but coming back Sylvia went in with her hindlegs, and you know how she loathes wet. She messed up the uphill fence after that though it wasn't really hard.'

Jack Winsley, one of Mrs Darcy's pupils went next. He was a very serious boy and rode so carefully it made you want to scream. He had no faults in six jumps, but he took ages over them and as he approached the seventh jump with the ditch on the landing side he realised he was losing time, which counted in this competition. He used his stick, his pony started to pull, crashed the jump and ran out.

Then a few more people we knew rode. Joan

Bishop fell off at the brook, rolled into the water, led her pony out and retired. John Finch beat his pony round and then got three refusals which he deserved. Lulu Brown who was the youngest competitor and only ten did a beautiful round and only came to grief at the last fence from sheer excitement at doing so well. April Cholly-Sawcutt, who had insisted on riding her new pony though she was far from ready, got fifteen faults and then retired.

We heard somebody say, 'Lead me away and lay me down!' and it was Captain Cholly-Sawcutt with his hand over his eyes.

Ann giggled but she soon stopped, as it was her turn.

'Jolly good!' said Diana generously as Ann cleared the first two fences.

'Her timing's always so good,' I said. 'Oh help!'

Ann's pony had taken off too soon at the first water jump and brought down bunches of gorse with his hindlegs.

However Ann had a lot of applause as she came to the finishing post and only had four faults.

'You're much the best so far,' I said, as she gave her pony oats.

'That's nothing,' said Ann. 'Look at Harry Forrester now.'

Harry Forrester was only two days off sixteen, and so was lucky to get into this event which was for *under* sixteens. He was a very experienced rider and had been in competitions since he was nine. His pony was a thoroughbred. All these things made us feel a bit nervous.

'But I've seen him do frightfully badly,' said James.

However Harry did frightfully well. He sailed over

everything and got the first clear round. Everybody clapped like mad.

'You were terrific, Harry,' said James.

'It was only a fluke,' said Harry, who wasn't at all conceited but a very nice boy.

There were two more good rounds, people seemed to get better as the event went on, and then it was my turn.

As I felt Rapide gather himself for the first jump I knew he was going to do it. He sailed over with inches to spare.

I touched him between the ears, which meant in our language, you needn't overdo it. He took me too literally, and I felt his fore-feet catch the gorse of the next fence which was one with water on the take-off side. The next was all right and so was the in-and-out and we came up to the brook for the second time. Rapide jumped too high and I was sure we were going to miss the edge, but somehow we were down and cantering on to the uphill hedge.

This time I saw the gorse fly. I didn't think I had a chance now, so I didn't worry about the final jumps and strangely enough cleared them.

When I got back to the others Ann said, 'I say! You were marvellous.'

'I got either four or six faults,' I said.

'You didn't,' said Diana. 'You only got two.'

'But at the second jump – '

'You didn't bring anything down,' said James, 'so I think you've been lucky.'

Then we heard the loud-speaker say, 'Number 27, two faults.'

'Hooray!' said Ann. 'You're second to Harry Forrester so far.'

Of the remaining competitors there were two

decent rounds. One looked to be clear, only there was some argument and we didn't hear the final result. It was done by a girl called Helen Moffat, one of Mrs Darcy's pupils, and the other good round was by Jean Smith from Lime Farm Riding School.

You know how it is in a competition, you get muddled up with the results and don't know where you stand. When the judges began to call in and I heard 27 called I was quite surprised.

'Go on!' said Ann. 'I told you you'd done well, Jill.'

Harry Forrester was first, I was second, Helen Moffat was third, and Ann was reserve.

'I was certain Jean Smith had got it,' said Ann delightedly as we munched bars of chocolate and gave Rapide the petting of his life. We were joined by Mummy, Mrs Derry, Ann's little sisters screaming with joy over Ann's green card, Mrs Darcy and Captain Cholly-Sawcutt. Everybody made a fuss of Rapide who looked very smug.

'Did you see my April?' said Captain Cholly-Sawcutt. 'Wasn't she appalling?'

'You are really proud of her,' said Mummy, 'for being so plucky as to enter at all.'

'She's come on jolly well,' said Mrs Darcy.

'In spite of being so fa –' began Ann, and shut up suddenly.

Class 2 open class, was just starting and we were very interested in what would happen to James and Wendy. Two walls had now been included in the course.

'Mrs Woodhouse is sure to win it,' said Diana. 'She always looks as if she couldn't help winning.'

Mrs Woodhouse and her horse were a lovely sight as they quietly and efficiently did a clear round.

'I think it's so depressing for the others when the first competitor does a clear round,' said Diana, thinking of James who was dithering on his new mare, Maureen. 'Who's going next? Oh, it's Bernice Wishford. She tells everybody that her horse let her down. I suppose it never occurs to her that she let the horse down.'

'Well, this one has run out with her,' said Mrs Darcy.

'Oh, look, it's Susan Pyke next!' shrieked Ann. 'In full hunting kit with white breeches. She looks about eighteen.'

'I hope she falls off,' said Diana. 'She's the biggest faller-off in the world. She can't jump a horse that size anyway. Gosh! She *has* fallen off.'

'She'll get on again,' I said, but Susan got up limping, and leaving somebody else to retrieve her horse she retired.

'Isn't it lovely?' I said. 'Everybody we don't like is doing badly.'

'I think you're disgusting,' said Mummy.

Two or three men did good rounds and one of them, Major Pitts, got only two faults, but we weren't pleased as he was rude to other people and used his stick too much.

'Oh, it's James!' shouted Diana, and we all watched breathlessly.

But James was unlucky and did a bad round. Funnily enough the jumps he did brilliantly were the difficult ones and he got his faults at the ones which looked easy.

'I was awful,' he said despondently as he joined us, patting Maureen and saying, 'It wasn't your fault, old girl.'

'Your timing wasn't too good,' said Diana.

'For the love of Mike don't tell me!' said James.

'Stop arguing, you people,' said Mrs Darcy. 'Wendy's started.'

Wendy was just clearing the second jump, and away she flew, her horse, Clarion, beautifully collected and taking the brook in his stride. It seemed only seconds before Wendy was coming up the hill, going steadily and confidently. She cleared the next two fences in lovely style, even the difficult one with the ditch on the landing side, and increased her speed for the last jump.

She's going to do it! I thought. Wendy's going to do a clear round!

Then a groan went up from the crowd. I shut my eyes, opened them again, and saw a rail of the last jump lying on the ground.

'Three faults,' said Mrs Darcy. 'Well done, Wendy.'

'It's Mr Brill, just coming up,' said James. 'He always does well, unfortunately.'

Mr Brill was a very experienced rider on a long-legged grey, but today he was very slow and had several refusals, and though he cleared his fences the time limit expired before he got to the last jump and he was disqualified.

Nobody else did better than Wendy, and when they were called Mrs Woodhouse was first, Major Pitts second, Wendy third, and a man called Harcourt reserve.

'I was certain I was going to fall off,' said Wendy modestly as we all pounded her on the back.

'None of the Lime Farm people have won anything,' said Diana with a lot of satisfaction.

She spoke too soon, because the next event, for novices, was won by Mrs Drafter on a wicked-looking bay with a white blaze and docked tail.

She did a clear round. However, we didn't care much, as everybody knew by now that the Drafters were leaving and that Mrs Darcy had so many new pupils that she was buying more horses and taking on stable staff.

The only exciting thing about the novice competition was that James, on a borrowed horse, entered at the last minute and got the reserve. He and Wendy hadn't entered as they didn't possess second horses and it was too soon to jump Clarion and Maureen again, but a friend of James's father came to the rescue with an experienced chestnut called Frisk, and though James was nervous he rode beautifully and we clapped like mad when he was called in.

After that was the lunch interval, during which we fed the ponies and ourselves and talked about the events. The children's partnership was coming on immediately after lunch, and then the main event, the Swift Cup for horses that had hunted not less than three seasons.

'I'm scared blue about the partnership,' said Diana, who was riding with a girl called Gwen Snow. 'Gwen and I haven't practised together much, and Val and Jackie Heath have done nothing but practise together for weeks. It makes all the difference when the ponies are friends and will follow each other's lead.'

'Oh, shut up,' said Ann. 'We're all equally bad anyway.'

When we were called into the collecting ring the steward explained the course. All the jumps except the in-and-out were too narrow for the ponies to jump together, as they do in pairs jumping, so we had to jump in turn, but the partnership had to be together when they reached the finishing post which meant that if you completed the course three jumps ahead of your partner you had to wait for her to catch up.

Diana said gloomily that she couldn't think of anything worse than Gwen standing waiting while she floundered in the brook three jumps back.

'You might still be floundering in the gorse at the first,' said James in a helpful brotherly way, as we waited for the first number to be called.

It wasn't very encouraging that the first round should be an excellent one, by Val and Jackie Heath. It was an education to watch their ponies cooperate, jumping nearly nose to tail, and finishing the course with only two faults between them and in an incredibly short time. I think they got the loudest applause the crowd had given that day.

There was a big entry for this event and some funny things happened as you can imagine. In one partnership of two sisters on a grey pony and a chestnut, the grey could do nothing wrong and the chestnut nothing right. In the end both competitors finished up weeping. There were several violent rows too. One boy who finished the last jump far ahead of his partner went back and administered a sound slap to the other pony's flank, whereupon the laggard rider dismounted and pulled his patner's cap off and they fought. It was terribly unsportsmanlike but rather funny.

When it got to my turn with Ann I knew that at least I could rely on Black Boy who was very steady and experienced. I was a bit afraid for Ann's George who was a nappy pony; Ann's mother liked nappy ponies.

As I feared, George rushed his jumps and got two ahead of me. I was so worried counting his faults that I forgot Black Boy, and perhaps this was a good thing, for my kind pony took control of the situation and I found myself with a clear round. Ann had managed to collect George by the time they reached the in-and-out, and finished with only four faults after all.

I had the feeling we might be in the running for a place, though the event went on for a long time as there were thirty-three entries.

Diana's fears were groundless and she and Gwen did a very good round.

When the judge called in, the Heaths and two brothers, farmer's sons called Bryce, both had clear rounds, but Jackie and Val were placed first as they had a lead of eleven seconds, and the Bryce boys second.

The big event of the day was coming up now, in fact a lot of the grown-up competitors had taken a dim view of having to wait until after the children's partnerships.

There were some magnificent horses and riders in the collecting ring, but our eyes were on Mrs Darcy on Blue Smoke and Mr Bush, James's father on Tiger Cub.

'Will you look at that!' said Ann, watching an enormous man being heaved into the saddle by a groom. His horse looked a real weight-carrier. 'Can you imagine that pair following hounds? They look as if they couldn't follow a tortoise.'

However, the fat man rode first and he certainly knew how to extend that grey of his. They lumbered home with only two faults and in quite good time.

Then we saw some really brilliant riding and I dreamed of a day to come when I too should be riding a hunter of three seasons in the Swift Cup. We all thought Mrs Darcy was going to do a clear round on Blue Smoke until she knocked one block out of the second wall. Everybody groaned. Mr Bush's horse was unfortunately in a refusing mood and he didn't do a good round, which we felt was a pity, as the Bush family were all skilled riders and should have taken something home besides two reserves.

Susan Pyke was entered on her father's hunter which, as usual, was far too big for her. She rode very showily and a lot of people clapped, but she didn't look so good when she finished the course with her arms round Matterhorn's neck and slowly clasping him like a necklace she slithered to the ground.

A man called Wilson who was a great comedian gave the crowd the laugh of its life. Mrs Darcy said it was a pity that he would fool about as he was really an excellent rider and one of the best men to hounds in the county, only on an occasion like this he couldn't resist fooling. He pretended to fall at every jump and then recovered at the last minute, he made faces and pretended to be frightened, and finished up sitting in the middle of the brook while the crowd roared and he took his hat off to them. Some of the older people thought this exhibition was bad taste, but it certainly brightened things up and we were all helpless with laughing.

Then the master's wife, Mrs Swift, did her round. This was sporting of her as she had no intention of taking a prize even if she won one in the event in which her husband was giving the prizes. However, she didn't stand an earthly. I think she was the slowest person round the jumps I ever saw in my life and I couldn't imagine what happened to her out hunting. She crawled up to every jump as though it was going to say 'Boo' to her, she was quite prepared to allow her horse two refusals whenever he wanted them, she lost her riding hat and went to look for it herself instead of leaving it to a steward and when she had completed a jump she looked so overcome that she and her horse had to stand still and have a rest. However, everybody liked Mrs Swift and when she finally finished, minutes after the allotted time when anybody else would have been disqualified, the crowd gave her a cheer and she looked beamingly happy.

'I suppose you realise,' said Wendy hopefully, 'that nobody has done a clear round?'

'Come to think of it,' said James, 'they haven't. I believe Mrs Darcy has a chance.'

In the end Mrs Darcy and a man called Captain Tuft both had two faults. We stood on tiptoe and joggled about to see what was happening.

'Hooray!' yelled James like a foghorn. 'They're placing her first. Her time must have been better.'

Mrs Darcy was first, Captain Tuft second and two unknowns took the next two places. We yelled with joy, and when Mrs Darcy rode up to take the cup I should think the cheers nearly carried her along.

'What an absolutely wonderful day it has been,' said Ann.

Mrs Darcy came up to us with the cup under her arm and we all crowded round Blue Smoke.

'I never thought I'd do it,' she said modestly, but you could see it was probably the most thrilling moment of her life. Then she congratulated us all on what we had done.

'And good luck to these two fellows!' she said, touching the cheeks of my Black Boy with his yellow rosette and Rapide with his blue one.

'Doesn't he look proud with his first rosette!' said Mummy. 'Dear old Rapide!'

'It's an extraordinary thing about Rapide,' I said, 'that he's a different pony now. He's completely changed his character.'

'Oh well,' said Mrs Darcy nodding wisely, 'ponies sometimes do.'

JILL AND THE RUNAWAY

Jill and the Runaway

Ruby Ferguson

Hodder
Children's
Books

a division of Hodder Headline plc

Jill and the Runaway

Copyright © 1954, 1993 Hodder and Stoughton Ltd.

First published in a single volume in Great Britain in 1954
by Hodder and Stoughton Ltd.

Originally published as *Jill Enjoys her Ponies* in 1972
by Knight Books

Revised single volume edition published 1993 by Knight Books

Contents

1 A disappointed jumper

I was sitting on a pile of gravel outside a field gate feeling absolutely browned off. I don't mean a bit fed up, I mean practically crying like a small kid. I wouldn't have wished my worst enemy to feel so awful, not even Susan Pyke or my cousin Cecilia, and they are the worst blots I know.

It was the day of Chatton Show, the biggest event of the riding year in our part of the world, and every single person I knew would be there – except Me.

I had got a strained wrist. Not anything really bad like a fracture or even a sprain, but just a stupid strained muscle; and I hadn't even got it out riding, I had got it by swinging the bucket too far when I came back from feeding Mummy's unspeakable hens.

I always swing an empty bucket, and I dare say you do too, and all I can say is – don't, if you want to have any chance of riding your pony for days after.

The only thing I had thought of and talked about for a long time before this vile and shattering accident was Chatton Show. (That is to say, I had thought in slight spasms about the end-of-term exams, though not very much, according to my headmistress, who wrote unsympathetically on my report, 'Jill can do anything she gives her mind to and would be advised to give it more consistently to Mathematics, History, and

French.' What I admire about Miss Grange-Dudley
is the marvellous way she expresses herself, like
Shakespeare.)

It was my last chance to win the fourteen-and-
under jumping, so of course I intended to do it.
Next year I would be fifteen and competing with a
crowd of very hard sixteen-year-olds who had gained
all their experience in bigger shows than Chatton.

When I swung the bucket and my arm hurt, I just
said Ouch! and took no more notice, but you can
imagine my feelings when I woke up on the morning
before the show with an arm like a Swiss roll.

I rushed into Mummy's room with a face lined
and drawn with horror, as it says in thrillers, and
cried, 'Mummy! Do something about my arm. Get
it down or scrape it or something!'

She looked at it and said, 'Oh, dear. I'm afraid
it's not much good, Jill. You should have gone
to the doctor last night, as I seem to remember
suggesting.'

'It wasn't bad last night,' I mumbled. 'It hardly
hurt at all.'

I didn't want to admit that Mummy had known
best, as she usually did.

'I'll go to the doctor now,' I said hopefully.

'Yes, do,' she said, not so hopefully.

So I went. I wore my jodhpurs and my fawn coat
and my new red and fawn checked tie to show that I
was a serious-minded person, and I sat in Dr Fisher's
waiting-room for half an hour with two old women
who were doing a sniffing duet, and a dim sort of
boy with a dirty bandage on his leg, and some other
faded-looking characters.

At last it was my turn. When I got home, Mummy said, 'Cheer up, Jill. I was afraid it wasn't going to be good news.'

'It isn't going to be any use for four days,' I said, and added, 'I don't want to go on living.' I then rushed upstairs and lay across my bed and wondered if anybody in the world had ever been so miserable before.

Mummy shouted upstairs, 'Are you coming down, Jill? Ann and Diana are here.' (My two riding friends.)

I yelled, 'Tell them to go away.'

But they didn't go away. They came up and said all the usual things. The more people tell you how sorry they are for you the worse you feel and the more you want to slay them.

'How dreary having to stand by the rails and watch us ride,' said Diana.

'I shan't,' I said. 'I'm not going.'

'Not going!' said Ann. 'You don't mean you're not going to Chatton Show?'

'I'd die,' I said.

'Well, you know best,' said Diana, 'but if it was me wild horses wouldn't keep me away. I mean, missing Chatton Show!'

I told her she needn't keep saying it.

'If you don't go, you'll wish you'd gone,' said Ann.

'I shan't,' I said.

'But what on earth will you do?' said Diana. 'I mean, there isn't anything on earth to do tomorrow but go to Chatton Show.'

'I'll read a good book,' I said bitterly. 'And I wish you'd both go away. I hate you.'

'Oh, we are sorry for you,' said Ann. 'We think it's the most awful bad luck that ever happened to anybody in the world.'

'And it's your last chance in the under-fourteens,' said Diana.

'Really?' I said sarcastically. 'I hadn't thought of that.' (Actually I hadn't thought of anything else.)

When I told Mummy I wasn't going to the show she said, 'I think you're being awfully silly.'

'I couldn't bear it,' I said in a sort of night-must-fall voice.

'But wouldn't you like to go with Mrs Lowe and Martin and me in the car and watch, and have a chicken lunch and ices, and see the Open Jumping?'

'No,' I croaked.

'Oh, Jill, you are a fool.'

'OK,' I said.

'But what will you do? You can't just hang about the cottage alone. Everybody will be at the show. You'll be bored stiff.'

I gave an awful gulp, like an expiring cow, and dashed upstairs again to bury my head in the pillow.

Of course the day of the show had to be the most gorgeous summer's day you ever saw. I tried not to notice the blue, blue sky and the bits of cottonwool cloud, and the sunshine spilling gold on the fields and the warm smell of grass and flowers. I wasn't quite such a beast as to wish it was raining to spoil the show for everybody else, but I did think Nature needn't have been quite so mean to me.

I got up and put on my gingham school dress and some pretty-far-gone gym shoes, and tried not to think of my beloved riding clothes hanging spruce and brushed in the cupboard.

At a quarter past ten the Lowes drove up in their car to call for Mummy. There were Mr and Mrs Lowe and Martin, all in light summer clothes. I tried to look cool and don't-carish. I thought, if they tell me to Look on the Bright Side and Some-girls-haven't-got-any-arms-at-all I'd burst into flames, but they didn't.

Mrs Lowe said, 'Not going, Jill?' and Martin said, 'Well, nobody's going to make you.'

Mummy got into the car in her cool cream silk jacket and skirt and pretty straw hat, and said, 'Now do eat a proper lunch, Jill, it's all in the fridge, not just toast and jam,' and I said, 'All right,' and looked heroic and waved them off with my good hand.

And the minute they were gone, believe it or believe it not, I wished with all my heart I had gone too and hadn't been such a fool.

I thought of a few other things as I walked slowly down to the orchard to my puzzled-looking ponies, who, of course, were wondering why they weren't going to the show for which they had been practising for weeks. Black Boy and Rapide lifted their heads from cropping the sweet orchard grass and fixed four lovely dark eyes on me. I was remembering how when I was a raw kid of ten and had just bought my first pony, and couldn't afford riding lessons and didn't even know how I was going to stable and feed Black Boy in the winter, Martin Lowe had made himself my friend and taught me to ride and helped me to solve all my problems. And he did it from a wheel-chair too, because he was paralysed and couldn't walk.

Mr and Mrs Lowe had been marvellous to me too, and invited me to their beautiful horsy home where there were lovely papers lying abut, like *Horse and Hound* and *Riding*, not the dreary magazines you find in most people's houses, all about knitting and love and how to make puddings.

So by now I was feeling the pangs of remorse, and I didn't even want the block of milk chocolate which Mummy had left on the kitchen table for a surprise for me.

The ponies looked a bit ragged, but I didn't see how I could groom them with only one hand. I fetched them some water, after sloshing a lot of it over my feet, and listened to them happily blowing into the bucket.

Black Boy was a bit small for me now but I could still make him do anything I wanted. I knew he would have won the under-fourteen jumping for me, and I had entered Rapide as my second horse, because on his day he could be brilliant. They were both trained to the last inch. But it wasn't much good thinking about things like that.

I waggled my wrist. It felt a bit better. I thought, *it would*! And I'll be jumping again in a week when it doesn't matter.

The morning seemed endless. I tried to read a thriller, but could only think what a din our help, Mrs Crosby, was making with the Hoover. Every time she passed the sitting-room door she shoved her head in and said, 'Having a nice read, dear? Why not go out and get a bit of fresh air? It don't do to brood.'

I said sarkily, 'Are you addressing a hen?' and she said, 'You don't know what real trouble is, you don't,' and I said, 'Oh, dry up!' – for which Mummy would have given me a good telling off if she had heard me.

That infuriated Mrs C. who said, 'And you've left your room in a shocking mess, I must say,' and I said, 'Well, what can I do with only one arm?' and that was asking for it, because she began to tell me about the daughter of the woman that her sister worked for who had both arms in splints for months and taught herself to paint pictures with her toes – 'lovely lifelike apples, ever so rosy' – and in the middle I got up and walked out, and Mrs Crosby said, 'If there's one thing I can't stick it's a great baby!'

In spite of what Mummy had said I didn't want any lunch. I took a pear and some biscuits and walked along the lane until I got to the heap of gravel which the road-menders had dumped outside a field gate. I sat down on it and thought, Help! There's hours and hours to wait yet.

And this is where you came in.

2 Other people's luck

After what seemed a lifetime I thought I had better go home, because apart from anything else there were the ponies and hens to feed. You might think that in the country it would be possible to get somebody to come and help with one's hens, but such is not the case. Most farm workers, having millions of hens to look after as part of their daily toil, take a dim view of going out of their way to feed and clean anybody else's mere eight.

It is surprising what you can do with one hand if you have time, and when I had done the feeding, and spilt more than the unfortunate creatures got, I went into the cottage and had some tea and toast, and waited for the car to come back, and every minute seemed an hour like it does in novels.

The sun still poured down and it had been the most perfect afternoon, and I had pictured it all in my mind, the spacious ring and the white-painted jumps, the stands crowded with spectators, the collecting ring and my friends waiting on their ponies under the trees feeling like one does while waiting for one's number to be called, and horses everywhere, flying tautly over the bars or swishing their tails in the paddock, or having coloured rosettes pinned to their cheekbands by lucky winners.

It was past seven o'clock when I heard sounds outside, ponies' hoofs, not the car with my returning mother. It was my friends, Ann and Diana, who knew I would be longing for news and had come straight from the show to tell me about it.

They both looked hot and dusty and happy.

'Are you still alive?' cried Ann as they came up the path. 'Everybody was saying, why hadn't you come.'

'Was it good?' I managed to say.

'Oh, the best ever. Don't think I'm being beastly, but it was. It was marvellous.'

'Who won the under-fourteen jumping?' I managed to gasp.

Diana pulled the knot of her yellow tie from under her ear, and said, 'A boy called Marshall that nobody had ever heard of. They're new people who've taken Mile End Farm. He was pretty hot, nobody else stood an earthly. He did three clear rounds, the competition round and two jumps-off. It literally paralysed you to see him. You know, one of these wonder-jumpers! Then he entered for the under-sixteens and was first in that too.'

'He wasn't! Not first in both classes?'

'Yes he was. He was great!'

'Then I don't suppose I'd have had a chance, even if I'd ridden?' I said.

'Well, even if you'd done a clear round in the competition you'd have had to have jumped it off, and jumped it off with this Marshall boy for ever and ever.'

'How old is he?'

'Just thirteen,' said Ann. 'He's got another year

in the under-fourteens, so what a hope for any-body else.'

'And if he's already won the under-sixteens too,' I said, 'what a hope for us next year! Go on, tell me some more. What did everybody I know do?'

'Wendy Mead was second in the Class C jumping on Mrs Darcy's Cocktail.'

'Oh, jolly good!' I said, feeling a bit more like myself.

'And I was third in the Child's Pony Self-Groomed and Schooled,' said Diana modestly.

'Nice work!' I said. 'Who was second in the under-fourteen jumping, anyway?'

There was a slight pause.

'Me,' said Ann, going red under her dust.

'You dope!' I shouted, frightfully pleased. 'Why didn't you say so before? Where's your rosette?'

'I took it off George,' said Ann, opening her pocket enough for me to see the blue ribbon. 'I didn't want to look showing-off when you were having such a terrible disappointment.'

'I feel all right now,' I said. 'I was a fool not to go. I wish I'd gone.'

'How's the wrist?' said Diana.

'Better,' I said. 'Too late to be any good, of course.'

'Well, there's Moorside next Saturday.'

'Moorside!' I said scornfully. 'All kids from riding schools.'

'Well, who isn't a kid from a riding school?' said Diana. 'I like that, coming from you! Who do you think you are?'

'You wouldn't have a cold drink handy?' asked

Ann in a dusty sort of voice, and I took them in the kitchen and they drank four glasses of water each, and there was only enough orange squash in the bottle to go into two of them, and even then it was weak.

Suddenly the Lowes' car drew up, and we all rushed to the garden gate.

'Congratulations, Ann,' said Mrs Lowe. 'You rode beautifully and you should have won. That Marshall boy was hardly human. You would hardly expect to be up against competition like that in the under-fourteens.'

'Ann was awfully good, Jill,' said Mummy, looking at me to see how I was taking all this, and I said, 'I'm jolly glad,' and everybody looked relieved.

'I've never seen better open jumping,' said Mr Lowe, 'and I've been going to Chatton Show ever since I can remember. Harvey Smith won it, he was superb. And we all saw Summertime.'

'Oooh!' breathed Diana. 'I wish I was a famous rider and could go all over the country with a famous horse, jumping in open competitions.'

'You may be some day,' said Martin Lowe.

'But Daddy would never let me go and work in a famous stable,' said Diana. 'I've got to be a dreary physiotherapist.'

'But you've still got two more years in the juvenile classes,' said Ann, 'and so have I and so has Jill, and one never knows, the Marshall boy's farmer parents might be ruined and have to leave the farm before next Chatton Show.'

'If you were my daughter,' said Mummy severely, 'I should feel compelled to point out to you that opposition is a challenge, not something to wish removed by the hand of Fate.'

'Gosh, Mrs Crewe!' said Diana. 'Anybody can tell you are an author. You talk just like a frightfully learned book.'

Mrs Lowe took me on one side and said, 'Would you like to do something interesting these holidays, Jill?'

I nearly said yes, but not quite. I said Um, because you know how it is with grown-ups, their ideas of what is interesting are often quite different from yours. I mean, Mrs Lowe is a very good sort, but I certainly didn't want to learn hand-weaving or go to French classes or take somebody's baby out.

'Would it be anything to do with horses?' I said doubtfully.

She laughed and said, 'I wouldn't dare suggest anything to you that wasn't to do with horses. I know you too well. You'll probably be hearing from a friend of mine in a few days. She asked me to suggest some people's names to her, and I gave her yours.'

She wouldn't tell me any more, but I thought as long as the interest was horsy it couldn't be too bad. Anyway, it couldn't be sewing or prams.

In a few days my wrist was all right, and I was riding again. Then the postman brought a letter for me. I am always so excited when I get a letter that I can never open it properly, but tear the envelope across, which infuriates Mummy who uses a paper knife even if she has to go and find it first. This is known as Patience, which is a virtue I haven't got.

I looked at the beginning of the letter, which said

'Dear Jill,' and then at the end which said, 'Yours sincerely, Phyllis Whirtley.'

I said, 'It's from somebody I never heard of. Perhaps it's an aged crone that I once helped across the road, and she's left me a Highland castle or something in her will.'

'Oh, I do hope it's a Highland castle!' said Mummy. 'Jill, that's no way to treat a letter. Flatten it out and read it properly.'

I propped the letter against the coffee pot (we were in the middle of breakfast) and the coffee pot fell over. You wouldn't think a light little thing like a letter could knock over a coffee pot, but then you don't know the kind of things that happen to me unless you have read my previous books. The funny thing was, there was about ten times as much coffee all over the table as there had been in the pot. I sat thinking how this could be, while Mummy mopped frantically and tried to save the butter and marmalade from the flood, and then she said, 'Do read it! What does it say?'

'It's from somebody called Phyllis Whirtley,' I explained. 'I think she must be that friend of Mrs Lowe's. She says, "Blossom Hall, August, Dear Jill" – what a nerve!'

'What a what?' said Mummy, in surprise.

'Oh, that isn't in the letter, only I do think people are the utter depths to call you Jill when they don't know you, as if you were about six.'

Mummy said she had had her doubts about that Highland castle, and could I possibly bear to read the letter without any more interruptions.

It said, 'Dear Jill, I am trying to collect a group of

young people who are keen on horses to help me in
an interesting project I have in mind.'

I stopped at this point, and said, 'Gosh! She sounds
like our English teacher.'

'Go *on!*' said Mummy.

I read out, 'I should be so pleased if you would
come and meet the others at my house on Friday
afternoon of next week, and stay for tea. Come on
your pony if you like, but do try and come. We have a
mutual friend in Mrs Lowe who says you are just the
kind of person I want.' 'Sounds a bit sinister, don't
you think?'

Mummy asked, what was the interesting project?
and I said, 'She doesn't say. She is probably afraid of
putting me off. She says, "If you have a friend of like
mind with yourself, do bring her along." What on
earth does "like mind" mean?' I began to giggle.

Mummy said that either Ann or Diana would do.

'It will have to be Ann,' I said, 'because Diana will
be in London next week. I suppose I'll have to go.
But what on earth do you think it's all about?'

The summer holidays only come once a year after
all, and you spend the greater part of the year looking
forward to them, and then they seem very short. In
our part of the world there are pony shows each
Saturday in August, and one trains hard for these
all through the early part of the summer. After all,
they are the real test of what you and your ponies
can do, and you compete with other people of your
own age who have also been schooling hard all the
year round.

I wasn't at all keen on the idea of anything interfer-
ing with my August programme. It's a funny thing,

but grown-ups always seem to think you're short of something to do in the summer holidays. I hate being organised, because I am perfectly capable of planning every single thing I am going to do in the summer holidays, and so I could if they were twice as long, and so can any other person who has a stable with two perfectly good ponies in it.

My friend Ann Derry wouldn't welcome outside interference either. Though unfortunate enough to have the kind of mother who employs a groom and cannot bear to see her darling daughter with a dandy brush in her hand, from the first Ann firmly insisted on doing her pony, George, herself and he was one of the loveliest ponies I have ever seen. I felt she hadn't quite the knack of showing him to the best advantage – showing was not her strong point – but George was particularly good at jumping and gymkhana events and had a full August programme in front of him.

So you can see why I wasn't wild with excitement at getting mixed up with this Mrs Whirtley. However, I was willing to view the prospect with an open mind. Anyway, I didn't let it worry me.

3 My frightful pupil

Black Boy and Rapide were badly in need of some jumping practice. Their week of idleness hadn't done them any good. They had put on weight and become lazy, so I took them up to the riding school where they proceeded to play me up in fine style.

Neither of them wanted to jump, and each in turn refused at the first fence. Then they went on to amuse themselves by pretending they didn't know what the jumps were for. Black Boy, who was always a bit of an actor, would sidle along in a very stagy way, tossing his head and swinging his rump, and suddenly arriving at the jump would look at it in pained surprise, widening and rolling his eyes affectedly, while Rapide, tied to the fence, stood looking on and making faces. When his turn came he copied Black Boy – as he always did for better or worse – and gave an even more ham performance.

I made them both go right round the seven jumps, while top bars went clattering down, and after Black Boy had eaten half the three-foot hedge while I was tightening Rapide's cheek strap which he had loosened by throwing his head about, I tied them both and walked back across the paddock red with shame and fury.

'I'd disqualify you at sight,' said Wendy Mead,

shaking with laughter. She was the girl who helped Mrs Darcy with the riding school, and her father's farm was nearly next door.

'I'd disqualify myself,' I said in disgust. 'What an exhibition, and I thought my ponies were foolproof! This is what comes of a week's rest out at grass.'

'I've come to the conclusion that any pony is capable of anything,' said Wendy. 'They've played you up thoroughly this morning, but you'll soon get them in hand again. By the way, Jill, if you've got half an hour to spare I wish you'd do me a favour.'

I told her I was boiling hot so I hoped it was something cool that she wanted me to do, and that I had to be home by twelve.

'Well, would you take a lesson for me?' she said. 'I don't know what I was thinking about, but I've booked two lessons for the same time.'

'Honestly,' I said, 'at the present moment I don't feel capable of teaching a four-year-old to sit on a seaside donkey.'

'Well, this is quite unimportant. A beginner. She rang up and booked a course of six lessons, and this will be the first.'

'Oh, all right,' I said without much enthusiasm. 'Only you know what beginners are. They bounce up on an unschooled pony, and want to gallop and jump before they can walk properly.'

'This one isn't bringing a pony, so you can put her on anything you like.'

'Well, can I have a look at Blue Smoke first?' I asked.

We went round to the stable, and in her stall stood Mrs Darcy's beautiful grey hunter, shining like satin, and turning her lovely head for our caresses. I made a lot of flattering remarks about her beauty, and thought that if I could ever own anything like her my life's ambition would be achieved.

'Do you remember that awful time when James Bush rode her, and she was ill afterwards, and we thought she was dying?' I said.

Wendy was just opening her mouth to reply when I thought I heard a sound like a shuffle of feet.

'What's that?' I said, and as we both listened we saw a small dark shadow move somewhere at the end of the line of stalls.

'There's somebody there,' said Wendy, 'who has no business to be there.' She called sharply, 'Come out, you – whoever you are!'

The weirdest little person appeared, and came sidling towards us, looking scared stiff. She looked about eight, and she had on a school skirt and washed-out tee-shirt, with black tights, and her hair hung over her eyes which peeped out from under her fringe like two black buttons in a bird's nest.

'Who on earth are you?' said Wendy.

The kid looked terrified, and said she was sorry but she just wanted to look at the horses.

'Well, you shouldn't be in here, you know,' said Wendy. 'Now run along home, quick!'

'But I've come for my l-lesson,' said the kid.

Wendy gave a groan, rolled up her eyes, and extended one hand dramatically towards me.

'Methinks 'tis your pupil,' she said. 'Take it, Jill, it's all yours.'

'Murder!' I said, under my breath. But Mrs Darcy had always insisted on extreme politeness to clients however off-putting they might look, and as one who has had a lot of experience of riding schools I can tell you that new pupils often look very off-putting indeed. (As a matter of fact, I did myself when I was a new pupil.) So I pulled myself together and said to the kid, 'Good morning. Will you come outside and tell me what you want? What's your name, by the way?'

'Dinah Dean,' said the kid, who looked even smaller and thinner when we got out into the daylight.

I asked her how old she was, and she said she was nearly thirteen. I looked surprised and said, 'Have you done much riding?'

She looked a bit miserable and said, 'I – I'm afraid I haven't ever been on a pony. I expect you won't want me here, not knowing anything about riding.'

'Oh, we'd much rather,' I said. 'We hate beginners who think they know everything before they start. Give me raw material every time.'

I got that last remark out of a book called *Raoul the Riding Master* and it came in handy and the kid looked very impressed.

'What shall I put her on?' I asked Wendy, and Wendy said, 'Oh, Ninepins, I should think.' Ninepins was the riding school's nice old slug, fifteen years old and very understanding with beginners.

'Come on then,' I said to the kid. 'First we go to the harness room and fetch the tack. Would you know anything about a pony's tack?'

'I suppose it would have a bridle and a s-s-saddle,' she stuttered.

'Look, would you mind not being so shy?' I said.

'You're quite right. I've known beginners who didn't even know what tack was.'

I collected Ninepins' tack, and then went along, followed by the kid, to get the pony.

'Oh, isn't he sweet!' she said, throwing her arms round his neck. I felt a bit more taken with her, because she obviously loved ponies, and Ninepins who hadn't been called sweet for years looked very bucked up.

'I suppose you haven't the slightest idea how to put the bridle on?' I asked.

'I wouldn't know anything,' she said, with a shy grin that got lost in her floppy hair.

'Well, let's get cracking,' I said. 'First we slip the reins over his head and neck, and next we stand close to his head and pass the right arm round and under, taking hold of the crown piece with the right hand and the bit with the left.' I went on with the usual instructions, and finished up, 'It sounds complicated when you say it, but it's awfully easy really, when you get the knack.'

She looked a bit doubtful and said, 'How does the saddle go on?'

I showed her how to run the stirrups up the leathers, and how to fling on the saddle and fasten the girths properly, and she watched so closely that I could feel her breathing down my arm. I slid my fingers down the girths to smooth out wrinkles, and she said, 'I think that's a good idea. I'd like to learn to put the tack on properly' – which was better than most beginners who think that saddling a pony is just like tying up a brown paper parcel.

'Have you any idea how to mount?' I said.

'I don't know anything,' she said, 'I expect you think I'm awful.'

'Don't be silly,' I said. 'I'll put you up the first time, and then I'll teach you to mount properly by yourself.'

To my surprise she went up quite lightly, and did all I told her, and sat straight with her knees and head up and her hands well down. Apart from looking so awful she didn't look bad at all – if you know what I mean.

'Ooh, this is gorgeous!' she said. I suddenly realised that the kid was having a sort of dream-come-true feeling, and I felt a bit sympathetic. Actually the first time I got on a pony I was far worse than Dinah Dean.

I started Ninepins off at a slow walk, and Dinah looked thrilled. She seemed to have those naturally light hands that people are born with, and she must have watched people riding because I could tell she was copying what she had seen and was trying to do it right.

I said, 'What school do you go to? I think I've seen you somewhere before.'

She turned red and said, 'I don't go to school. I sort of keep house and cook and all that for Daddy.'

I said that I thought people had to go to school, and she said, 'You see, we're always moving, and nobody notices me. Can I get off now, and learn to mount by myself?'

I was quite surprised and impressed, because the last thing most beginners want to do is to get down and learn to mount properly. They usually want to gallop and try a few jumps.

I showed her how to mount, and she soon got the idea. She really was the best beginner I'd ever had anything to do with, if she hadn't looked so awful and made me cold inside in case anybody I knew would come along the lane and watch us and think what a terrible advertisement she was for the riding school. Then I suddenly remembered where I had seen her before. She had once come up and patted Black Boy when I had tied him outside the Post Office, and I had shooed her off.

If she recognised me she hadn't shown it. I let her do a complete round of the paddock by herself and she did quite well and looked to be in a sort of daze of joy, and then I thought, Thank goodness the half-hour's up!

I brought her in and said, 'Well, that's all for now. I suppose you've arranged with Miss Mead for your next lesson?'

Dinah went bright scarlet, and I thought she was going to cry.

She blurted out, 'I'm not coming any more.'

'Well, that's up to you,' I said, surprised. 'But you're not bad at all, and you'd be quite good after a few more lessons.'

'It was a lovely lesson,' she said, 'but – well, I can't pay for it. I thought I'd have the lessons and then find some way of paying for them, but I can't. I expect you'll feel like sending me to prison.'

I thought, that's the limit. People who run a riding school or any sort of business, do occasionally come across characters who think it is clever to do cheating things like that. I remembered how when I was helping some friends of mine to run a stable and hire out hacks, there was a woman who got a pony for a whole week for her child for nothing, by giving us a false name and address. I suppose she thought because we were only young she had twisted us very cleverly, and we were sorry for her child for having a mother like that.

Up to then I had been feeling a bit sorry for the Dean kid, but now I was just plain furious. I didn't know how I was going to tell Wendy Mead, and I hoped she wouldn't think I was in any way to blame.

I said very coldly, 'You shouldn't have come. We don't teach people to ride for the fun of it. Now get out of here and don't ever come back again.'

I led Ninepins away and never looked back to see what Dinah was doing. I said to Wendy, 'That was a wash-out. The kid had a lesson and then calmly said she couldn't pay for it.'

'The little beast!' said Wendy. 'We've had that kind before. And she'd the nerve to book six lessons! Well, I'll be on the look-out for her if she ever turns up here again. Thanks, Jill, I'm sorry your time has been wasted.'

I collected my ponies, and Wendy said, 'Don't worry about them misbehaving. They know perfectly well what they're supposed to do. When are you using them again?'

'Saturday,' I said, 'at Moorside. It's rather a kiddish affair but it's all practice.'

'It was rotten luck missing Chatton Show.'

'You're telling me!' I said. 'By the way, congrats on winning the Grade C jumping.'

'Oh that was just a fluke,' said Wendy modestly. Black Boy and Rapide looked as meek and innocent as if they had done a perfect morning's work.

'Oh, come on, you two perishers!' I said.

4   This pride and fall business

I was late home, which annoyed Mummy as she had planned an early lunch so that she could catch a bus to Rychester, and I had to explain. When I told her about Dinah she said, 'That must be the child I was hearing about. Everybody seems sorry for her. Her father does some kind of research and keeps this child cleaning the house and cooking. He could be made to send her to school, but I believe they never stay anywhere long and she wouldn't be much better off. They live in one of those hard-looking little houses on the new estate.'

'She had a perfectly good riding lesson for nothing,' I said, 'and wasted half my morning.'

Mummy looked thoughtful and said, 'I don't like to think that a child wants a lesson so badly that she'll cheat to get one.'

'Oh, some kids would try anything on,' I said, feeling at the same time a sneaking feeling that Dinah wasn't really that type of kid. I added, 'I never had anything I didn't pay for.' But the minute I'd said it I remembered that I had had practically everything without paying for it, just because Martin Lowe had given me my first lessons and my feeding stuff and a lot of other things.

I said, 'Well, anyway, I did jobs to pay for Black

Boy's winter keep, and I bought my first riding coat and jodhpurs secondhand at an auction.'

'And it was my money, if I remember rightly,' said Mummy musingly, and added, 'How much would a lesson cost like the one you gave Dinah Dean?'

'Ten pounds,' I said.

She took some money out of her purse and said, 'Give that to Mrs Darcy. Then the riding school won't be the loser.'

'You needn't – ' I began, but she already had on her faraway look which means she is thinking about some of those very whimsy characters she puts into her children's books. I sometimes think it's a good thing that the children in Mummy's books don't go to my school or they'd be murdered. She had just had her latest one published, called *Angeline, the Fairy Child*, about a person who was only six and brought joy and gladness into the heart of her bitter old grandfather, and there had been eleven frightfully good reviews of it in eleven frightfully good papers, and Mummy was thrilled, but it just left me cold.

I went around to see Ann that night and found her fussing and fuming over a slight cut on George's knee that you could hardly see.

'Our kid Pam did it,' she said. 'She'd no business to ride George, I've told her a million times she's not to touch him. Now he'll lose joint-oil. He'll be scarred for life.'

I told her it was nothing and you could hardly see it.

'He'll be stiff on Saturday for Moorside gymkhana,' fumed Ann.

'He won't,' I said. 'Gosh, you are a fusspot,

Ann. Put some penicillin powder on it. It's only a scratch.'

'I bet it turns septic,' she grumbled.

'If it does I'll lend you Black Boy for Saturday,' I said. 'Anyway, Moorside is nothing. You know we only enter for it because Mrs Darcy says it looks unsportsmanlike to shun the smaller gymkhanas just because we're good.' Then to cheer her up I told her about Mrs Whirtley and the Interesting Project, and asked her if she'd like to go with me as my other horsy person.

'But what's it all in aid of?' said Ann suspiciously, just as I knew she would.

I told her I hadn't a clue, she knew just as much about it as I did.

I added, 'The Whirtley woman is a friend of Mrs Lowe's, and Mrs Lowe is so decent and knows how I feel about the things I do in the summer holidays that I don't think she'd deliberately get me mixed up in anything I didn't care about.'

'The summer holidays are so jolly short,' said Ann. 'I mean, we don't want to do anything but ride, do we? I mean, supposing it's getting up a Bring and Buy Sale! We tried that once and we weren't so hot at it. Even Mrs Lowe likes Bring and Buy Sales, and so does my mother and yours too, if it comes to that. I can't think of anything drearier.'

'We could go to Blossom Hall,' I said. 'The Whirtley woman mentioned something about tea. And if we don't like the Interesting Project we can always wangle out of it.'

'If we go,' said Ann, 'we'll be in it up to the neck.'

'*You* don't have to come,' I said. 'I'll get somebody else.'

Actually I wanted Ann to come with me more than anybody, and I had a feeling that her sense of curiosity would make her come, especially if I suggested that she needn't, and I was right.

'Oh, I'll come,' she said. 'If you can bear it, I can.'

'It might be jolly good,' I said hopefully. 'She might be going to offer us the use of her parkland for practice gallops. That would be super! She may have had it revealed to her in a dream that she ought to take all the poor little ponies off the road and give them some lovely parkland to gallop in. She may be frightfully rich and burning to do something for the cause of equitation.'

Ann said gloomily that she was quite sure there would be a catch in it.

'She probably wants us to do a flag day,' she said, 'and you know I never dare ask people to buy flags. I did it for the orphans, and I just slunk into a doorway and got nothing, and Daddy had to put five pounds into my box all in small change or I wouldn't have had anything at all.'

'OK,' I said. 'If it's a flag day we're out.'

Saturday came, and as I had predicted you couldn't tell that George had a scratch, though Mrs Derry still fussed about and said she was sure he was going to limp at any minute, and darling-do-be-careful.

Ann and I hacked to Moorside with our lunches, oats, grooming tools, and everything else we needed neatly packed up. We weren't particularly interested, so for once we hadn't that cold and hot sensation of excitement that one gets before a pony event. It was hot, so we wore our new shirts, mine was yellow and Ann's blue, and our well-brushed jodhpurs and boots, and we took our black coats for the Grand Parade and for going up for any cups we might win.

On the road we saw a lot of other people also making for Moorside, in fact there was a complete traffic block where some girl's pony was planted firmly broadside across the road and she had no idea how to pull or push it round. Nobody else seemed to have much idea either, in fact Ann had to get down and encourage the pony to move, which he did, recognising the hand and voice of experience. The girl remounted, and Ann gave the pony a whack, and the girl lost her stirrups and went on to his neck.

'Golly,' she said as she came back to me. 'Most of these people look as if they were on a pony for the first time in history.'

'Don't criticise the entry until after the competition,' I said, and she said, 'Well, look at them. I ask you!'

We reached the ground, which was merely a large field belonging to a farm, and decided that the whole thing was rather crude. The ring was not fenced but was made by running a rope round some stakes, and there were a few benches for spectators but no proper seats. There was a Scoutish kind of tent marked Stewards, and a St John Ambulance tent with a nurse standing by the flap looking hopeful. The ponies were on the far side of the field, and a few people were exercising up and down.

Ann and I went and joined them but found very few people there we knew. Besides ourselves there only seemed to be about half a dozen experienced riders, and the rest were obviously in for their first or second competition, and fond mothers were all over the place tying numbers on, in some cases upside down. One mother even held up a child's number to me and said, 'Where does this go?'

Ann said, 'Gosh, why did we come?' I said, to encourage the other entry, and she said would I kindly stop quoting out of books, as I had done nothing else since we left home.

The first class, for ponies under thirteen hands, was called into the collecting ring, and you should have seen the small kids scrambling about and backing into each other, while half the ponies were calmly cropping grass regardless of frenzied rein-pulling, and several others walked straight across the ring and out at the other side.

However, by then a few older and more experienced-looking people had begun to arrive, which we thought was a good thing as we hadn't liked the idea of snatching all the prizes from the hands of these babes.

I was mainly interested in the 14–2 showing class in which I had decided to show Rapide. He had not Black Boy's natural aptitude for showing, so I wanted him to get some practice and had given him a lot of schooling for this purpose. I thought Moorside would be a good small show for him to take a first or second, and it would give him confidence for bigger events. He looked beautifully groomed and sure of himself, and I patted his nose and said, 'Now you do as well as you did yesterday in the paddock, and we're home.'

Rapide made a face at me. He was given to making faces and I never quite knew what they meant. The only time he ever won me a cup he made a face at the woman who was presenting it, and she turned quite pale and nearly dropped it. She didn't understand Rapide, and probably thought he was about to take a bite out of her hat. Gosh, I was embarrassed.

However, to return to Moorside. I glanced over the other ponies in the 14–2 class as we waited to go into the ring, and there didn't look to be any frightening opposition, apart from Ann's George who was the sort of eye-catching pony with a long stride and dignified action beloved by certain judges, though George wasn't very light in hand and was apt to become unbalanced at critical moments.

There was a very neat farmer's daughter on a very neat pony. She looked frightfully serious and wore a dark blue coat. There was also a boy in a tweed hacking jacket on a long-backed bay, who looked so confident that for the first time I felt a twinge in my middle. Before I had time to see any more the ring steward called us in and we began riding round.

Now that Class Two was in action I saw that it was a more competent lot than I had expected. This shook me, and I had Rapide on rather a tight short rein which he resented. Hastily realising that he was inclined to overbend I let him walk out for a little and collected him. He went calmly into his trot and I felt that all was well at last.

In front of me Ann was riding George like the book, but so was everybody else riding like the book. I never saw such a lot of correct riding in my life. Nobody crowded anybody and nobody ran out. Then the ring steward told us to canter and things began to happen. A girl on a dashing pony whizzed past me, her pony bucked, and she came off. Two other people couldn't get their ponies to canter. One resorted to whacking and was stopped by the judge, the other just gave up trying and trotted on. I noticed that the farmer's daughter in dark blue was going beautifully, so was the boy on the long-backed bay and a few other people, in fact I was noticing the others to such an extent that for an instant I forgot it was Rapide I was riding and not Black Boy until to my dismay I found he was blithely cantering on the wrong leg. I tried to change him, but it was too late. He crowded George in front and for one humiliating moment I thought he was going to run out.

By the time I had collected him I saw that the neat dark blue girl had been called in, also the competent boy. Ann was called in third. Seeing my chances melt away like this completely upset me. Another boy was called in, and by now there was no opposition of any kind left and I was called fifth.

I had enough presence of mind to rein back well and Rapide obliged by standing squarely, but honestly by then I was so unsure of myself and of him that I found myself looking down to see what his legs were doing, and of course the judge's eye was on me as I did it, further jeopardising any chances I had left.

I sat quietly and watched the others do their shows. The neat little blue girl was terribly good, so was the boy. Ann's figure of eight didn't quite come off, and I could tell that she was a bit flustered at the way things had turned out after the way we had criticised other people before the show began.

The boy in fourth place was called Leonard Payne and was one of Mrs Darcy's pupils. He wasn't particularly good and I could not bear the thought of being beaten by him. Such, however, was to be my fate on this dark day of my history. Leonard had practised his show many times under Mrs Darcy's eye and it went off beautifully.

It was my turn. I walked a circle, trotted, cantered slowly, came back to a trot, then cantered on the other leg. It seemed to go all right, only Rapide was obviously not happy. I went back to my place and dragged off the saddle, and by now I felt so dim and low that I wouldn't have been surprised if the judge had found saddle galls or anything else on Rapide.

However, he made the usual vague muttering sounds and told me to lead out in hand at a walk and trot back. This went off quite decently and I hoped it was not too late.

The judge then told the first five to walk round in a circle, showing that he was not yet satisfied with the placing. While we did this I tried to sum up my chances. There was still hope. Ann was moved from third to second, displacing the tweed boy, and I could not think I would not displace Leonard Payne and get the Reserve (which was bad enough when I had foolishly counted on being first or second). But they called us in, and there was I, still fifth and unclassed, and the rosettes were given out. I retired feeling very dim indeed.

The next class we were interested in was of course the fourteen-and-under jumping. Showing the state of conceit we were in when we arrived, I must confess that we had both been certain of getting clear rounds.

We didn't get clear rounds! Actually we tied for third place with four faults each. By now we were both thoroughly snappy. Ann said that it was George's scratch that was to blame, and I said it was Rapide's bad luck to be having an off day, but the truth was as we very well knew that we had started off much too confident and careless and that is fatal in riding. One should be just as keyed-up at a small affair as a big one.

'Here I go!' said Ann grimly as we rode out of the ring. 'Second at Chatton Show last Saturday against some real riders, and third at Moorside today among a lot of kids from riding schools.'

'Oh, dry up!' I barked, not liking to have my rash words thrown back at me. 'We certainly shan't be needing our black coats to ride up for cups, and strange as it may seem, not having won any firsts we shan't be invited to ride in the Grand Parade.'

Just for something to do we went in for the Musical Chairs, and I was first and Ann second, though that didn't soothe us much. We fed the ponies and gave them drinks, and after partly quenching our own misery with about six ices each we rode home. I knew Mummy would merely shrug her shoulders and say, 'Nobody wins all the time,' whereas Mrs Derry would probably weep copiously over Ann and nearly let all the blinds down, being that sort of mother. I was sorry for Ann's young sister Pam, because I knew she would never hear the end of that scratch she let George get.

It had been a shocking day, and I have told you all about it because it served us jolly well right for thinking we were too good for Moorside. It taught me a lesson, and I have never since thought I was too good for anything, so I hope you will not do so either, however good you may be.

5 My rash deed

Being the summer holidays, I went up to the riding school for the weekly cross-country ride, and as we all clattered out of the gate a dark shadow flitted across the hedge and somebody's pony side-stepped and bucked.

Wendy Mead rode up and said, 'What's happening here?' Then she said, 'Oh, it's that awful Dean child. Get away with you! And don't come round here again, slinking in hedges.'

I saw then it was Dinah Dean, and she gave me a longing look, but I looked the other way. We went for our ride, and it was wonderful, over Neshbury Common and through the pinewood glades, and we did a bit of hedge-jumping and the sort of things you do in Handy Hunter competitions. But all the time I had a weird feeling about Dinah that I couldn't shake off. Don't get the idea that I am a Noble Character, in fact if you have read my other books you will already be saying Far From It, but it seemed to be a slur on the glorious cause of equitation that a person without any money to pay for it should want a lesson so badly that she would cheat a riding school to get it. And as you know, if you have survived after reading my aforesaid earlier books, the cause of equitation is the main object of my life. I felt as if I ought to Do

Something About It, but I didn't know what, and I didn't want to bother anyway.

When I got home Mummy was out, and Mrs Crosby had gone home, so I made myself a beaker of cocoa and a pile of toast, and brought all my tack into the kitchen to clean it, which in the ordinary way I am not allowed to do, as when I have finished there seems to be Brasso and saddle-soap all over the chairs, floor, etc. I took my time over getting everything clean, and then lugged it all back to the tack room and went upstairs.

In a box on the top of the cupboard where I hang my clothes were my very first check coat and jodhpurs, now much too small for me. They were secondhand when I bought them at an auction four years ago, but they were good quality and had been kept clean and mended, so there was lots of life in them yet for somebody small enough to wear them. Actually I was keeping them for my descendants in the hope that I would one day have some horsy daughters, but now I told myself hastily that any daughters I might have would probably be quite unlike me, and very earnest about fossils or Alsatians or ballet and have no use for riding things, and I would be sorry I had kept them for such unworthy creatures.

I bundled the things under my arm, wrote a note for Mummy saying 'Back for supper', and stuck it on her typewriter, so that if – as usual – she came back bursting with inspiration for a new chapter of *Basil the Bird-Song Boy* (which was the off-putting title of the new book she had begun to write) she couldn't fail to see it.

Then I got out my bike and dashed off to the new estate where all the houses were the same, and just like the houses that children of three draw, boxes with lids and flat fronts.

I asked a kid where the Deans lived, and she showed me the house. It looked even horrider than the others as it wasn't very clean and there was a lopsided blind upstairs.

I knocked at the door and Dinah answered it. Before she had time to fall down dead with shock, I shoved the parcel at her and muttered, 'Here, these are for you, and perhaps someday you'll be able to get some riding lessons.'

Then I dashed off before she could thank me or anything. When one does a deed like this one is supposed to glow with happiness, but I must say I didn't. I only began to think that probably the noble cause of equitation would have got along just as well if I had kept my coat and jodhs for my descendants as I had originally intended, especially if one of my daughters turned out to be horsy after all, as she very well might, because of course I should do all I could to put her off fossils and Alsatians and ballet while she was a helpless infant.

So I felt that as usual I had been quite mad, and that Mummy was right when she said you should never do anything drastic in cold blood. Or was it hot blood? Anyway, I'd done it, and I couldn't go and snatch the things back, so I started thinking about something else which happened to be Mrs Whirtley, and wondering if Ann would prove to be right about the flag day and if so, how we could get out of it.

I arrived home, and Mummy asked where had

I been, and I said nowhere – as one does – and after supper I took Rapide into the little paddock behind the orchard and gave him some very intensive schooling indeed, because I was so annoyed with him over Moorside.

I kept him at the slow trot, then changed gradually to an extended trot, and back to slow. Then I rode some circles, and crossed my stirrups and trotted again. Then I rode him at the loose rein walk and the ordinary walk, and tried a quarter turn to either side, and put him through a complete imaginary show. Believe me, he did everything beautifully – as he would when it didn't matter – and looked at me as much as to say 'I know I'm good.' I said, 'Well, why did you let me down on Saturday?' I felt furious, but patted him all the same for doing well, which a pony naturally expects, and took him in and rubbed him down and gave him his supper.

The next evening Mummy had some letters to post and said she would walk down to the post office with them as the box in our lane is a bit unpredictable.

She had been gone ten minutes when there was a knock at the door. I was reading the new copy of *Riding* which Mrs Lowe kindly passes on to me, so I didn't like to have to uncoil myself or break off in an exciting bit about stable management.

On the doorstep stood a person in a neat coat and jodhpurs. Mine! It was Dinah Dean.

She blurted out, 'I never thanked you for these. I was so stunned. It was marvellous of you. I don't know how to thank you. I mean – '

'That's all right,' I said, running my eye over her. Apart from the decent coat and jodhs she looked frightful. She had on some very scruffy shoes and the same washed-out pink tee-shirt, and her hair was more lopsided than ever.

I said, 'If you don't mind me saying so, you ought to wear a shirt with a collar and tie, and couldn't you shove your hair back and stick a grip in?'

She went bright red and said, 'I'm s-sorry.'

'Look, you'd better come upstairs,' I said, feeling like slaying her but somehow driven on by my Better Feelings. 'I've got a white shirt that's too small for me and I can probably find you an old tie and some grips.'

She followed me up to my room, and when I opened the door she said, 'Ooooh!'

My room did look smashing. On the tallboy were my cups and prizes (which I happened to have cleaned that morning) and all round the room was my Pony Frieze. This frieze consists of a green line which I painted right round the walls about four feet from the ground, and all along it are stuck pictures of horses cut out of magazines, standing on the green line or prancing along it as though it were the grass in a paddock. There was just about a yard of the line without any horses because I still hadn't got enough to fill it up.

'Oh, it's wonderful!' said Dinah, and rushed up to the frieze and started patting the horses with her finger.

'What a lovely idea.'

'It's not bad,' I said.

She said, 'I've got an old *Country Life* that Daddy brought home wrapped round something. It's got pictures of horses in it. I'll bring it for you, for the unfinished bit.'

I said rather squashingly that she needn't bother, I could get some myself. Then I found the old shirt and said, 'It isn't too clean but you can wash it.' I found an old fawn tie too that had gone stringy, and about six grips. Dinah looked as if she was going to have a fit, and started muttering thank you about a million times, but I wanted to get rid of her and get back to *Riding*, and anyway Doing Good always makes me feel hot and bothered, so I bundled her downstairs.

'Now look,' I said. 'You buzz off and don't come here again. I don't want you.'

'Oh, please could I come and muck out your stable?' she said. 'I'd come every morning before I get Daddy's breakfast. I'd like to, because you gave me all these things.'

'No, you can't,' I said. 'I just don't want you here! Can't you understand?'

She said, 'Well, do you think I could go and muck out Mrs Darcy's stable? I feel so awful about what I did. I didn't mean to cheat.'

'I know you didn't,' I said. 'But I advise you to keep away from Mrs Darcy's or you'll be well and truly slain. Now go away, and stay away, if you can understand plain English.'

She got the idea and gave a sort of gulp, so I shoved her out and shut the door thankfully. I had been terrified that Mummy would come back before the kid was gone.

Next morning when I went down to unlock my tack room I found someone had been there before me. It had all been tidied up to such an extent it nearly hurt you to look at it. I know my tack room usually looks as though a tornado has gone through it, but the point is that when it is in a muddle I know just where to put my hand on everything and when it is tidy – although it looks good – I can't find a thing. On the bench was a note which read, 'I got through the window. I hope you don't mind. Dinah.'

I wrote on the bottom of the note, 'Yes, I do mind, and it'll take me ages to get the place back into the kind of muddle I like, so if you come back here again, buzz off. Jill.'

The last thing I wanted was to get mixed up with Dinah Dean. I don't think she came back. The note stayed where it was.

6 Blossom Hall

Ann and I were a long time making up our minds what to wear to go to Mrs Whirtley's.

'The point is, are we going to ride there?' said Ann.

I said, 'Of course we are. Otherwise we shall have to go in school-ish cotton frocks and look like a couple of kids. The point is, shall we wear just shirts and jodhpurs as it's rather hot weather, or our tweed coats, or our blacks?

Ann said our blacks would be too hot. I said, yes, but jolly sophisticated, and it was better to make Mrs Whirtley think we were a couple of hard women to hounds than just two more child riders, and anyway if we put some of Mummy's powder on our faces it would stop the hotness showing through.

Eventually we decided on our black coats. We plastered on the powder, and a lipstick called Flame-Thrower that Ann found at the local chemist's, but we had to rub a lot of that off as it was rather frightening.

We started off early on Black Boy and George, and rode slowly so as not to arrive practically on fire.

Blossom Hall was a great big shabby Georgian mansion with wonderful parkland all round it, and a lawn in front that looked about a mile square.

Ann said, 'Think of living in a place like this and being able to ride round the park all day. Some people are jolly lucky.'

'If ever I'm rich,' I said, 'this is what I'll buy, but I never will be.'

Ann said we might both marry millionaires and I said, 'Don't be so feeble,' and she said, well somebody had to marry millionaires and it might as well be us.

Then Mrs Whirtley came down the imposing steps and said, 'Come along, girls. Welcome to Blossom Hall.'

We rather liked the look of her, because actually she was exactly like a horse about the face, even to the forelock and big teeth.

We tied the ponies where she showed us, and went into a large drawing-room full of big bouncing settees and oil paintings and looped-up curtains, where four other people of about our age were sitting round. Two of them were boys in shirts and trousers, and the others were girls in cotton dresses and sandals. They looked at Ann and me rather awesomely as if we were grown-ups. Nobody said anything and we all sat there feeling dumb. Soon five more people arrived, three boys and two girls, and then another girl who was in a black coat . . . with large round specs and long plaits. She glared at Ann and me.

Mrs Whirtley said, 'Now we're all here. To business, I think, don't you, people?'

As none of us knew what the business was we all looked quite blank, and one girl giggled out loud.

Mrs Whirtley had a very fluty voice and kept patting the side of her nose while she was talking.

I daren't look at her for fear of having hysterics. She said, 'Well now, people, I must tell you why I asked you to come here.'

('Flag Day!' Ann muttered.)

'We have just come to live at this wonderful old house with its fine park, and I feel that some good use should be made of it.'

('Shouldn't think it is,' I muttered back.)

'Mr Whirtley and I feel that it is up to us to make a real effort for some good cause – '

('There you are!' muttered Ann.)

' – and this park and garden will make a wonderful setting for the kind of effort we have in mind.'

('Shut up, you're off the beam!' I muttered back.)

'What we are thinking of,' said Mrs Whirtley, 'is a kind of fête, and that is why you riders are here today, because the fête is to be in aid of various societies for the protection and care of horses, and we propose to hold it next month, on the second Saturday in September, just before you all go back to school.'

I began to brighten up a bit.

'I have always been of the opinion,' went on Mrs Whirtley, 'that young people have the best and brightest ideas, so I decided to form my committee from people like yourselves, representing young horse lovers from various parts of the county. Are you all willing to be on my committee and help me to arrange the fête?'

Everybody looked at everybody else and nobody said anything, we were all paralysed.

'Oh, don't be shy,' said Mrs Whirtley, and the girl with specs and plaits grinned rather sickeningly and said, 'I think we're all willing, Mrs Whirtley.'

She said, 'Splendid, splendid!' and beamed, and went on, 'Now what you have to decide is what we are going to do at the fête. Don't think about the food or anything like that because that is my affair. But if we get a thousand people here, how are we going to amuse them? It's got to be lively and appealing to everybody of all ages. Now, let me hear some of your ideas.'

To my horror she looked straight at me and I wished I hadn't made myself look so sophisticated. I sucked off a bit of my lipstick and it tasted awful.

'Do tell me your name,' said Mrs Whirtley.

'Jill Crewe,' I said.

'Oh, of course, I've heard a lot about Jill Crewe. Well, come along, Jill, what do you suggest we do at the fête?'

'C-could we have a pageant?' I stuttered feebly. 'Ponies Through the Ages, or something?'

'That's one idea,' said Mrs Whirtley. 'A pageant. Anything else?'

One kid chirped up that her mother had a Queen Elizabeth dress, so she would like to ride her pony and be Queen Elizabeth in the pageant.

'Well, dear, we haven't got as far as that,' said Mrs Whirtley, looking very snootily at the kid who went a sort of pale green. 'Any more ideas? What about you?' And she looked at the girl with specs, who promptly said her name was Clarissa Dandleby, and what about a point-to-point?

Mrs Whirtley looked a bit stunned, as well she might, and said, 'Of course, dear, we're not all point-to-point riders,' and Clarissa Dandleby said she had ridden in her first point-to-point when she was only eleven and hoped she would soon be steeplechasing, and Mrs Whirtley said, 'I think we'd better not have *too* big ideas,' and Clarissa said, 'Well, what about some Hunter Trials?'

'Couldn't we have just an ordinary gymkhana?' said a boy, and Clarissa Dandleby glowered at him and said, 'How jolly tame,' and another boy said, 'Well, let's have a gymkhana *and* Hunter Trials *and* a pageant,' and about five people said 'Gosh!'

'I do think,' said Mrs Whirtley, 'that perhaps a gymkhana would be the best idea. It lets everybody in, doesn't it? Even the tinies.'

'Of course, if it's going to be a kids' thing – ' began somebody, and Clarissa Dandleby interrupted, 'It wouldn't be too bad if we could have dressage and cross-country too.'

'Oh that's much too ambitious,' said Mrs Whirtley.

'I want to be in a pageant,' said the kid who wanted to be Queen Elizabeth.

'I want to be Dick Turpin,' said another kid.

'Couldn't we have an open jumping event?' suggested Ann, 'and get some famous riders and horses to enter?'

'I'm afraid that might cost so much to organise that it would swallow up all the profits,' said Mrs Whirtley, 'and after all we do want to make a lot of money for the needy horses.'

'Couldn't we do a play?' said a very fat girl in a too-tight cotton dress. 'I could write one. I've written about eight plays. One's called *With Drake on the High Seas*, only I could alter it a bit and call it *With Saddle in the Sierras* or something like that.'

'Your plays are mouldy,' said the boy sitting next

to her who looked like her brother. 'They did one at your school and everybody was nearly sick.'

'That isn't very kind, dear,' said Mrs Whirtley, and the boy said, 'Well, Moira's plays *are* mouldy. I wouldn't mind doing a play if it could be a decent play like *Murder on the Stairs* or an Agatha Christie one.'

'If a play's in the open air it might as well be a pageant,' said somebody else, and everybody yelled, 'Now we're back at the pageant again!'

'I'll tell you what we'll do,' said Mrs Whirtley, 'we'll have tea, and meanwhile you can all be thinking and then we'll have some brilliant ideas.'

I must say the tea cheered us all up no end, it was simply smashing. There were four kinds of sandwiches, and buns and meringues and jam puffs and chocolate cake. Mrs Whirtley proved to be the most decent kind of hostess and didn't pass the best things just once but several times, and there was enough for everybody to have about three of everything if they wanted.

However, her hopes must have been dashed to the ground, because far from developing any brilliant ideas after tea nobody could think of anything new to say, except a frightful kid with a lisp who said, 'couldn't there be a fanthy dreth parade with decorated ponieth?'

Most people turned pale green at the idea, but one person said, 'I think fancy dress would be a good idea, and we could have collecting boxes and shake them at people and get a lot of money. We could dress up like pirates.'

'I know! We could sell pirate flags!' yelled some

ghastly-minded boy. Ann and I looked at each other and shuddered.

'I have already decided,' said Mrs Whirtley. 'We shall have a gymkhana. It isn't very original, but it appeals to everybody and we may be able to get some good riders for open jumping.'

Clarissa Dandleby gave a snort, and said that Mrs Whirtley simply wouldn't get anybody who was any good to come for an ordinary gymkhana.

'My dear child,' said Mrs Whirtley in a blistering voice, 'I don't remember your name, but let me tell you that I have been getting up gymkhanas for years and I have never yet had to complain about the attendance.'

'Squash for Clarissa,' muttered a girl behind me. 'She thinks she's the best-known girl rider in the county.'

Somebody said, could there be a novice hack class, as she had a novice hack she wanted to enter, and Mrs Whirtley said there could be.

She then added, 'The tickets will be printed in a couple of days and I shall send them out to you. I want you each to sell two dozen to start with.

Ann made a face at me, but everybody seemed quite satisfied except Clarissa Dandleby who, in spite of her squash, still went on muttering that simply nobody would come to a gymkhana unless there was a dressage test and open jumping with large prizes, and as for her she couldn't be expected to compete along with a lot of kids on ponies.

That was the end of the meeting, and we wandered out on the drive and sorted out our ponies who by now had all made friends and got their ropes mixed.

Clarissa's pony was a lovely dark chestnut mare with four white socks, and Clarissa did a lot of frantic kicking before she got away at an extremely uncollected canter. She was obviously the kicking type.

7 We *must* sell tickets

'About these awful two dozen tickets that we've each got to sell,' I said a few days later, sitting rather uncomfortably on a turned-up box, watching Ann give a lesson to her young sister.

'I've just realised why Pam's so ghastly,' she said. 'She doesn't ride at all. She just sits and uses her hands.'

'She's what they call a passive rider,' I said. 'Tell her to use her legs and seat.'

'I have,' said Ann. 'She won't.'

'Well, cross her stirrups and make her.'

'She'll fall off.'

'Well, let her,' I said. 'What are we going to do about selling these tickets?'

Ann told Pam that she could get down and added, 'I think you're absolutely hopeless.'

I pointed out that she shouldn't tell people that, because all the books on equitation said that the pupil must be encouraged until a spirit of accord was established between man and horse.

Ann said she couldn't care less, and went on, 'I'm not having the ponies out again till it stops raining. I'm sick of cleaning sodden tack and drying ponies after every ride.'

'You might suggest something about these awful

tickets,' I said. 'I mean, two dozen *each* – '

'Oh, it's not too bad,' said Ann. 'I'll sell Mummy about four, and about ten to people in our form, and Diana and James – that's two more – and Mrs Darcy will buy one for herself and one each for Wendy and Joey – '

'Gosh!' I said. 'You have a nerve. Half those people are mine, anyway. If you sell one to Diana then I ought to sell one to James, and as for Mrs Darcy, it's a bit much to think you can bag her *and* Wendy *and* Joey.'

Ann said, 'Twenty-four times two pounds fifty works out at sixty pounds. We'd better have a Bring and Buy Sale after all and raise enough money to pay for our own tickets.'

'Let's go and see some people,' I said. 'Now, before we rub down the ponies. Let's walk up to their doors dragging sodden ponies and looking pathetic and ask them to buy a ticket for downtrodden horses. That ought to shake them.'

Ann said, where should we start? and I said, what about her next-door neighbour? and she said that wasn't fair, as Mrs Ponsford was practically hers and would have to buy one from her anyway.

'You old Scrooge,' I said. 'All right, let's go along *my* road and start at Mrs Norton's. Come on.'

We oozed up Mrs Norton's drive and knocked at the door. The rain was pouring off our riding hats and down the necks of our macs, and the ponies were plastered with mud and looked extremely downtrodden. We didn't look at all nice.

Mrs Norton came to the door, and I said, 'Oh, would you like to buy some tickets for a – '

'No, thank you,' said Mrs Norton very sweetly, and shut the door.

'Help!' said Ann. 'It's *worse* than a flag day.'

'Well, let's try the next house,' I suggested. 'We're so wet already that a bit more doesn't matter.'

We toiled up the drive to West Lea, and the housekeeper said Mrs Jones was out, so we toiled down again, and the ponies made snorting noises expressing their fed-up-ness, and I could feel the rain coming inside my mac, which was depressing as I couldn't see Mummy buying me a new one if I wanted to hunt in the winter.

'Let's go to Mrs Pugh's,' I said, 'and if we don't sell any there let's throw them away and not go to Mrs Whirtley's any more.'

Strangely enough, Mrs Pugh bought three tickets, and as we rode back under the dripping trees we argued about who had sold the odd one.

'It's mine,' I said. 'I asked her, the minute she opened the door.'

Ann pointed out that it was she who had said what the ticket was for.

'OK,' I said. 'Call it three pounds seventy-five each. Let's go home, because it's going to take hours to rub the ponies down and clean the tack and we'll never get a polish on it.'

When I got to our cottage Mrs Crosby was in one of her worst moods and said I was for ever filling her kitchen with dirty sopping wet saddles, and I said I didn't make the weather, and she said, if I was her girl she'd find me something better to do, and so we went on and on as we had done a thousand times before.

It cleared up for Saturday, and we went to a Horse Show at Mitby, and Ann's father let us use the horse box and travel properly, so we arrived dustless and smart with everything polished and the ponies looking super.

This show was divided into two parts. There was a dressage and cross-country event, and also a gymkhana.

We watched the dressage and wondered if we would ever be good enough to go in for it, or if we could get somebody to coach us. Then we entered for one or two of the gymkhana events, and I won the potato race, mainly because everybody else was cockeyed and couldn't get within miles of the bucket, and my potatoes must have been a better shape than usual because I hurled them madly about and they went in, so I wasn't too proud of my achievement.

Ann was a certainty for the Bending until she was beaten in the final heat by a girl who missed out two poles, and the judge didn't even notice, which didn't say much for him.

We had had enough, so we went back to the main ring to see the end of the cross-country, and I shoved my red rosette into my pocket because I was a bit ashamed of what I had won it for. There is something definitely sordid about potatoes when all around you are magnificent people who do dressage tests on blood ponies.

'Look over there,' said Ann. 'It's Captain Cholly-Sawcutt.'

The famous British Team rider was surrounded by a small crowd of friends and admirers, and as usual he looked very friendly and jovial, and a bit like royalty look on grand public occasions.

'I'll tell you what,' I said suddenly. 'I'm going to ask him to buy a ticket for the Whirtley massacre.'

'You can't!' said Ann with a yell of horror.

'Yes, I can. After all, I did give his fat daughters a riding lesson while Mrs Darcy was away' – (this happened in a previous book of mine) – 'and he rode Petronelle round our jumps, and signed our autograph books.'

'He won't remember you,' said Ann. 'Look at all those terrific people he's with, judges, and the hunting crowd and everything. You can't!'

If I had thought about it in cold blood I don't think I could, but I just pushed a few ends of hair under my hat, and picked a bit of hay off my coat, and rubbed my boots on the backs of my jodhs, and marched across to where the great man stood, and gave a cough.

At first he didn't notice me, and then by a bit of luck he turned round and practically fell over me.

After we had both reeled about and got on our feet again, he said, 'If it isn't Jill Crewe!'

I felt so bucked that he had actually remembered my name that I went a sort of boiled colour, especially as all the famous people around had been looking at me as if I was something too mere for words.

'Having a good time?' said the great man in a very friendly way.

'Terrific,' I said.

'Won anything yet?'

'Well, not actually – ' I began, going redder than ever, and just at that moment I dragged my hands out of my pockets where I usually keep them when I don't know what to do with them, and out came that awful red rosette and fell plop on the emerald turf, and a very noble-looking man in immaculate tweeds stooped down and handed it back to me in an impressed kind of way.

'Nice work,' said Captain Cholly-Sawcutt. 'Honestly, I didn't notice you in the dressage.'

'It's for the potato race,' I blurted, and there was one solid yell of laughter. I felt ghastly.

'Well, it takes a good eye to win a potato race,' said the great man pleasantly. 'I bet you I couldn't win one. How's that good pony you rode in the Hunter Trials last spring?'

'Rapide?' I said. 'He's not too bad. But what I wanted was — I mean to say, do you know the Whirtleys at Blossom Hall? Because they're having a fête in aid of charities for horses, and I've got to sell twenty-four tickets, and honestly I never shall, it's practically a physical impossibility, but oh, Captain Cholly-Sawcutt, do you think you could possibly bear to buy one? Because if you do everybody else would buy one too.' Having got this out I stood there looking completely screwy.

'I hope they're not fifty pounds each, or anything like that,' said the Captain, smiling at one or two of his superlatively horsy friends. 'This girl,' he added, meaning me, 'could get away with anything.'

'They're two pounds fifty,' I said, 'and I believe there's going to be a jolly good tea.'

'That settles it,' he said. 'Give me a dozen.'

I nearly passed out.

'Sorry,' he said, 'is that too many?'

'Gosh!' I said. 'Thirty pounds. It's terrific. Oh, I say, it is decent of you.'

'How many do you want to sell?' he said.

'Oh, another dozen,' I said, mentally deciding with great presence of mind that Ann would then be able to foist hers off on to Mummy and all the rest of my intended customers.

'Done!' said the Captain. 'It's a deal. Come on, Colonel, take a dozen tickets for a fête in aid of horses. That'll be the best thing you ever did in the cause of equitation since you got twenty-four faults at Richmond Horse Show in 1904.'

'I repudiate your insults,' said the Colonel, 'but I'll pay for the tickets.' (I looked up 'repudiate' after in the dictionary and decided to use it myself later, as I like a new word.)

Dumbly I folded the ten pound notes which were handed to me and put them in the pocket of my jodhs all mixed up with the potato rosette. When I became conscious again, I said, 'Thanks. Thanks most frightfully. I'll post the tickets to you the minute I get home.'

When I got back to Ann she didn't believe me. She thought I was making it up until I showed her the ten pound notes. Then she said, 'Well, while you were at it you might have sold them another dozen. That would have got rid of a few of mine too.'

'What colossal nerve!' I said. 'You can have all my customers now, Mummy and the Lowes and Mrs Darcy's crowd and everybody.'

So she calmed down, and I swaggered across the trodden, warm-smelling turf swishing the tail of my best black coat, and soon we got to the horse box and watched Ann's father's man leading the happy ponies up the ramp, and I felt very thrilled and decided that even if it meant never having another Christmas present as long as I lived I would have a black coat and boots next Christmas.

When I got home and told Mummy all about it, to my surprise she put on one of her non-co-operative looks.

'I don't know that I approve of it, Jill. You put Captain Cholly-Sawcutt into a position in which he couldn't do anything but buy your tickets. I don't think it was very sportsmanlike.'

'But if he hadn't liked it,' I pointed out, 'he needn't have bought a whole dozen and made his friend buy another dozen. He could have bought just one or two.'

'You seem to have an answer for everything,' said Mummy, 'but I do hate people who thrust themselves forward, and thank goodness it is something you have never done, so don't start it now.'

I went upstairs to put the two dozen tickets in an envelope for Captain Cholly-Sawcutt, and I wrote a note saying, 'I hope you don't think I pushed these on you and it was dreadful cheek, because I didn't mean it like that, and if you do, send the tickets back and I'll send you the sixty pounds.'

Then I came downstairs feeling better, and blow me down! Mummy had discovered the potato race rosette which had fallen out of the pocket of my jodhpurs and had some bits of dusty straw sticking to it, and she was much more thrilled than she need have been, and after all the prize was only ten pounds, but I had earned it myself and that always meant a lot to Mummy.

8 In the cause of equitation

When I went up to the riding school for my lesson Mrs Darcy was very excited to hear about Mrs Whirtley's fête. Being August it was fairly quiet up there, as a lot of people were away at the seaside, and only the keen ones who didn't want to miss any of the shows were going as usual for their lessons. Normally Mrs Darcy was so busy that she had a waiting list of people who wanted lessons, and she was so popular that no other teacher stood a chance at all. Also, practically every child for miles around now rode. People's mothers – including my own – used to talk about 'when this pony craze dies down', but I didn't see it dying down in my lifetime.

As you know, ponies have a spell of jumping perfectly and then all of a sudden get the idea of taking off too soon, or going spectator-shy or something like that. This is known as temperament. Rapide was off his jumping, and I thought it must in some way be my fault, because if you are a serious rider you should always blame yourself before you blame your pony, so I was putting in some hard work on him, under Mrs Darcy's eye.

I never got tired of her jumps or the neat look of her stables and well-kept ponies, and since some of my friends and I had practically run the place during its owner's absence – as I related in a previous book – I always had a feeling about the riding school that it partly belonged to me.

'It ought to be a good show,' said Mrs Darcy. 'Mrs Whirtley is a first-rate organiser and does things on a big scale.'

I told her about how I had sold the tickets to Captain Cholly-Sawcutt, and asked, 'Do you think there's a chance he might come? If he does, and jumps Petronelle for an exhibition, we'd need a tank regiment to keep the people away. It would be jolly good for the fête.'

'I don't think there's a hope of him being there,' she said. 'He'll be away, jumping with the British team, possibly on the Continent. But he might give his tickets to some of his friends and persuade them to enter for the open jumping. That's such a big attraction, if you can get well-known riders and horses.'

'If only he would,' I said.

'Tell you what,' said Mrs Darcy, 'I'll mention it to him myself. He's such a good sport. You haven't seen his place, have you? Marvellous training stables – breaking young horses – dressage – hunters – everything. Just your cup of tea.'

'Gosh!' I said with a sigh. 'I'm as likely to see the inside of Buckingham Palace.'

'Tell you what,' said Mrs Darcy again, 'if you say there's a class for novice hacks, how about you showing Sandy Two for me?'

I blinked several times. I had never dreamed in my wildest dreams – and believe me, some of my horsy dreams are extremely wild – of being asked

to show a horse out of Mrs Darcy's stable. I came
to earth when she made the blighting remark 'You
needn't if you don't want to.'

'Want to!' I yelled. 'Help! I'm not good enough.'

'That's up to you,' said Mrs Darcy. 'It's time you
stopped thinking you're a beginner. I'll give you the
necessary coaching if you'll struggle up here in your
spare time.'

'Actually I don't have any,' I said, 'but I'll make
some, even if it's in the stilly watches of the night.'

'Come and have a look at the fellow,' she said.

Sandy Two was out at grass in the little paddock
behind her bungalow. He was a roan of fifteen
hands, with black points, a lovely head, and large,
intelligent eyes.

'I'd love to show him,' I said, 'if you think I could
do him justice.'

'Don't worry,' said Mrs Darcy. 'Come up tomorrow night about eight and I'll run over what you need
to know.'

I went home feeling very excited, and dreamed
that night that I was showing Sandy Two and his
legs were getting longer and longer, and I couldn't
even mount him, and somebody picked me up with
a crane and put me in the saddle, and I tried to rein
back and Sandy Two sat down on the judge who
turned out to be my form teacher. She shouted,
'Remember what happens to people who think they
can ride horses too big for them!' I thought of a girl
at my school called Susan Pyke, whom I will not
call a friend, who in theory saw herself at her best
on something about sixteen hands but in practice
finished up in every collecting ring swinging on

her horse's neck like a monkey and arguing with the judge!

Was I glad to wake up!

After all this I thought it was time that Ann and I got busy boosting the fête, so we decided to go and see all the people from school who weren't on holiday. We went first to see two friends of ours called Val and Jackie Heath (whose actual names were Valerie and Jacqueline, only they had had the good sense to abandon these by the time they were about three).

Val and Jackie had been doing very well with their riding lately, in fact being lucky enough to have a horsy aunt in London they had ridden at Windsor Horse Show and Jackie had taken a first on one of her aunt's ponies in the 13–2 class. It had rather turned her head and given her ideas of grandeur, and even Val had bathed in the reflected glory and had never been quite the same since. Also Jackie had got David Broome's autograph, and she kept it wrapped in silver paper in a cigar box, and only showed it to special people.

The Heaths were quite glad to see us, and when we had had some lemonade and buns we had to stand for ages watching Val doing half-passes until we were nearly screaming, especially as Jackie said that their father was going to arrange for them to have some coaching in dressage from a man who had been trained in Italy by a man who had been a cavalry officer.

'Well, what about this fête?' I said at last, when I could get a word in. 'You'll both come, won't you? I mean,' I added sarkily, 'if it doesn't interfere with you jumping at Wembley, or anything like that.'

It is funny how some people never know when you are being sarky. Jackie said, 'Oh, we're not riding at Wembley, at least not this year,' and Ann said, 'Really? I'm frightfully surprised, but at least it will give the others a chance.' Then Val chased us both round their yard (living at a farm they have lots of room) and nearly laid me out with a dandy brush which caught me on the ear, and we all finished up by crashing into the door of a shed where there was a sick calf that had to have absolute quiet, and the door gave way and Ann sat down practically on the calf, and Mr Heath came out and was livid.

'You can buy two tickets from Ann,' I said when the noise of battle had died down.

'Is it just a gymkhana?' said Val. 'It sounds a bit tame.'

'No, it isn't just a gymkhana,' I said. 'It's a noble effort in the noble cause of noble equitation.'

'Gosh!' said Jackie. 'That's the first time I've ever known Jill to be short of adjectives.'

'I'm not short,' I told her witheringly, 'it's the only suitable adjective for anything so noble.'

'Oh, come on, be noble,' said Ann. 'Buy the tickets.'

Val said all right, they would buy two tickets and come if they could.

'You'll jolly well come,' I said. 'It's no good people buying tickets if nobody's going to be there on the day. And you'll jolly well enter for all the classes you can as soon as the schedules are out. Of course we understand that nobody else will stand a chance, but think what you'll be able to do with all that prize money.'

Again the sarcasm was wasted, as Jackie said seriously that it would be nice to buy some good hunting tack.

'Are you asking Susan Pyke?' she went on. 'I mean, she's always a bit of a sensation on one of her marvellous steeds, especially when she argues with the judges.'

Ann said that we'd better ask Susan, it always made one more, so we went along to her house. She was sitting in the garden, madly knitting, trying to finish a yellow polo-necked sweater, and was quite glad to see us.

'Daddy is buying me an Anglo-Arab mare,' she said when we told her about the fête. 'It would be a try-out for her, wouldn't it?'

'Oh, rather,' said Ann, 'and do get a lot of other people to come too.'

Susan promised that practically all her relations and friends would come to see her on the Anglo-Arab mare, and we said the more the merrier and she'd probably win everything hands down, and she said in a very Susan-ish way that she hoped the prizes were large, and I said in a rather sticky voice that this was a charity affair and its aim was rather to get money out of people than to give big prizes to the competitors, and Susan said she wouldn't mind that for just once, and she rather thought she'd enter for the open jumping and I said, do!

She couldn't have been nicer to us, if a bit condescending, and showed us how to do the neck of the polo-sweater so that it fitted and didn't look like a halter (as the ones I have knitted always do) and when we went away Ann said to me that

Susan would really be quite nice if she wasn't so sickening.

We toiled round all day getting people to promise to come to the fête, and we only hoped that everybody else on the committee was working as hard as we were, though we had our doubts about Clarissa Dandleby. I was so hot that when I got home all I could do was to totter into the larder and drink about a gallon of delicious orange fruit cup that was standing there. When Mummy came in I said brightly, 'I drank all the fruit cup, it was marvellous, it must have taken you ages to make with all that chopped fruit and mint and stuff,' and she said drily, 'It did, it took me about two hours to make it for three people who are coming in for a game of bridge tonight,' and I went cold with remorse. I mean, I just do these things and never think till it's too late. So I was peeling oranges and chopping apples and mint for ages after that, and my one consolation was that I hadn't noticed the sandwiches which were also ready for Mummy's bridge evening.

After all this I thought I was due for a little relaxation, so I got Black Boy out and went for a ride in the sunlit evening, all along the grass verges of the lanes. Birds in the trees were making the usual din they do make when they are going to bed, and as I watched the sinking sun I was so happy I wouldn't have changed places with anybody on earth.

9 Cecilia turns up

The next afternoon Mrs Whirtley rang up to say that there would be another meeting of the committee at her house on Tuesday afternoon, and she hoped I had been working hard, and would I mind letting Ann Derry know as it would save Mrs Whirtley a call as she had about a million to make.

Ann was in our cottage at the time, and she said at once, 'Whoopee! The tea the old girl gave us last time was what I call fantastic.'

'She won't keep it up,' I said. 'She'll let us down gently with weak orangeade and biscuits that have gone soft.'

Mummy chimed in that she thought we were the limit, and that working for a Cause was its own reward regardless of such earthly things as meringues, and I refrained from saying, 'That's what you think.'

Ann and I arrived at Blossom Hall, and soon we were all assembled in the drawing-room for the meeting, that is all except Clarissa Dandleby. I naturally hoped that she wasn't coming, as I had taken rather a dislike to her, but as though reading my anxious thoughts Mrs Whirtley said, 'We're all here except Clarissa Dandleby and she rang me up to say that she might be late, as she is coming by car and bringing a friend who would like to be on the committee.'

She had hardly finished speaking when a car was heard to stop outside, and Clarissa's somewhat foghornish voice was heard too, arguing with the driver about what time he was to come back for her. Then she came in and apologised for being late, but she had had to wait for her friend.

Then the friend came in and I practically collapsed.

It was my cousin Cecilia!

When I came round I found Cecilia sitting next to me with Clarissa in the row in front.

Cecilia said, 'Good gracious, Jill, what are you doing here? How on earth will the riding school manage without you?' and Clarissa turned round and looked at me through her enormous specs and said, 'Oh, do you run a riding school?' and I said, 'Of course not,' and Cecilia said, 'Oh, don't be so modest, Jill. You know you teach the sweet little kiddies to ride their dear little Shetlands and the nannies come too.'

Clarissa giggled, and I said nonchalantly, 'I'm starting a class for the under-twos, if you'd both like to join.'

Cecilia said, joking apart, she was quite surprised to see me on the committee, and I said, not as surprised as I was to see her as she was quite the most un-horsy person I knew, and she said one didn't have to be horsy to do Good Works, and in her set Good Works were all the thing just now, so she didn't care if it was worn-out

horses or suffering orphans or toothless Lithua-
nians.

Mrs Whirtley said, 'I see you two know each
other, how nice, but oughtn't we to get on with
the business?'

She then asked everybody what they had done
about boosting the fête and how many tickets they
had sold.

Ann and I were just thinking smugly that nobody
could have done as well as we had, when a boy got
up and said he had sold all his two dozen tickets on
the first day and had orders for four dozen more,
and a girl said, when were the gymkhana schedules
coming out, as twenty-three people she knew were
all dying to enter?

'Ah, the schedules!' said Mrs Whirtley. 'I've drawn
up what I think is a good list, and I'll read it to you
and then you can approve.'

A girl got up and said her mother wanted to know
if there could be a riding class for the under-sevens so
that her little brother could enter. He was only five
and so sweet and it would encourage him if he could
win a prize.

Mrs Whirtley looked a bit bleak and said there
would only be time for a few gymkhana events,
as there would only be the one ring for everything,
so she had planned just two classes for the younger
ones, Musical Chairs and Egg-and-Spoon for the
under-fourteens, and one showing class for ponies
and one for novice hacks, and one juvenile jumping
for under-sixteens. As there would be a big entry for
all these classes it would by then be the tea interval,
and after tea would be the open jumping. We would

be glad to know that she had already got some good entries, including George Glee on Poetry, Bernard Bushey on Charles Stewart, and Sonia Pretty on How Now.

Everybody clapped, and when the clapping had died down Cecilia got up and said, much as she disliked appearing a wet blanket, there would be people at the fête who might like to rest their eyes from such a lot of horsy happenings, and couldn't there be a marquee with an exhibition of handicrafts and perhaps a competition for decorated dinner tables?

Several people said, Help! and Mrs Whirtley said that was quite an idea, only it would need somebody good to organise it, and Cecilia said, 'Oh, I'll organise it,' and Mrs Whirtley looked a bit winded and said, 'Thank you, dear.'

She then finished reading the schedule, and everybody approved – or if they didn't they daren't say so – and Mrs Whirtley said she would get them off to the printers, and would we let her know how many we all wanted so that we could have them by the weekend.

Clarissa Dandleby said darkly, 'I'm afraid you'll be sorry, Mrs Whirtley, that you didn't take my advice and have dressage and cross-country,' and Mrs Whirtley said she thought she'd survive, and after that it was time for tea.

The tea was, if anything, even better than before. Cecilia chatted to me in a very friendly way, and said did I remember the time I had stayed with her and played with those awful children at the Rectory? I said I remembered doing a lot of jolly hard work at the Rectory, saving people's ponies from extinction, and she laughed and said, 'I do think you're weird.'

Just then a maid came in and said Miss Jill Crewe was wanted on the telephone. I started thinking of all the marvellous news I might be going to receive, but when I got to the phone it was Mummy.

She said, 'Is Cecilia there?' and when I said yes, and how did she know? she said that Aunt Primrose, Cecilia's mother, had rung up to say that Cecilia would be at Blossom Hall, and could I take her home with me for a few days?

I said, 'Oh!' in a strangled voice, and Mummy said she was sending a taxi at five o'clock for me and Cecilia and Cecilia's luggage, and perhaps Ann would be kind enough to take Black Boy home with her own pony.

I went back to the drawing-room and I said to Cecilia, 'You're coming home with me for a few days.' Cecilia said, 'How marvellous!' and I said, 'And I don't want any funny jokes about riding schools,' and she said, 'You *are* touchy. If you'd been at my school they'd have knocked all that out of you.' I said I couldn't think of a worse fate than being at Cecilia's school, where they do nothing but be top in exams and have crushes on the teachers and swap library books called *The Madcap of St Monica's*, and such ghastly titles.

Meanwhile a lot of horsy conversation was going on all round us, and snatches of it came drifting to my ears. I wished I could have shunted off Cecilia and joined in. I caught such interesting phrases as 'he didn't look as if he had ever jumped anything higher than two foot six in his life' . . . 'the judge ordered him straight off the field and that was the end of him' . . . 'not enough room to do the bending race at the gallop' . . . 'oh, but she always takes a groom with her everywhere, so no wonder – ' . . . ' – got eighteen faults, no I'm not making it up – ', . . . 'believe it or believe it not, those Bartram kids still ride with the backward seat' . . . 'I'll be back in time for the first meet of the season, that's the main thing.'

Ann was in a group of people talking about pony clubs and I could hear them discussing the possibility of getting up some inter-pony club contests. I heard somebody else say that their hunting prospects were dim as their new Master of Foxhounds didn't care for children and didn't encourage them to follow on their ponies, much less on bicycles or on foot, and somebody else said, what a frightful shame, but perhaps he'd resign or die soon and they'd get somebody more human.

Then Clarissa Dandleby started talking, and when her foghorn voice was uplifted nobody else's stood a chance. She said her father was going to take her to Ireland for the bloodstock sales. She said that she couldn't understand people who didn't attend bloodstock sales as it was always possible to pick up a bargain cheap. Somebody else said, what did she mean by cheap? and she said, for instance, her father had picked up a marvellous pony for only three thousand pounds, and everybody looked blank and said Oh.

My cousin Cecilia said, 'I used to like Clarissa when she went to my school but now I think she's quite mad,' and I said I couldn't agree more.

Mrs Whirtley then gave us A Look, and said, 'Tea

is over, you know, and we have such a lot of work
still to do.'

The work was mostly about who should run the
sideshows, such as selling ice cream and helping on
the Bring and Buy stall. Nobody was very keen to
do these sordid tasks, but Ann and I offered to do an
hour on the cake raffle as long as it didn't interfere
with any of the classes we were entering for in the
gymkhana. Nobody wanted to do anything after tea
except watch the open jumping, until Cecilia said in
a shattering way that she didn't give a hoot for the
open jumping, and as the handicrafts exhibition and
the decorated dinner tables competition would be
completely organised by then she would be glad to
do anything that Mrs Whirtley wanted. Everybody
stared dumbly at Cecilia, partly in horror at the
ghastly sight of somebody who didn't want to
watch open jumping, and partly in the realisation
that un-horsy people might even have their uses.

Then the meeting was over, and the taxi came
for me and Cecilia. Ann said, 'Good luck,' and
with a sinking heart I watched her ride off on
George, leading Black Boy who gave me a hurt
sort of look.

'To think I'm going to stay at your darling little
cottage again,' said Cecilia, 'and sleep in that sweet
little bedroom with the sloping roof.' She wasn't
being sarky, she really meant it, but my heart
slithered down another foot or so as I realised that
Cecilia would be having my room, and I would
have to go on the divan in the apple room, and
she would probably make rude remarks about my
pony frieze, but when we got home and she saw

it she merely said, 'Well, it's a change from Mickey Mouse.'

I didn't rise to this, as by now I was used to Cecilia trying to make me feel about six.

10 A novice hack

After Cecilia had unpacked and had told Mummy how much she adored her last book, *Angeline, the Fairy Child*, and asked if she was writing another – which is the way you talk to authors – I began to fidget about and Mummy said, what was the matter with me, and couldn't I think of any way to entertain Cecilia, good gracious she was my only cousin and I didn't see her often.

Cecilia said, 'I expect Jill's dying to go and have a riding lesson or something?' and I said, 'You never said a truer word. I'm supposed to go and get some coaching from Mrs Darcy for the novice hack class.'

Cecilia said she would just as soon read, so very relieved I tore off to get my bike and disappear before she could get the bright idea of coming with me.

Mrs Darcy was ready for me, with Sandy Two. I mounted him and of course fifteen hands felt tall to me. It wasn't as if I was like Wendy Mead, used to a stable where you had to ride anything. I trotted Sandy Two round the paddock. He was very well-schooled and answered my rather nervous aids, until he suddenly realised that I was not in complete control and began to snatch at the reins.

'Ride him, Jill!' Mrs Darcy yelled in her impatient

way. 'Keep him balanced. You've got your weight on your forehand.'

I brought Sandy Two back and managed a smooth halt.

'I wish you'd tell me exactly what I'll have to do on the day,' I said. 'I've been reading my equitation books and they say "the judges will expect you to do this-and-that-and-the-other". It's baffling.'

'The judges won't require you to do anything you're not perfectly capable of doing already,' said Mrs Darcy. 'You only need to use your common sense. Now come on, Sandy, show Jill what you can do.'

She mounted Sandy Two herself and demonstrated a collected walk, while I looked on. She halted, turned on the forehand, reined back and circled. Then she made me walk beside her and told me to notice how Sandy Two was using his hocks, and to see that he always did, and to use my legs to keep him up to the bridle.

'He goes well with you,' I said with a sigh like a furnace bellows. 'If only I could make him do the same for me.'

'Don't talk like an idiot,' she said sharply. 'You've been reading too many books. An ounce of practice is worth a ton of theory, even in – or especially in – equitation. Now let's have a show. I'll be the judge and you do your stuff.'

I mounted, and said rather feebly, 'Shall I start by entering the ring?'

'Well, where else would you enter,' said Mrs Darcy. 'The tea tent?'

I entered an imaginary ring and rode Sandy Two

round at a walk, trot, and canter. He went very well, and I was rather thrilled when Mrs Darcy as the judge called me in to stand in an imaginary first place.

'Now will you do a show, please,' she said. 'Anything you like.'

I wanted to giggle, because I couldn't think what to do, but I thought wildly of a book I had read the previous night, something about cantering on each leg in turn. So I tried that, and it partly came off and was partly a bit messy. The worst of it was I couldn't think what else to do, and just went cantering on.

'Could you possibly walk in and rein back?' said Mrs Darcy impatiently.

I thought I managed that rather well, and I dismounted and took the saddle off, and got Sandy Two's legs arranged, and waited for the 'judge' to look him over.

'We'll cut that,' said Mrs Darcy. 'Now lead him out in hand at a trot, and try and look a bit dignified yourself. There's no need to gallop alongside with your hat slipping.'

I tried to look dignified, which wasn't easy as Sandy Two seemed to be enjoying this bit and wasn't anxious to turn. I had a job to push him round, and we got back to the 'judge' with my hat straight but my collar up at one side. I pulled it round and settled my tie.

'It would look better,' Mrs Darcy said, 'if you could manage not to need to dress yourself until you get out of the ring. That'll do. You can stay on and practise a bit.'

'What place are you giving me?' I asked.

'Oh, I'd probably give you Reserve if the others weren't very good.'

I felt squashed, and said that I didn't think the competition would be all that hot in the novice hack class at Mrs Whirtley's fête, and Mrs Darcy squashed me still lower by observing that even if there was practically no competition at all, no real rider would think of aiming at anything less than perfection.

I stayed on and practised for another half-hour. Sandy Two was a lovely hack and made for showing, and I knew I was very lucky indeed to have such a chance, and that if we didn't do well it would be my fault and mine alone.

Wendy Mead came out and watched me. I asked her rather feebly what she thought my chances were on the day, and she said in a sinister voice, 'You'd better be first!'

This made me feel like the heroine in a thriller when she hears the mystery warning over the telephone, but I wasn't going to let Wendy see I was rattled, so I cantered up to her, did a beautiful halt, slid down, and said 'He's a lovely horse and he has a lovely long stride.'

'It'll be lovelier and longer when you get your knees to him properly,' was all that Wendy said, but as we walked in she said, 'By the way, did you give that Dean child your old riding clothes?'

'Why?' I said.

'Because she wears them all over the place, and it looks so silly. She told somebody you had given them to her. You'd have done better to give her a cotton frock.'

'She likes wearing them,' I said, wondering why on earth I was sticking up for Dinah Dean. 'I expect it helps her to pretend she's got a pony.'

'What a crazy idea!' said Wendy.

It was late, so I helped to rub Sandy Two down, and then I jumped on my bike and whizzed home pretty fast — as the brakes don't work anyway — and did a dirt-track swerve round the cottage to the back door.

Mummy and Cecilia were having cocoa and buns in the sitting-room.

'Gosh, I'm hungry!' I said.

'And how many poor ponies have collapsed under you tonight?' said Cecilia pleasantly.

'Sixteen,' I said. 'Seventeen if you count the donkey.'

Mummy told her that I was practising to ride one of Mrs Darcy's horses in a competition, and that flattened her down a bit, especially as Mummy laid it on about how good I was, which was flattering and kind of Mummy, if untrue.

11   A china pony

The next day Mummy said that she would take Cecilia and me to Rychester for a treat, and we would do the shops and have lunch and perhaps go to a cinema. I wanted to go, because there was a shop in Rychester where they sold little china models of horses and I wanted to gaze at these and see how much they were and wonder if I could afford one.

We went the twenty miles on the bus and it took an hour. My one idea was to get to the china shop, but before long I came to the conclusion that it is a mistake to go shopping with unsympathetic people. Now if I had been shopping with Ann or Diana Bush we should have made a beeline for that particular shop with the horses, but Mummy and Cecilia had vastly different ideas and I daren't tell them what I wanted without provoking some of Cecilia's most sarky remarks, while even Mummy would be apt to say, 'Must we have horses all the time, even in Rychester?'

The minute we arrived there Cecilia said she wanted to go and see the cathedral. I could see this appealed to Mummy, as she is very keen on architecture and ancient stones of a mouldering nature, and she knows an awful lot about the cathedral and loves to show people round it, so

I smothered my feelings and we walked round all the medieval tombs and admired the windows, and Cecilia went on about Gothic and Perpendicular until I was nearly choking. I kept thinking they had had enough, and then they would come across a case full of ancient documents and off they would go again.

When it was twenty past eleven, I said, couldn't we go and have an ice? Mummy said, 'But we've only just had breakfast. Good gracious, it simply can't be twenty past eleven!' and Cecilia said how funny it was that you never noticed the time when you were enjoying yourself.

We went to a café opposite the cathedral called *The Buzzing Beehive* and I had a rather soapy ice and Mummy and Cecilia had coffee. I ate my ice in about four seconds, but they were ages over their coffee. I said, weren't we going to the shops? and Mummy said, yes of course, she wanted to get some curtain lining at Smith's, and Cecilia said, was there a very good wool shop nearby? Mummy said that Smith's had a frightfully good wool department. I could see them in Smith's for hours choosing curtain stuff and knitting wool!

I said, could I go and do some shopping by myself? Mummy said in a dim and tactless way, 'What is it you want to buy?'

I said I just wanted to look at some shops, and Mummy said I'd better go to Smith's with them as while they were there it would be a chance to look at some school shirts for me for next term.

The rest of the morning passed drearily by, and soon it was one o'clock and we were all feeling hungry. We went to a café called *The Wagging*

Windmill for lunch, and had hors-d'oeuvre and rolls and fruit salad.

Cecilia said that if we were going to the cinema in the afternoon, could we go to the one where there was that film about African natives cultivating the jungle, called *Kibwa?*

I wanted to say Help! but I just said, 'I've seen it.'

Mummy said, 'Where?'

I said, 'At school last term. Some relation of Miss Grange-Dudley's came and gave a running commentary on it. It was ghastly.'

Cecilia said, 'You can't have seen it. It's absolutely new. It was only generally released about a week ago.'

I said, 'Well, I've seen it and that's that,' and she said again, 'You can't have,' and Mummy said, 'I don't think you can have seen it, Jill, it must have been something like it,' and I said, 'I know it was *Kibwa* because the relation of Miss Grange-Dudley was the man who took the film in Africa, and it was so deadly boring we all went to sleep.'

Mummy ended this argument by asking if there wasn't anything else we'd like to go to, and I said the only decent film ever made was *My Friend Flicka* and I wouldn't mind seeing it ten times.

Cecilia said I couldn't expect them to have a film about horses in every single cinema in Rychester just for my benefit, and I said, 'OK, you go and see that jungle stuff, and I'll go shopping.'

We were now back where we started, because Mummy promptly said, 'What do you want to go shopping for, Jill?' and I mumbled, 'Oh, nothing.'

In the end we went to a Walt Disney film, and it was very good, only I couldn't think of anything but those little china horses and how I was being frustrated at every turn by the Hand of Fate, like people in books.

When we came out of the cinema it was a quarter to five, and Cecilia said she would treat us to tea before we went to catch our bus at five thirty. I thought, I shan't be in Rychester again for ages, because Mummy doesn't like me to go there alone, and it has got to be like this!

Mummy led the way towards a café called *The Deadly Daffodil*, or some such sordid name, and I felt it was now or never, so I said I definitely didn't want any tea, and while they were having theirs could I possibly go to Pitt's the tailors about having my black coat let out, and then meet them at the bus?

To my joy Mummy said, 'Yes, you can if you want to, but you've only had that coat a year. You'll have to eat less,' and Cecilia said, 'All these hard-riding women have figures like feather-beds.'

I fled before Mummy could change her mind, and of course I had to go to Pitt's before I went to the china shop, and there wasn't much time. In Pitt's I had to wait while an ancient character with a droopy moustache dithered on about whether he wanted large checks or small checks on his new coat. It was ghastly waiting. He couldn't make up his mind, then he asked Mr Pitt which he would suggest, and Mr Pitt said the small checks were smarter, and the Trying Customer said he preferred the large ones, and so it went on, and after about another ten minutes he said he would think it over and come in again tomorrow.

My business didn't take long, as Mr Pitt said he would make time to do my coat any time I could spare it, and I said I would send it by post, and then I was galloping along High Street and looking for the turning that went down to the lovely china shop.

The horses were there and they were six pounds each. I decided to buy one out of the ten pound prize money that I had won in the Potato Race. It was thrilling to stand looking at them in the window and decide which one I would have. They were beautiful models, in six different positions, and the colours were very natural. The two I liked best were a bay hunter in the act of cropping grass – he had such lovely long legs – and a sturdier chestnut pony with an arched neck and a black mane tossed by the wind. It was awful trying to choose, because it was ten past five already and I couldn't linger, so I decided on the chestnut pony because he had a look of my own Black Boy.

I went in and bought him, and when I was getting out the money I saw a white china basket to hold about two roses and thought it would be nice for Mummy's room, if not too expensive. It turned out to be three pounds fifty, so I bought that too, and the assistant put both things into a parcel and I went charging off to the bus station.

My watch must have been slow because there to my horror was the Chatton bus, just starting up, and I saw the frenzied face of Mummy at the window with her mouth going, Hurry up!

I tore across the square and grabbed the bus handrail and jumped for the platform. The conductor grabbed me and pulled me on, and crash! down went my parcel at his feet. It was an awful crunchy crash of broken china.

Nearly choking with despair I said, 'It doesn't matter,' as he kindly picked up the sagging parcel and handed it to me. I shoved it just as it was into my coat pocket. I had gone through so much to get it, and now this!

Mummy hadn't noticed the crash. She said, 'This is ridiculous, Jill, I'm very annoyed with you. You know what time the bus leaves, must you always be late?'

I said I was sorry, and then sat wretchedly looking out at the ugly houses and dismal fields that slipped by the windows in endless succession. It was evidently my unlucky day and Fate didn't intend me to have one of those lovely horses.

As soon as we got home I rushed out to do the ponies' feeds. In the privacy of the shed while I measured out oats, I thought I could not bear to see the chestnut pony in bits and I would throw the parcel away just as it was, but then I thought perhaps I could do something with glue, though from the crunchiness of the parcel I hadn't much hope.

So I opened it. Mummy's china basket was smashed into a hundred pieces, and my little horse had hardly so much as a chip! He must have been on top of the basket and the basket took all the blow.

I was so excited I hugged him, and decided to call him Invictus, which in case you don't know means Unconquered.

But at the same time I felt that Mummy had been done out of her present, so I planned to go into

Chatton when I had some more pocket money and buy her something that would do instead.

I wrapped Invictus in a lot of paper and put him on the shelf behind the hens' meal bin. I couldn't put him in my room because Cecilia was there.

12   Fun on the common

The next morning Mummy said, 'What are you two girls going to do today?'

I said that Ann was coming round and we were going for a ride, and would probably meet Diana Bush and her brother James who were back from London. Cecilia said that in that case she would sit in the orchard and embroider something for the handicrafts exhibition.

Mummy said, 'Nonsense, you must go with the others, on Jill's bike, and have a ride on Rapide when you get to the Common.'

Cecilia (who in spite of all that she said about horsy people rather fancied herself as a rider, and held the weird theory that nobody needed lessons and all one had to do was to hang on to the pony and urge it to dash madly about) was taken with this idea, but said she hadn't any clothes. So Mummy produced her own very nice brown trousers and a matching silk shirt, and Cecilia put them on. They made her look very sophisticated, and she walked about in front of the long glass in Mummy's room until I felt sick.

I said cheekily, 'Come on, Horrible. Ann's been waiting for ages.'

Ann had George, I took Rapide, and Cecilia rode the bike. When we came to the steep hill we dismounted and led the ponies up, but Cecilia stood on her pedals and rode up to the top, where she waited for us in a very showing-off way.

'Do you walk up all the hills?' she said. 'You'll make the ponies soft.'

We said that we weren't anxious to start a morning's riding with blown and sweaty ponies, and Cecilia said that horses in good condition were never blown and sweaty, but of course riding grass-fed ponies we wouldn't know.

Ann said to me, 'Does she know anything about riding?' and I said, 'No, she makes it up as she goes on.'

When we got to the Common we met Diana and James, and strangely enough Cecilia took to them at once. Just as everything that Ann and I did was wrong, everything that Diana and James did was right. Diana was slim and tall and was riding a very graceful pony called Sylvia, and James who was seventeen was on a spirited cob which really belonged to his father.

I don't know if you have noticed how a boy always shows off when he is with girls. James showed off disgustingly. He did a circus trick of vaulting on to the cob, and then gave a rocky exhibition of the gallop with crossed stirrups and folded arms. Diana said, 'He is a fool, Daddy has told him not to do that,' but Cecilia was impressed.

James jumped a ditch and made a perfect landing, more by good luck than anything else, as I saw him clutch the cob's mane and nearly lose his seat, but Cecilia clapped and said, 'I say, you are most frightfully good!'

'Oh, I'm not so hot really,' said James looking conceited.

'If you ask me, James,' said Diana in a sisterly way, 'you did a rotten jump there. You always do take off too soon.'

James wouldn't have that, and they argued. At last Diana said, 'Well, let's have a competition. Canter to the funny tree with the lump on it, turn, and back on the other leg, and we'll do the timing with the stop watch. Who'll go first?'

'You,' said Ann. 'You made it up.'

Diana had chosen a competition that was just Sylvia's cup of tea, she had done it so often. She gave a perfect performance, but James who was timing said she was slow.

Ann went next, but George wasn't happy and didn't change legs at all, so though she beat Diana's time by eleven seconds Ann was disqualified.

Then it was my turn, but when we got to the tree Rapide didn't want to turn, in fact he carried me for twenty yards before I got him round, so I lost a lot of time.

James went last, and did the whole thing perfectly, and in the shortest time. He then asked Cecilia if she wouldn't like to have a try on the cob? Cecilia calmly said she'd love to. I went cold, and said, 'You'd better borrow George from Ann. He's the quietest pony.'

'Good gracious! Anybody would think I was forty and ready for a wheel-chair,' said Cecilia. 'And I don't want a pony who can't do the course properly.'

Ann went red, and began, 'It was my fault that George didn't change legs – ' but Cecilia was already mounting Marquis, or rather was being heaved up kindly by James. I shut my eyes and thought, Help!

Before Cecilia could get her second stirrup Marquis was off. He shot away, and finding himself completely uncontrolled broke into a gallop. I had visions of Cecilia either going right on into the next county and finishing up at the ocean, or else taking a most frightful toss, but actually Marquis was a sensible old hand at competitions, and when he got to the tree he turned and came back, looking like a steeplechaser. How Cecilia hung on I don't know. She certainly wasn't in the saddle when she got back, she was on the cob's neck with her arms round his neck and more or less gripping his hogged mane with her teeth.

She slithered off, sat down smack on the ground, and announced, 'I beat you all for time.'

'You're telling us!' said Ann, and Diana said, 'What you did can hardly be described as a canter.'

Cecilia got up and said she thought cantering was silly anyway, and only for riding schools, and she liked a pony to *go*, and Marquis was the best ride she had ever had.

'You're jolly lucky to be alive,' I said, and she said, 'Some people wouldn't know how to ride anything but a slug. Well, it's agreed that I won that competition. What shall we do next?'

'There's a lot of brushwood about,' said Ann. 'Let's strip some poles and stick them up and have a bending race.'

'Isn't that a bit kiddish?' said Cecilia.

'It's jolly good exercise for control,' said James.

We all began to collect long pieces of brushwood

and strip them and stick them up in two rows. This had necessarily to be done in rather soft ground, which would slow the race down and make us careful.

'Jill and Ann can ride off first,' said Diana. 'Then James and I, then the two winners, and Cecilia can ride with the finalist.'

Ann's George and my Rapide were old hands at bending. Neither of them got the speed they might have done, but they started well, turned at the end without losing ground, and zigzagged back beautifully. We finished neck and neck, and had to do it again. This time George's forward leap carried him ahead and he got into a gallop before Rapide, but paid for his extra speed by overshooting the turning-post, and I got home by a length.

Then Diana and James got away. James was apt to whack the cob round, which Marquis didn't like. He was really too spirited for a bending race and while he pranced Diana won by two lengths.

Then it was Diana's turn to ride it off with me. I had met her many a time in the show ring at this competition, and she usually beat me. I took it for granted that she would do so today, because Rapide wasn't at his best on the softish ground. I saw as we came up towards the finish that Diana was nearly a length ahead, but James shouted, 'You missed a pole!'

'I jolly well didn't,' I said.

'Not you, you dope. Diana. You've won, Jill.'

Diana panted, slapped her chest, and said, 'Well, it's you and Cecilia now, Jill. Which horse do you want, Cecilia?'

I was certain she would choose Marquis again and probably break her neck, and after all I was responsible for her, but to my relief she said she would have Sylvia, as she was sure Sylvia would have won the last heat easily if she hadn't missed the pole.

She lumbered up on to Sylvia and fussed over the stirrups. Sylvia looked bored with this, and when James shouted Go! She made a bad start. Cecilia kicked like mad and yelled, 'Get on, you! Gallop, can't you!' Needless to say this did not impress Sylvia who was used to aids, not shouting, and she was only turning the bottom pole when I finished.

'If I'd taken Marquis I'd have won,' said Cecilia, and we didn't bother to argue about this, though James said, 'You shouldn't neck-rein like a polo-player, you should use your legs.'

To my surprise Cecilia accepted this criticism meekly, and even said she supposed speed wasn't everything. This was amazing coming from Cecilia who had previously recognised no other pace than a gallop. I began to have hopes of her.

James said, 'Now let's each do a show, five minutes of anything you like, and Cecilia can judge who gets the Gold Challenge Cup and the Imperial Certificate of Magnificent Equitation.'

Cecilia looked pleased. James said that as he was already on Marquis he would go first. We all knew that this kind of thing was just up his street, as while he was staying in London he had done some practising in a covered school with a dressage coach.

James did everything he knew, and it looked terrific to see him making delicate intricate movements in the bright sunshine with the green Common all round, and even if he was more showy than accurate we would all have liked to be able to do as well. Then Diana had her turn, and of course she had learned a lot from practising with James, and Sylvia being rather a vain pony there was quite a lot of tail-flicking and neck-arching mixed up with the dressage.

Then I gave Rapide a chance to show what all his recent schooling had done for him, and he behaved beautifully and I only wished we could have been in a real show ring, and finally Ann did some perfect figures of eight on George.

Cecilia said that everybody was good, but actually she had liked Diana's show best, so we made Diana come up to receive the Challenge Cup – which was a spray of blackberry flowers – and bow to the judge, and she pretended to drop the cup on his toe and we all yelled.

The main point was that from that moment Cecilia realised that there was more in riding than clutching on to a pony and dashing about, and I never heard another sarky word from her, in fact when a bit later I asked her if she would like a ride on Rapide while I rode the bike she asked me if she was sitting properly, and how to do a collected walk, which was nearly unbelievable to anyone who had previously known my dear cousin.

We had a wonderful morning and as usual got home late for lunch and were flayed alive by Mummy, whose Thing is a morbid passion for being punctual at meals.

In the afternoon I found that Rapide had a loose shoe so I took him to the farrier's. I told Mr

Ramsbuckle about the fête and made him promise to come and bring the whole of the local farriers' union, or whatever they call themselves.

Just then Wendy Mead rode up on one of her father's farm horses, with tack that needed repairing slung round her shoulders.

While we waited she said, 'Your friend Dinah Dean has done it now!'

I went cold, and said, 'She isn't my friend, and I wish I'd never given her the clothes, and what's she done anyway?'

'She's been riding a pony in the middle of the night – quite a lot of nights, I gather. It's in a field at Watson's farm, in fact it's Mary Watson's pony. Mary had an idea several nights ago that something queer was happening. Then she looked out of her bedroom window about midnight and thought she saw somebody riding the pony in the field, but it wasn't a clear night and in the morning she thought she must have dreamed it. However, the next night the moon was up, and Mary distinctly saw somebody riding her pony. She told her father, and the next night Mr Watson lay in wait and caught Dinah at it.'

'What did he do?'

'He couldn't do much,' said Wendy heatedly, 'but he gave Dinah a fright and sent her packing, ar.d Mary says if it happens again Dinah will be jolly sorry.'

'And I suppose you're going to tell me that she was wearing my clothes?' I said, and Wendy said, 'I wouldn't know, but it looks to me as if you've started something. That kid's a menace.'

I didn't say anything, but I knew the whole village would be talking about the Watson affair, and I wished I could get hold of Dinah and find out what she was up to, and stop her.

The next day Cecilia went home. In the morning she went down to Chatton on my bike and bought presents for Mummy and me. She bought Mummy a painted tile to stand a teapot on, and she bought me a book about arranging flowers. I thought it was very kind of her, and Mummy was reading my book for days after and saying what good ideas it had, like having sprays of carrot tops in an old saucepan with a few gladioli mixed in, and everybody was happy so that was all right.

13 A pony for sale

The more I thought of it, the more I felt I had got to see Dinah Dean. It wasn't easy to find time, as in the holidays I usually arrange with my friends to spend all the days doing something with the ponies, and also I get let in for the usual domestic chores, as doubtless you do too. However, there came a wettish afternoon, and Ann had a cold and her fussy mother wouldn't let her ride, so I put on a mac and found myself whizzing off to Dinah's house.

Dinah opened the door. When she saw me she went red and looked as if she was going to cry. She said, 'Will you come in? I'm just doing some cooking.'

We went into a horrid dark kitchen, and Dinah took a rather messy cake out of the oven and started scraping the burnt bits off.

I said, 'What on earth have you been doing? You'll get into prison, and everybody will know they're my clothes.'

She said, 'Well, I had simply got to learn to ride, and I can now, and it didn't do the pony any harm.'

'You can't call that riding,' I pointed out.

'Yes, you can,' she said. 'I watched people, and I got a book out of the library and copied nearly all of it out and learnt it off by heart.'

'But you didn't have any tack, did you?' I said.

'No, I learnt bareback which made it harder, but I sat properly and did everything as it said, and the pony liked me and she was marvellous.'

I told her that Mary Watson was going to murder her, and so would I if anybody did that with one of my ponies. She just looked at me, and said, 'Could I possibly have a ride on your pony some day?'

'Gosh!' I said. 'What frightful cheek!'

'I wouldn't do him any harm,' she said, 'and I'd pay for it by cleaning out hens or anything you like.'

'You don't want much!' I said. 'Mary Watson would think I was backing you up and she'd murder me too.'

'I suppose it wouldn't do,' said Dinah, looking miserably at the horrid cake. 'But the only thing I want to do in the world is ride and I do adore ponies so.'

'Wouldn't your father pay for some lessons for you?' I said.

She shook her head and said, 'Whenever I ask him he always says, "Don't bother me, can't you see I'm busy?" He's always doing figures and making charts and things, and he never really notices anything in ordinary life. I take him his supper and he reads papers all the time he's eating it, and then about an hour after he says, "Aren't we going to have any supper tonight?"'

'Well, I'll have to go,' I said, 'but honestly, Dinah, you'll have to stop doing awful things, especially in my clothes.'

She started to cry and said, 'I wish I'd never had them, you can take them back if you want.'

I felt sorry for her, because having been poor and proud myself once I knew what it felt like. I suddenly wanted to say that she could come round one evening and have a ride on Black Boy, but I thought the whole village would hear about it and think I was backing Dinah.

The next day I told Ann all about it, and she said she thought I was really mean and ought to have offered her a ride, as whatever the village thought it was the duty of a true sportsman to encourage the young entry, and I said you couldn't really call Dinah the young entry as she was more of a gate-crasher.

However you know how awkward one's Better Feelings are when they get hold of one, one just can't do anything about it, so I went back to Dinah's. When she opened the door I blurted out, 'You can have a ride on Black Boy.'

She lit up like a Christmas tree, and said, 'Oh. How gorgeous! When?'

I said, 'I don't want anybody to see, so we'll have to be a bit conspirator-ish. You know that crossroads on the Common with a broken-down cottage on one side and the beginning of the woods on the other?'

She said she did, and I went on, 'Meet me there in about an hour and I'll bring the ponies. We can ride in the woods where nobody will see us.'

I dashed off and got the ponies, and felt a bit like Guy Fawkes starting out to blow up the Houses of Parliament, and when I got to the aforesaid crossroads it was all quiet and deserted, and there was Dinah, waiting. I got her up on Black Boy, and I must say she sat very well and knew what to do. I never knew a kid improve her riding so much under what are known as Adverse Circumstances.

We set off into the woods. She kept saying how marvellous it was, and she did look happy. I led the way on Rapide.

She said, 'This is something I've dreamed about, cantering down a forest ride into the romantic depths of the mighty wood.'

I said, 'Well, as a matter of fact these woods are very deep and people never come here. I know a way that nobody on earth knows, I discovered it by accident when I was a kid, and I'll show you.'

I hadn't thought about it for years, but there was a secret way I had never told to anybody, not even my own friends. You broke through what looked like a dead end of hazel brush, and there a grassy ride opened out before you and you could go on winding about among trees for a mile or so till you came to a sort of fairy clearing in the heart of the woods.

I took Dinah, and she was very excited. When she saw the little clearing she said, 'Wouldn't it be wonderful to live here for ever? Nobody would be able to find you, and there's grass for the pony and you could eat nuts and blackberries.'

I said, yes, it would be rather gorgeous, but I didn't see myself having the chance to do it, and we'd better be turning home.

When we got back to civilisation again she started thanking me for the ride till she was nearly blue in the face, and I was glad I had done it for her. I said perhaps someday when I had time I'd let her have another ride, only she'd have to jolly well behave

herself meanwhile, and she looked rather thoughtful
and opened her mouth to say something and then
shut it again, and I said, 'What's the matter?' and she
said, 'Nothing,' then she said, 'Thanks a million,' and
went dashing off.

I went round to Ann's to tell her I'd given Dinah
a ride and that the Good Deed was over, thank
goodness, but when I got to the Derrys' house it
was only to find a scene of wild drama, as Ann's
little sister Pam had been riding Ann's old pony
Seraphine and had been bucked off at a jump and
was in bed with concussion.

Mrs Derry was so fussy she behaved as if she
wasn't quite all there, and proved to be the most
hopeless kind of mother for any horsy person to
have, as one minute she was saying that Pam must
never ride again, and the next minute that Ann must
never ride again, and that she would sell Seraphine.
Ann looked furious, and I pointed out to Mrs Derry
that every single rider who ever lived took tosses and
that Pam would probably have dozens before she died
– as I had had myself in my long experience as a rider
– and the whole point was that Pam had never learned
to fall properly, but she would in time.

Unfortunately this only made Mrs Derry worse,
and after breathing out a lot of dire threats she said
that Seraphine was dangerous and would definitely
have to go.

At this Ann began to cry, as she was fond of
Seraphine who had once been her pony when she
was smaller, but she had to admit that Seraphine's
temper had been a bit uncertain lately and if she didn't
want to jump she was apt to buck. That, however,

was no reason for selling her, as one would not sell one's aged aunt for similar reasons.

Pam was all right in a day or two, and Ann told her she would slay her if she didn't say it was entirely her own fault that Seraphine threw her. Pam did say it, but it was no good, Mrs Derry was adamant. She began to draft an advertisement for the *Rychester Weekly*, a worthy but stodgy paper which is read all over the county by persons who want to buy houses and antique furniture and to sell things like sewing machines and – unfortunately – ponies.

Ann and I had hoped that we might be allowed to draft the advertisement, as we had planned to make it so unattractive that nobody would want to buy Seraphine, but we were not allowed. The morning after the advertisement appeared Ann had visions of the postman staggering under a load of offers for Seraphine, but such was not the case. There was not a single letter and our spirits rocketed up. The next afternoon Mrs Derry went out in the car, and I went to tea with Ann. While we were sitting in the dining-room arguing about something or other, the doorbell rang.

We looked at each other in a bleak sort of way and said, Seraphine! Then we rushed to the front door. A farming character stood there, and I instantly took a dislike to him. He had funny little eyes and the kind of hair which looks like a badly thatched cottage, and I have noticed that persons with hair like this are not fond of animals.

He said, 'Name of Derry? My name's Mr Towtle. I read in the *Weekly* that you've got a pony for sale. Like to have a look at it, if it's cheap.'

Ann went red and said, 'It isn't cheap.'

I said quickly, 'It isn't for sale, it's all a mistake,' and shut the door before Mr Towtle, left outside, could think what to say next. We peeped through the glass, and after scratching his head a few times he went away.

'Gosh, Jill, you were marvellous,' said Ann, and I said, 'That's the only way to do it, and we've got to get rid of everybody who comes the same way.' Ann said that her mother wouldn't be out every afternoon, and she couldn't be sitting all the time waiting to get to the front door first, so we made a lot of plans to keep Mrs Derry out of the way, like getting Mummy and Diana Bush's mother and a few others to invite her out to tea every day, but actually we hadn't much hope.

Nobody else called that afternoon, and Mrs Derry came home and fortunately didn't ask if anyone had called about the pony. I went home, and Ann told me next morning that she had lain awake most of the night dreading what the postman might bring in the chilly dawn. However, in the chilly dawn she fell fast asleep, and didn't wake till nine o'clock and got into a row for being late for breakfast. There were several opened letters by Mrs Derry's plate, and Ann managed to get a squint at them and saw to her relief that they were only bills and effusions from distant relations, which was comforting.

We began to hope again, and to cheer ourselves up by remembering that the end of the summer wasn't a good time for selling ponies, and so on.

Then the blow fell. A woman in a camel coat arrived one afternoon with a boy of about ten and

Mrs Derry opened the door herself, and we heard the woman say, 'I believe you have a pony for sale.'

Ann pushed her fingers in her ears, which I thought was a feeble thing to do as one might as well know The Worst. The next thing, we saw Mrs Derry taking the woman and the boy down to see Seraphine, and I had a feeling that All Was Lost.

'I think she looks rather nice,' I said, trying to look on the bright side like the awful children in Mummy's books.

'The boy looked fairly OK, too,' said Ann miserably. We both sat biting our nails, picturing the sordid scene that must by now be taking place in Seraphine's loosebox.

About twenty minutes later Pam burst in and said that Seraphine was sold. The woman's name was Mrs Arden and the boy's name was William, and he was having riding lessons and his father had promised him a pony for his birthday. He was very taken with Seraphine and had always wanted a grey, and had told his mother he wouldn't look at any more ponies because that was the one he wanted, and he was going to work hard at his riding and win a lot of prizes next summer.

When Pam stopped for breath Ann said, 'I think you're beastly hard-hearted, Pam, to sound so bucked about it,' and Pam said she thought Ann was feeble to make such a fuss, and Ann picked up the nearest thing and threw it at Pam and it happened to be Mrs Derry's mending basket, and socks and darning wool and needles and buttons flew all over the place, and we had to pick them up by crawling all over the floor and jam them back in the basket any old how.

Then Mrs Derry came back and told us the sordid transaction was completed and she was pleased at the price Seraphine had fetched, and Mrs Arden was going to send a horse box tomorrow. Ann said, 'The only thing I care about is that Seraphine should go to a good home,' and Mrs Derry said, 'As if I shouldn't be satisfied about that!' and added that Mrs Arden was fond of dogs and a leading light in the Women's Institute, which hadn't anything to do with the pony really but sounded vaguely comforting, especially as the Women's Institute had recently passed a resolution against sending ponies to slaughterhouses.

So we felt less gloomy, though we took care to be out of the way when Seraphine actually left. I mean, there are some things one cannot stand. I regret to say that beastly little Pam, who must have had a heart like a stone, was very interested in the horse box and even helped the man to shove Seraphine up the ramp. It was only when Seraphine was gone that it dawned on Pam that she hadn't got a pony at all now, and wasn't likely to have one, and when Ann firmly refused ever to let her ride George she cried and yelled, and it served her jolly well right.

14 That dreadful Dinah

I went up to Mrs Darcy's and practised every night on Sandy Two. I was doing much better now, and had gone over the ground a lot of times, but one never has to slacken when schooling a pony or he will get the idea that he can slack on The Day. I worked very hard, though Mrs Darcy was still not satisfied and always seemed to turn up to watch just when I was doing something badly.

She herself had entered for the open jumping at the fête on Blue Smoke, and there were a lot of other entries coming in, including some from friends of Captain Cholly-Sawcutt who would be worth watching. At our next committee meeting at Blossom Hall, Mrs Whirtley was very bucked about this, and when she learned that I knew Captain Cholly-Sawcutt and had sold him tickets she went boiled puce colour with joy, and Clarissa Dandleby's eyes popped out like organ stops, and afterwards two kids actually asked me for my autograph. The tea was as good as ever and everybody was in a good humour and dying for the actual fête to happen and Cecilia had had entries for heaps of handicrafts and decorated dinner-tables so she was happy too, and altogether our Joy was Unconfined as Shakespeare or somebody says.

I rode home thinking that life wasn't too bad at all, but I had hardly got into the house when Mummy came out of the sitting-room and said, 'Oh dear, Jill, that unfortunate Dean child has got into really bad trouble this time.'

I nearly sat down flat on the floor. I just said, 'What?'

'Well, it's rather awful,' said Mummy. 'They say she's stolen some ponies.'

'She's — what?' I gasped.

'She's stolen three ponies from a shed in some farmer's field and she and the ponies have disappeared.'

'How do they know it was her?' I said.

'Because apparently the farmer has had to warn her off his land several times. He was always noticing her hanging about the shed and looking in through the window. And once in the evening he saw her try the door and chased her, but she got away. She's very thin and quick, you know. And as I said, she's disappeared. Her father hasn't seen her since seven o'clock last night. In a way I think it serves him right for not looking after her better, and I think he's learnt his lesson and when he gets Dinah back he'll make her happier at home.'

'Oh,' was all I said, as I walked off to the orchard to think. I just couldn't understand it, and neither could anybody else. Everybody was talking about this strange affair, and thinking that Dinah would soon turn up, but she didn't. She and the three ponies had completely disappeared and it was a first-class mystery in Chatton, as you can imagine. I felt that being more or less mixed up with Dinah's doings, she and I might end our days shut up in some dungeon.

This quite put me off riding, which wasn't a good thing at all with the fête so near at hand. I tried to convince myself that nobody could really blame me, as I had only tried to be encouraging to the young entry in the manner of a true sportsman, and that the best thing I could do was to forget it and concentrate on Sandy Two and the under-fourteen jumping and the other things I had entered for at the gymkhana. However, as you probably know, when you have something on your mind it does jolly well put you off, and I wished I had never set eyes on that beastly little Dinah or done Good Deeds to her.

Ann and I practised competitions together all day long, and every time I did anything badly she said, 'What's gone wrong with you?' and I said, 'Oh, dry up!' and so it went on. There was I with my guilty secret – if you can call it a guilty secret, merely having given Dinah a ride on my pony – but it felt guilty to me, what with the clothes and everything. I honestly rather hoped that she had been whisked away by the fairies and would never appear again, but the fact was that she had run away from home and taken three of somebody else's ponies with her, and everybody was asking where could she be? Also by now the police were looking for her. It was awful.

And then in the middle of the night, which is the time when one's best ideas often come to one, I woke and sat straight up in bed. Gosh! I thought. The fairy glade in the woods, the place I showed her. I wonder!

I had got to get there and see.

It was jolly difficult, as I had planned a busy day for next day. About six of us were going up to Diana's and James's farm to do jumps and competitions, and we were going to take sandwich lunches and have a picnic in their orchard. There were my sandwiches to make, the ponies to feed and groom, and I had to be off by nine thirty. What on earth was I going to do?

All I could do was to get up frightfully early and be off to the woods about six, before anybody was around. I set my alarm clock for six, and it worked, and I jumped clean out of bed on the first buzz, and it was jolly cold as lovely summer days often are before they start, if you know what I mean. I put on my shorts and a wool sweater and tiptoed out. I was terrified that Mummy would hear me and ask where I was going, for she would certainly think I had gone mad, as early rising and skipping about in the dew are not among my strong points.

But there wasn't a sound from her room. I slipped out of the back door and went to wake up Black Boy, who was very surprised indeed. Soon we were off, and we had the world to ourselves and it was very pretty, as it is at that hour of the morning if you are brave enough to try it.

The air smelt good, everything glowed with a goldy light, a lot of larks were singing madly in the pinkish sky, and other little birds jibbered and jabbered happily in the hedges. Not that I was feeling very birdy. I was wondering what I should do if I didn't find Dinah where I thought I should find her. Then I thought, why worry? If she isn't there she's probably disappeared for ever and ever. I cheered up and said good morning to some passing farm workers who didn't look at all surprised to see me riding so early.

I got to the woods and rode on and on into the depths, far beyond where people usually go, and I broke through the hazel thickets and found the secret ride, and went on and on winding among the trees the way I knew until I came to the edge of the clearing and there I stopped.

In the clearing were three horses, two fast asleep and one nosing the fine grass. There was a big percheron, an old pony, and a young wildish-looking pony. Black Boy gave a little whicker when he saw the other horses, but I told him to be quiet and I slid down and tied him.

I found Dinah in a dry cosy spot between the roots of a big beech tree, curled up fast asleep on the beech mast, wrapped in two grey blankets. She looked as happy and peaceful as could be. Beside her was a basket containing half a loaf of bread, a cup, and three apples.

I said, 'Dinah!' She gave a sort of terrified squeak and jumped right up in one bound. When she saw it was me she just said, 'Oh.'

I said, 'Gosh, you are awful!'

She just said calmly, 'I thought you might turn up. But you're quite right, absolutely nobody else in the world can ever find me here.'

I said, 'Goodness! How long do you think you're going to stay here?' and she said as calmly as before, 'For ever, I should think.'

I said very angrily, 'Now look here, Dinah, I'm not standing for this kind of thing. I mean, stealing horses – '

She went into an absolute fury and yelled, 'You beast! I don't steal! I didn't steal them, I rescued them.'

'What on earth are you talking about?' I said. 'Those are the horses you stole from a farmer's shed, aren't they? Everybody's talking about it.'

'So you don't know?' she said. 'Well, I'll tell you. It's that beast, Mr Towtle. He's going round buying up horses and ponies cheap and selling them to be slaughtered and making a lot of money out of it. *Nice* horses, like those! He keeps a crowd of them all jammed together in that horrible shed in his field, and they're terrified and hungry, and he doesn't even feed them. I wish I could have got them all out instead of just three.'

I gaped at her, and said, 'What did you do?'

'I saw what was going on through the window,' she said, 'and I turned out to be a very good detective. The door had a Yale lock. I fetched a ladder from the farm in the middle of the night and broke the window and got in and opened the door from inside. I told you I could only manage three, one to ride and two to lead, so I picked the hungriest, the ones that had been there longest. When the shed is packed full a van comes in the middle of the night and loads them up. The Towtle beast is afraid of what the neighbourhood would say if they knew.'

'Which one did you ride?' I asked, looking at the three horses.

'The percheron,' said Dinah, and I said, 'You would!' I was struck dumb by this amazing kid.

'You'd have done it yourself,' said Dinah calmly, and I said, 'I wouldn't have had the nerve.'

'I wish I could get three more,' she said, 'but he's guarding the shed now, and I've been out each night and the van has been and fetched a load away. He's got to be stopped, the brute. Those poor horses!'

I honestly didn't know what to say or do. It was all too big and daring for me, and I thought, well if Dinah can cope, let her.

I said, what was she going to do next? and she said, 'Nothing for the present. I'll just stay here. We're all quite happy, but I'll tell you what you can do, you can bring me a loaf of bread now and then and a few apples and leave them on this side of the hazel thicket, and I can fetch them.'

I said, 'OK, I'll do that, but honestly you can't stay here for ever and ever,' and she said, '*Can't* I!'

I said feebly, 'They're awfully nice horses,' and she said, 'I know they are, and that old pony's a lovely ride, he's been somebody's pet. It makes your blood boil. Fortunately there's grazing for them here, and a stream.'

I said, 'I'll bring the bread and things, but it's going to be awfully difficult for me to get away, so don't expect to see me when I come. I'm booked up all the time, getting ready for this fête at Mrs Whirtley's.'

She grinned and said, 'Oh, that's all right.' She gave a little chirrup, and all the horses woke up and came to her and nuzzled her shoulders, and she gave them each one of the apples, leaving herself the dry bread for her breakfast. I shuddered when I thought of them being cruelly treated and sent to some horrible horse butcher. I had to take off my hat to Dinah.

So off I went, and rode home feeling more mixed up than ever. I got home and fed my ponies and the

hens, and went in for my own breakfast without any
remarks being made.

Then I went round to Diana's farm and made an
awful mess of all the competitions, and they said they
couldn't imagine what had come over me and I would
have to do something about myself before The Day.
How true!

15 Wonderful, wonderful stables

I thought I had better pull myself together (as
aforesaid) and get the worryful Dinah out of my
mind, and strangely enough I did, because Black
Boy in some peculiar manner got colic and rolled
about on his back in a most hysterical way, and I
rang up the vet and he didn't come for ages, and it
was only a fortnight off the fête, and I was frantic
and had Mummy and Mrs Crosby and everybody else
running round in circles. However, the vet came and
gave Black Boy a draught and got him into his stall,
and I sat with him nearly a whole night, watching the
hands of my watch go round so that I shouldn't miss
giving him his medicine at the right time. Mummy
came out at intervals and said I must come in and go
to bed, and she thought I was idiotic and all the rest
of it, and I said, You little know! Every time I left
Black Boy for even a few minutes he seemed worse
when I got back, and he rolled his eyes at me so
pathetically. However, when the vet came again he
said, 'This animal's playing you up,' and surprisingly
enough Black Boy was immediately much better and
got up on his feet and looked sheepish.

He was fairly seedy for two days, and it was only
when he was all right again that I remembered Dinah
and the bread and apples. I thought if she had died

of hunger it would be my fault, but she didn't strike
me as the sort of person who would die of anything,
she was extremely resourceful. I asked Mrs Crosby
for a loaf – we always have plenty – and I picked a
whole bag of apples from our orchard where there are
thousands. They didn't look very ripe, but I guessed
Dinah wouldn't be too particular, and I took the lot
and left them on her side of the hazel thicket and sped
back like the wind.

After that I got on with my ordinary life, which
really I hadn't been able to do for quite a long time,
what with Cecilia and Dinah and Black Boy's colic.
The things one could do if one was left alone to do
them! I had planned to do all kinds of things in the
summer holidays and here they were whizzing by
and hardly anything done at all. At the beginning
the eight weeks had felt like a year, and now they
felt like eight minutes.

I got the ponies back on their routine of careful
schooling, and had a few rides in the evenings with
Ann and Diana Bush. Then I reorganised my tack
room for the winter ahead, and cleaned some of the
stuff that had got pushed into corners, and mended
everything that needed it.

Mrs Crosby grumbled and said I used all her cleaning stuff, and she didn't know what had come over
me, and give her sure and steady all the time instead
of here today and gone tomorrow, and I retorted, 'A
rolling stone gathers no moss and likewise a stitch
in time saves nine, and now think of another one
if you can!' and she said if I was her girl she'd
have something to say about that mending basket,
so just to show her, I reorganised all my clothes too

and mended everything and ironed all my shirts and pressed my jodhs, and she said it *would* be just when she was needing the iron herself! You can't please some people.

Then I remembered Dinah again and thought it was about time she had some more food. You can't think what a job I had to get away for half an hour. Everybody all of a sudden seemed to take such an interest in where I was going. I got a loaf out of the bread bin and had to put it back again. Next time I got it out I met Mummy and she said, 'Darling, I told you only to use the broken bread for the animals.' Finally I managed it, and galloped all the way to the woods and dumped the bread and apples where Dinah would be able to find them.

I didn't stop to see if she was alive or if she had acquired any more horses. But on the way back I suddenly thought, Towtle! That was the horrible man who nearly bought Seraphine! Gosh, what an escape!

I then stopped thinking about Dinah's doings because I had loads of other worries, mainly having to revise my ideas about the fête so as to give Rapide the major part of the work, though the vet had said that Black Boy would be quite fit for his classes. I didn't want to take any risks.

A day or two later Mrs Darcy came cantering up the lane on Blue Smoke and stopped at our gate. She called out, 'Nice weather for the fête!'

I was more or less standing on my head, weeding the path under Mummy's orders, so I said something that sounded like OO–er–ah–um.

'I say!' said Mrs Darcy. 'I've got to go over to the

Cholly-Sawcutt place this afternoon. I wondered if you'd care to come. Ask your mother if you can.'

I was so thrilled that I straightened out in one jump and nearly turned a somersault. I asked Mrs Darcy to wait, and rushed into the cottage where Mummy was sitting at her typewriter with a furrowed brow.

'Mrs Darcy wants – ' I began.

Mummy said, 'Oh, darling! I've been wanting to do this bit properly for about an hour, and just when I get the right sentence you've got to come and drive it right out of my head. What is it?'

I told her, and she looked a bit bleak.

'Stables!' she said. 'I suppose this is what they'd call the Higher Horsemanship. Well, don't get any ideas, will you, Jill? Because I've set my heart on your doing a decent secretarial course when you leave school.'

I looked uncomfortable, because the prospect of going to see the Cholly-Sawcutt stables didn't mix with secretarial courses, and the last thing I wanted was to discuss my future. I just said, 'Oh, Mummy, please say I can go. I want to so much.'

She said I could go, and I tore back and told Mrs Darcy. We set off in her car at two o'clock.

I don't know if you have ever been to a big training stable, but it is the sort of place where if you are a horsy person you could wander about in a dream for hours. The long rows of beautifully kept loose boxes, the broad paved yard, the green paddocks and the jumping field simply dazzled me. We drove into the yard. A lot of people looked very busy, and I couldn't drag my eyes away from the beautiful heads of two hunters looking out over their half doors. There was so much to see, my head kept turning from side to side and I wished it was on a swivel and would go right round.

A manager person came out to speak to Mrs Darcy, and I hoped the business was going to take a long time. It would be awful if it was over in five minutes and I never got any further than this. I wanted to go and look into all those loose boxes and peep into the harness rooms, and wander across the paddocks and examine the jumps, and I was madly excited by the glimpse of a man in the distance who seemed to be breaking in a pony. Just then the vet arrived in his car, and was met by a groom in khaki overalls who led him to a small building in the yard. My feet were itching to follow them and see what was going on there.

The manager said, 'Excuse me a minute,' and went away. I said to Mrs Darcy, 'Gosh, there must be a lot going on here!' and she said, 'Plenty of hard work,' and I said, 'Plenty of fun too.'

'Well, they do a bit of everything,' she said. 'The Captain is particularly good with young horses, and his hunters are noted. He usually has one or two beautiful foals.'

'I expect those are his own practice jumps over there,' I said, in a voice of deep awe.

'They're snorters,' said Mrs Darcy. 'But so beautifully made. I've been round them, but I don't suppose anybody but the Captain has ever jumped a clear round in that field.'

The manager came back and after a few words all seemed to be over; then all of a sudden who should walk out of the house but Captain Cholly-Sawcutt himself.

'Goodness!' called Mrs Darcy. 'I thought you were miles away.'

He greeted us cheerily, and said, 'It just happens that I have a free weekend. In fact I've promised to go to this fête on Saturday and do an exhibition round before the open jumping begins. I rang Mrs Whirtley up and told her I'd come.'

I said, 'I hope everybody knows, then millions will be there.'

'Don't worry,' said Mrs Darcy laughing. 'If I know Phyllis Whirtley she'll have spread the news all over the county by now.'

'Have you sold any more tickets?' said the great man to me in a very friendly way.

'Oh, Jill's been working like a beaver,' said Mrs Darcy. 'If the fête isn't a success it won't be her fault. And she's showing Sandy Two for me in the Novice Hack class.'

'Good for you,' said the Captain. 'You'll have a couple of tough judges in Colonel Brown and Tom Beasley, so it won't be a walkover for anybody. For a small affair this fête is going to be a very big affair, if you get my meaning.'

I stood on one leg and scratched my other ankle and said, 'Oh!'

Mrs Darcy smiled and said, 'I notice that Jill can't keep her eyes off that man of yours who is lunging the colt. I think she'd like to know the sort of work you do here.'

The Captain asked me if I took it that seriously, and I could only go boiled puce colour with excitement and stammer out that I took it more seriously than anything else in the world.

He said, 'If you like, I'll find a boy to take you round,' and I said, 'How absolutely wonderful.'

He said, 'Well, we have about two hundred acres here. At present we're schooling some five- and six-year-olds, and getting the hunters ready for next season. We always have young horses on hand, and it's quite a job finding time to school them. Of course my people ride my horses in all local tests and competitions, and go far afield for dressage tests and cross-country events and road and track events. It means long hours of work for them, so needless to say the only people I employ here are those whose whole life is horses. This isn't just a job, it's a whole way of life. I've got three full-time grooms here, and a new girl who's as keen as mustard, and a boy who's come for experience in making and breaking. I'm away such a lot, I have to have people I can trust absolutely to see that everything goes on as I would have it if I were here.'

'Now you know!' said Mrs Darcy. 'This makes my place look like a baby's playground, doesn't it?'

It did, but I couldn't very well agree without appearing rude.

'By the way,' said the Captain, 'what's all this about some girl in your part of the world walking off with three horses and disappearing?'

I went cold, and Mrs Darcy said, 'Oh, it's the local mystery. She's an odd sort of girl, but where she can have got to with three horses is past imagining. I mean, the police are on the look-out on roads for miles round; she must have daubed herself and the horses all over with invisible paint. It's a nine days' wonder.'

'I hope she isn't one of your pupils,' said the Captain.

'Oh, good gracious no, not likely.'

I edged away while they were talking as I didn't want to hear all this, and was only just in time, as the Captain said, 'It's a bit thick, I mean stealing horses – ' and I opened my big mouth and nearly found myself saying out loud, 'She says she didn't steal them, she rescued them,' and only just stopped myself in time. It was a sticky moment.

The Captain called out, 'Harry!' and a boy of about sixteen came out of a door. 'Take this young lady round and show her everything she fancies to see.' I could hardly believe that this was happening to me.

Harry proved to be an awfully good guide. Soon my ambition was realised, as we went round all the loose-boxes and saw the hunters, and went into the neat professional-looking tack rooms, and he also showed me a new foal a week old whom he said was destined to be a great steeplechaser some day.

I said, 'Do you get any riding here?' and he said, 'Oh, yes! The Captain is a wonderful employer and gives everybody a chance of doing some riding and getting all kinds of experience. I wouldn't have come here otherwise. At some stables you don't get any instruction at all, but here – although I'm actually only the lowest form of life on the place – I'm being taught how to prepare a horse for a cross-country event, and I've also been allowed to ride in one or two showing classes. It makes the life so frightfully interesting.'

'It must be marvellous,' I said, 'to do nothing but horses from morning to night all day long.'

He nodded and said, 'All day long is right. Counting the actual work, and the training I get, and taking the horses to shows, I suppose my average working day is about fourteen hours, but I love it and I don't count it in hours. I mean, there simply isn't anything I'd rather be doing.'

'I'd feel like that too,' I said.

He asked me, was I a girl groom at Mrs Darcy's? and I was so flattered at being taken for one that it was an awful come-down to have to admit that I was still at school. Harry said, 'I expect you're dying to leave and get cracking with horses,' and I said in a very dim sort of way that on the contrary I was going to take a secretarial course, and my mother wanted me to go to a family in Switzerland to get French and German. Harry just said, Oh.

I could hardly tear myself away from the horses, and when I saw a groom at work on a beautiful black hunter it was all I could do not to seize a stable rubber and join in. I felt I would gladly have run about with buckets from morning to night in a place like that.

I asked Harry what he was going to be in the end, and he said of course he was going to be a famous rider and go all over the country competing in shows, and have a partnership in a good stable.

Meanwhile the Captain and Mrs Darcy had gone into the house, and as they came out I could hear shrieks and yells and out rushed the three Cholly-Sawcutt girls, April, May, and June.

I had had some experience – as I have told in a previous book – in teaching these three to ride, but like their father I had come to the conclusion that it was a hopeless task. It seems almost unbelievable that the daughters of the great Captain Cholly-Sawcutt should have been born incurably ham-handed, bouncing, and completely without a sense of balance. But such was the case. And like other people with such hideous natural drawbacks they didn't realise how awful they were – at least, if they did they didn't let it worry them – but jogged happily about on their ponies and entered for lots of competitions, and were excited if they finished up anywhere but last. Their father used to cover his face with his hands when they were jumping, not in fear lest they might be thrown but in horror because they looked so awful.

You couldn't teach them. Nobody on earth could teach them. They were the Local Joke.

'Have you seen the foal, Jill?' yelled April.

'Isn't he a pet?' shouted May.

'We're going to the fête on Saturday,' shrieked June. 'We've entered for everything.'

Their father gave a sort of hollow groan, and Mrs Darcy said, 'Well, I've no doubt you'll all enjoy yourselves.'

'Daddy said I was improving,' said April. 'You did say so, didn't you, Daddy?'

'Did I?' said the Captain. 'I must have been mad.'

I thought, wasn't Fate funny to put three girls like that into a home like that, when they would have been so happy with somebody like Mrs Derry, going out to tea and doing the flowers and learning tennis.

'Do come and see our ponies,' said May. 'That is, if you're not in a hurry.'

Of course I am the sort of person who would go with anybody to see anybody's ponies, but I wanted to be tactful so I looked at Mrs Darcy first, and she nodded as much as to say it was all right for me to go.

You will probably think I am going to tell you that the Cholly-Sawcutt girls had blood ponies of overpowering beauty, but such was not the case. Their father wisely realised that anything good would be wasted on them, so they had pleasant but very ordinary ponies of a strong and untemperamental kind, suited to their bouncy natures. And if you think these ponies were called by imaginative and romantic names you will also be disappointed because April, May, and June were not like that. The ponies were called by the dim and mere names of Tom, Bess, and Lad. They were kept in a small paddock of their own, but they had a nice little stable of their own too, and they each had their own stall and manger. Over each stall was a little wooden plaque with a letter painted on it in white paint, T, B, and L, and on three pegs hung three dark blue rugs, each having a white-embroidered letter, T, B, and L. I thought this was rather nice.

We gave the ponies sugar, actually far too much sugar as they were quite fat enough already, and June said, 'We've been doing quite a lot of schooling for the gymkhana on Saturday, much more than usual. I shouldn't be surprised if we won something.'

May said, 'I should! We never have yet.'

April said, 'It's awful having a famous rider for your father because the judges daren't give you a prize or people would think they were sucking up to Daddy.'

I was so taken aback by this absolutely preposterous idea that I could only open my mouth and stare at the frightful April. When I became conscious again I simply had to say, 'If you won a competition they'd have to give you the prize. Don't be silly.'

April said, 'Well, we never do win anything, so shucks to you.'

'We never win anything because we're rotten,' said June cheerfully.

I rather liked June. I said, 'Well, why don't you do something about it?' Only I really hadn't much hope for these poor girls, because of having been born the wrong shape for riders.

'It's too much bother doing anything about it,' said May, 'so we just go on being awful.'

And, believe me, this was true, they were content just to go on being awful, and if you are riders you will shudder at the thought just as I did.

Then June asked me to sign her autograph book, which she kept conveniently handy in a small corn bin, and she had got Ringo Starr in it and other world-shakingly famous people, in fact I wrote my name on the same page as Ringo Starr and it made me feel terrific.

I felt I had had the most wonderful afternoon and I hardly spoke all the way home.

Mrs Darcy said, 'I thought you'd be impressed, but you'd better come back to earth.'

16 The big day at last

It was a wet morning on the day of the fête, but everybody went round saying things like 'Rain before seven, fine before eleven', and funnily enough this turned out to be true.

I was busy all the morning, grooming the ponies and washing tails and hoofs. Then I packed all the grooming kit and the ponies' 'rewards' in the shape of oats and sugar. I don't know why I was so conceited as to think they would need a lot of rewards.

Then I ironed over my best shirt and tie, and brushed my clothes for the umpteenth time, and polished my boots, and as usual I couldn't find my riding hat and Mrs Crosby said, 'It's just the same old story about that hat of yours. If I were you I'd sleep with it tied round my neck,' and I said, 'I left it in the hall on its peg and I bet it was you who moved it,' and she said she wouldn't touch the silly thing with the tongs, not if it was ever so, and I said the whole point was to find it instead of arguing.

'It's all the same on these gymkhana mornings,' she grumbled. 'You just lose your head.'

'You mean my hat,' I said, not very cleverly.

I finally found it myself under a mac in the harness room and remembered that I had thrown it down there the day before, and Mrs Crosby

– who was a good sort in spite of being so fond
of a wrangle – brushed it for me and did it over
with some mysterious witch-like concoction which
she said 'brought up the black'.

I spent a long time dressing. We were all going
to travel in state in the Lowes' car, and Martin
Lowe had arrange to have my ponies taken over to
Blossom Hall.

The phone rang several times during the morning.
Everybody seemed to be going to the fête, and
everybody said exactly the same thing, 'Isn't it an
awful morning? But they say rain before seven fine
before eleven,' and I said, 'I jolly well hope so.'

At five minutes to eleven there was a bit of blue
in the sky, and at five past the sun was shining with
that steady look which means it intends to keep on.

Mrs Darcy rang up to say that she was setting off
at twelve thirty and would see me at the fête, and that
Sandy Two looked lovely and was in great form. I
dithered a bit at this. It meant that whatever happened
in the Novice Hack class it wouldn't be Sandy Two's
fault. I was thinking far more of Sandy Two than I
was of my own pony class.

I was dressed too soon and couldn't keep still, and
at twelve our cold lunch was on the table and Mummy
had stopped wondering what to put on and had gone
all summery in her cream silk.

When the Lowes drove up, Mrs Lowe said, 'All
roads today seem to be leading to Blossom Hall.
Everybody in the neighbourhood must be going.
It nearly seems to be rivalling Chatton Show as an
attraction.'

Martin gave me an encouraging smile and said,

'You look jolly good, Jill. I think you're going to have quite a day.'

I said that I had already been told that the judges were tough, and he said consolingly that the toughest ones were usually the fairest, which was something.

We set off, and it was an exciting journey as we kept passing horse boxes and parties of riders, all making for Blossom Hall, and I kept recognising people and waving.

When we turned into the gates of the park I saw that it had been completely transformed. There were marquees and little signposts and Scouts directing the traffic, and crowds of people everywhere. There was a turnstile with a long queue waiting to pay for admission, which was encouraging. Although the fête had hardly begun, the refreshment marquee looked to be full of people eating, and I thought how funny it was that when you are enjoying yourself it makes you hungry.

Mr Lowe parked the car, and their man was waiting at the car park with Martin's wheel-chair. We thought we had better go and see how the ponies were after the journey.

Just then I saw Ann calmly riding across the turf and yelled, 'Ann! Over here!'

She came over to us and said, 'So you're here. Golly, everybody's here! I should think Chatton'll be the original deserted village. I've seen Susan Pyke on her new half-Arab mare, and I nearly turned back because I don't think anybody else will stand a chance, except that she'll probably finish up with her arms round its neck and the judge having fourteen fits all over her. And Val and Jackie have each brought two

ponies and they've got new black coats. I mean Val
and Jackie, not the ponies. And James Bush is
riding his father's Gay Prince in the open jumping and it's the biggest thing he's ever been in
for, and his knees won't stop wobbling. Oh, and
you'd scream! I've seen the Ghoul and the Zombie.'

These were two of our teachers from school and I
said, 'Oh, yes, they've got a cottage near here,' and
Mummy said, 'You really are the limit, why can't
you say Miss Brace and Miss Peters?' and I said,
'Did you call teachers Miss Brace and Miss Peters
when you were at school?' and she had to admit that
her teachers had had other names too.

By now we were getting over towards the ponies,
under the big trees at the side of the park. They all
looked beautiful and their owners were busy putting
the final touches. All our friends were there.

Black Boy and Rapide looked knowing and happy
which always gave me confidence before a gymkhana.
While I was fussing over their girths and bridles, Mrs
Whirtley appeared, all in rose pink with an outsize
pink hat. She was shaking hands with everybody all
along the line of ponies, and saying how marvellous
everybody looked and what a marvellous day it was,
and when she got to Ann and me she handed us both
a white satin rosette with a white streamer with
Committee printed on it in gold letters, to pin on
our lapels.

Ann said it was the first time either of us had ever
been an official at a pony show, and Martin said,
'Who knows? You may be a judge some day,' and
Ann said that as most judges appeared to be about
eighty years old she wasn't very keen.

Just then two of the Committee boys came by pushing a yellow ice cream cart – which was their spell of duty – and they more or less blackmailed us into buying from them, so we each had an ice, and George got most of Ann's, which I thought was a bit rash as I wouldn't normally give ponies ice cream before a competition. But Ann said that if George was at all frustrated he didn't do his best, and if he wanted ice cream he just had to have it.

Mrs Whirtley said she had put in an extra showing class for the under-tens, as there was such a demand for it by infatuated parents who liked to see their infants looking so sweet on their ponies, and that was just about to take place, so meanwhile would Ann and I sell some raffle tickets for a superb iced cake?

We said we would, and it gave us a chance to wander round and see what everybody was doing. We sold a lot of tickets, though some people said they would have liked to see the superb iced cake before spending fifty pence, and why weren't we carrying it round with us? I said, 'Gosh, it weighs about a ton!' and Ann said, 'How much of the superb icing do you think there would be left on the superb iced cake if we carted it round with us in this heat?' Which seemed to satisfy them, and they paid their fifty pences, in fact a lot of people took one pound's worth, and we got over thirty pounds. Actually, we hadn't seen the cake, but if Mrs Whirtley said it was superb then it was, and in the end it was won by an old woman called Mrs Mains who was nearly ninety and lived in a one-room cottage in Billet Lane and hadn't any teeth, and some people thought she was a witch.

Mrs Whirtley brought the cake out of the house

on a lordly dish and everybody gasped and said Ooooh! and Mrs Mains said 'Lawks-a-mussy', and Mr Cuppleheaver the carrier offered to take it to the cottage for her on his lorry, and I'm quite sure that when the cake got into the cottage there wouldn't be any room for Mrs Mains. I often wondered what she did with it.

It is funny how people always win the wrong things in raffles.

Meanwhile the children's showing class was going on, and you couldn't get near the rails for the proud parents. There were some people who were only five, on Shetlands, and some frightfully efficient cool and collected ones of nine or ten. Ann said she would hate to be the judge. We both picked out the ones we thought would be placed first, second, and third, and we must have been pretty good judges because we proved to be right in two out of the three places, and it all ended up as baby classes often do end up, with some people in tears and others falling off their ponies with excitement at having won prizes.

The next was the under-fourteen Egg and Spoon, but though I had entered I didn't compete, as Mrs Darcy got hold of me and suggested that I should exercise Sandy Two. She tied on my number for me, and said, 'The ground is just right. Sandy is putting his feet down well, he likes it.'

I mounted and at once felt at home. Mrs Darcy came with me across the park to where several other competitors were exercising too. There were some lovely hacks, and one young man on a lean chestnut looked too incredibly good for words.

I walked, trotted, and then cantered Sandy Two

on a loose rein. I said to Mrs Darcy, 'Everybody else looks terribly good.'

'Now don't be silly,' she said in her forthright way. 'You're on the top of your form and so is Sandy. The novice test is quite easy and you know your stuff. I'm not asking you to win, I'm only asking you to do your best, and you're quite capable of perfection. You wouldn't want to compete against a lot of slugs!'

'He's a bit fresh,' I said, collecting Sandy Two who was trying to side-step.

'Of course he's fresh. The judges expect him to be.' Mrs Darcy added, 'You get down now, and I'll walk him about. This Egg-and-Spoon thing seems to be going on for ever.'

I began to wander across the park, and soon I noticed a large marquee, and full of curiosity peeped inside.

'Oh, hello,' said a voice, and there was my cousin Cecilia. It was her marquee. She was standing behind a long table covered with the most dismal articles of which she looked disgustingly proud. These were the handicrafts and Cecilia had made a lot of them herself and was waiting for them to be judged. There were a lot of knitted things, and some teacups with fat red roses painted on them, and some hideous brooches made out of acorns, and a lot of stuffed toys. There was a giraffe with staring eyes and a tiger made out of somebody's old pullover, and some chickens made out of grey blanket with combs of red flannel, and there were dozens of knitted woolly lambs. There was a very rickety stool with Bide-a-Wee painted on it in an awful shade of pink, and a purple satin cushion all frills, and some hard-looking bedroom slippers, and of course tons of Cecilia's own embroidery.

'Gosh!' I said. 'Do you have to stop in here all the time?' and Cecilia said she'd much rather, she was loving it. She said, 'Your coat collar's up at the back and you've got too much lipstick on.' I said, 'I haven't got any lipstick on at all,' and she said, 'Goodness! Do you mean to say your lips are that awful colour naturally? You'll terrify the judges.'

I said, 'I've just been exercising Sandy Two and I'm hot,' and she said, 'I thought good riders always stayed cool, I've heard you say so yourself.'

You just couldn't argue with Cecilia.

She said, 'If you can tear your mind from horses, come and look at the decorated dinner tables.'

What she meant was, come and look at the dinner table she had decorated herself. She led me past a lot of sweet peas and roses to her table. She had done it all in yellow flowers and it looked terribly impressive, though I couldn't help wondering what the food would look like with all that yellow round it. If you had been sitting at the table eating your dinner you wouldn't have been able to see anybody else who was sitting at the same table for all those flowers, but I suppose that doesn't matter in a competition.

I said, there didn't look to be much room for the stew and the vegetables and all the plates, and Cecilia said witheringly, 'Don't be silly.'

There were quite a lot of people in the tent, and you could hear what they said, and they all seemed to be admiring Cecilia's table very much. Of course the tables were numbered, and nobody knew who had done them.

Just then Ann came in, and said, 'Oh, there you are. Diana Bush won the Egg-and-Spoon and Jackie Heath was second, and I had the most awful luck, I lost my egg in the first heat. It's our showing class next, but there's heaps of time while they get the ring ready.'

Cecilia said, 'Oh, is that Ann? You look a bit of a wreck too.'

Ann said, 'Are you stopping in here all the time? Aren't you riding?' and Cecilia said she hadn't had any practice since she left Chatton, so she had decided to concentrate on the handicrafts, etc., and weren't they gorgeous? Ann said, absolutely terrific, but if any nervous kid saw that giraffe it would probably have a fit.

Then we both said good luck, we had better be getting along to the ring.

Black Boy was ready for the fray, and very nice he looked. There was an enormous entry for the under-sixteen showing class, and we looked like the Canterbury Pilgrims when the collecting steward called us into the ring. Half the people there I had never seen before.

I found myself riding behind Clarissa Dandleby, on a dashing blood pony. She sat too far forward and held it on a tight rein and was bright scarlet in the face. Behind me was Ann, on George, and I caught sight of Diana Bush on a new chestnut pony that was a bit too much for her.

We walked on quietly, except for the few people who didn't seem to know what a collected walk was, then we trotted and followed up with a canter.

At this point I saw Clarissa Dandleby in front of

me use her stick, and give her pony a whack that
you could hear across the field. He bucked and then
cantered on the wrong leg. The judge said, 'Number
31, stop using a stick,' and I thought, well that's the
end of Clarissa.

Black Boy was going very nicely with his neck
arched. Though he looked lively he felt very con-
trolled and to my delight we were called in third.
I didn't know the people in first and second place,
but Ann was fourth.

Then the fun began. The boy who was placed
first was riding a lovely grey pony of eye-catching
showiness, long stride, and impressive action, and
nobody was surprised he had been given first place,
but when it came to reining back this pony proved
impossible and would not stand in line. The judges
waited for him for what seemed ages, and at last when
he backed violently into the girl who was quietly
sitting in second place a judge came over and said,
'Line up and stand, please.' At that moment he had
to skip for his life, and his patience being exhausted he
then told the girl and me to move up one, and sent the
boy into third place. I was so pleased at being second
that I didn't notice what happened next, because the
girl was now doing her show. She did a very correct
one, though I thought she was rather slow and and apt
to swing off her balance, but it is a foolish thing in a
competition to let yourself think another person is not
doing too well, so I concentrated on keeping Black
Boy standing squarely until it was my own turn.

My show seemed to go off quite well, and I looked
round, to see that the boy who had been first had
now given up even trying to control his too-fresh

pony and was prancing off the field, and Ann was in third place.

The unsaddling and leading out went off without incident, and then the judges went into a huddle. They took ages deciding, but eventually left things alone and came up with the rosettes. I was very excited to get second, it was much more than I had hoped for, and I was so glad that Ann was third, in fact I wouldn't have been surprised if our positions were reversed. We cantered gaily round the ring with our rosettes, and when we got outside I remembered Susan Pyke and the half-Arab and wondered why she wasn't placed, but apparently she had found the pony too much for her, had crowded everybody else, and finally ridden right out of the ring.

17 Riding at the fête

The next class was Musical Chairs and I had entered Rapide, but I decided to scratch from it as I wanted to be fresh for the Novice Hack class which followed.

Ann said, 'Well, don't stand there for the next half-hour mooning over Sandy Two and getting the needle,' and I said I had no intention of mooning and would enjoy standing at the rails and watching the fun. I went and joined Mummy and the others, and Martin said, 'You did very well in that showing class, but I think you had a lot of luck. I never saw so many nappy ponies in my life. It beats me why people enter for showing classes when they can't even ride.' I said, 'I'm glad you weren't the judge or you'd have probably said that I couldn't even ride,' and he said that what I wanted to aim at was more elegance, and I said, 'Help!'

I was quite glad I hadn't entered for the Musical Chairs because it was murder. There were so many people in it that they had to do it in three goes, and even then the ponies were nearly in a stampede and people emerged from the scrimmage weeping.

All the parents round the ring were yelling and encouraging their own frightful offspring, and even ponies who knew their stuff from A to Z gave up trying and backed out of the mêlée to crop grass.

There was a thwacking of sticks, and the judges got furious and sent people out of the ring. Small red-faced kids kept crawling up to their mummies and saying it wasn't fair, the big ones had pushed them off the stools. Honestly, you couldn't hear the band half the time.

Eventually the whole thing was won by Clarissa Dandleby. She *would* win! She looked to me the sort of person who would win any war single-handed, being a born shover. I heard afterwards that she bit the boy who was left in with her at the end, and everybody was yelling so they never heard him shriek with pain and let go of the stool, and there was Clarissa sitting on it without a plait out of place and her glasses still on.

Martin said, 'Anybody who won that ought to go into the SAS. Who is she, anyway?'

I said, 'She's called Clarissa Dandleby and she's on the Committee and she hunts five times a week all through the season, and she's going to be a steeplechaser some day.'

Mummy said, 'She looks it,' and Mrs Lowe said, 'Well, she's not what I call a ladylike rider,' which was so understating the case that we all burst out laughing.

However, Clarissa was so thrilled to have won that you could see her gooseberry eyes popping right across the ring, and when she galloped round with her red rosette in her teeth her pony was covered with foam and we all felt very sorry for it.

Thank goodness I had kept calm and collected, because the next class was the Novice Hacks. Mummy held up her mirror for me to see that I was quite neat

and then I went in search of Mrs Darcy who said
coolly, 'Oh, there you are. Well, you look all right,
but weren't you going to ride in your black coat?'

I gave one yell. Think of forgetting to change
my coat! I absolutely flew to the Lowes' horse box
where I had parked my things, and changed, and
flew back again.

There was Sandy Two with his tail brushed out
and his plaiting beautifully done. Even then I nearly
went off without my number and Mrs Darcy had to
tie it on for me.

'Will Class 4, the Novice Hack class, please come
to the collecting ring?' said the loudspeaker.

As soon as I was actually up and riding I felt all
right, though a bit dreamlike. Sandy Two was very fit
and walked with a long, free stride. As we went round
the ring I had a good look at the other competitors,
and felt almost sorry that the competition wasn't very
strong. Some of the other horses were bucking and
some jogging instead of walking. There was only
one outstanding one, and that was more of a hunter
than a hack, ridden very competently by a farmer's
daughter called Jean Nelson who always won a lot
of prizes each season. I guessed Jean would probably
be first.

However, I had to admit that Sandy was on top
of his form and wasn't putting a foot wrong. He felt
even more light in hand than usual, and went into
his trot and canter with the utmost smoothness.

Jean Nelson was called in first and I was second. My
rein back was good and Sandy Two stood squarely, so
I resisted the fatal impulse to look down at his feet.

Jean Nelson's show was, I thought, perfect, but

mine seemed all right too. Actually I wasn't doing a thing, Sandy Two did it all himself. He took his inspection with a look of 'Find anything wrong with me if you can', and was perfect to lead in hand.

Then we waited while the judges made their minds up, though I couldn't think there was anything to ponder about. To my amazement when they finally approached I got the red rosette because they had decided that Jean Nelson's horse was more of a hunter than a hack and had given me the benefit of the doubt.

I rode out still feeling dazed, and Mrs Darcy met me and said, 'Thanks very much.' This was terrific praise from her, but I didn't deserve any as she had provided me with a perfect horse. I patted Sandy Two for ages and gave him sugar, and I felt very thrilled.

The next class was the Juvenile Jumping and there was a huge entry. A lot of people were in it just for fun, including April Cholly-Sawcutt who said she had been practising and could get over anything. Actually she was putting away ice creams up to the very last minute, and when her number was called she said, 'Golly! I forgot to show Tom round the jumps!'

We all watched Tom go over the bush jump in fine style, except that you could see the whole of the county through April's legs and she bumped down into the saddle with a thud that made Tom quiver all over, but he was strong and used to April. I guessed her father was groaning if he was watching. Then the crowd roared. Tom turned calmly round and took a bite out of the succulent top of the bush. April pulled him round and went for the wall at a mad gallop. Tom had by now decided that everybody concerned was out to play the fool, so he stopped dead, April shot over his head and landed on the turf with a resounding wallop. She grinned and got up, but Tom was by now halfway out of the ring, tossing his head about and trailing the reins. So that was the end of April's career, and we got down to the real business.

There were six jumps and none of them was very easy. Rapide had inspected them without showing any concern, but when it came to the point he didn't jump well. It just wasn't his day. He took the wall in a positive shower of bricks, and though he let me collect him he brought down the triple. I was very annoyed with him, but one doesn't show it in the ring, and he got his pat just the same as we left the ring. These things will happen.

I had plenty of time to watch the other people. Ann only got four faults, and up to then there hadn't been a clear round, but after that there were six clear rounds done by Val Heath, Susan Pyke (on the half-Arab, who certainly was a jumper), Clarissa Dandleby, and three unknowns. Clarissa went out at the first jump-off, and in the end Val was first, an unknown boy second, and Susan Pyke third. The standard had been high and the competition very keen, but when I congratulated Susan afterwards she wasn't at all pleased and said her father would consider it very *infra dig.* to be third on a pony that cost nearly three thousand pounds.

I said, 'What on earth has the cost of the pony to do with it? It's the riding,' and Susan said her father didn't look at it like that, so I began to feel sorry for Susan for having that sort of father.

Susan said in a nettled sort of way, 'Val's pony can't have cost a penny more than twelve hundred pounds,' and I said, 'Val is a jolly good jumper, she'd get the best out of any pony,' and walked off before Susan could annoy me any more.

It was now teatime and we had a wonderful party, sitting on the grass. There were loads of sandwiches and luscious iced cakes, and we topped it off with an ice cream or two and I don't know how many cups of tea. Our riding responsibilities were now over, and there was the open jumping to look forward to as well as Captain Cholly-Sawcutt's exhibition.

Meanwhile Mummy said she would like to see Cecilia's marquee so I took her over, and immediately we saw Cecilia in the middle of an admiring circle, being photographed by the local press. Her mother and father were there, and quite a lot of people who seemed to be her nearest and dearest.

She was standing by the stall and holding up a large piece of pink embroidery with a red card pinned to it saying First Prize.

'Isn't it nice?' said my Aunt Primrose, spotting us. 'Cecilia has won the first prize for handicrafts, isn't it marvellous?'

Honestly, the fuss that was made you would think Cecilia had won the open jumping at Wembley. Meanwhile the judges were making up their minds about the floral dinner tables, and while everybody in Cecilia's circle was still nattering on about her sordid embroidery, I was the one who came up and told her that her yellow flower arrangement had been placed second. So she had to go over and be photographed in front of that, holding up the blue card, and I thought Aunt Primrose was going to burst into flames with maternal pride. She kept saying she always knew Cecilia had it in her to do Great Things.

(When it came to giving the prizes later on it was an absolute scream, because being a charity affair they turned out to be articles not money prizes, and Mrs Whirtley had chosen nothing but horsy things for horsy people, so Cecilia got a riding stick for her embroidery and a hoof-pick for her dinner table, but Aunt Primrose said it didn't matter, they would come in for Christmas presents for somebody.)

By the time we got back to the ring there were thousands round it waiting to see Captain Cholly-Sawcutt's exhibition. In the middle of the ring was the local Silver Band, playing away like mad. We didn't get a very good view, but we could just see him when he rode in on Petronelle and the crowd went mad and gave him the most magnificent applause. The band melted way, panting a bit under their instruments, and there was the beautiful mare and the supreme rider alone in the vast green ring in the dazzling sunlight.

The Captain rode right round once so that everybody could see him. Then he dismounted and led Petronelle round the jumps. The ones we had used in the under-sixteen's had been taken away and the difficult ones erected in their places, and all we younger ones were dreaming of the day when we too should unflinchingly face jumps like these in open competitions.

Then the Captain came in for his exhibition round,

which was of course effortless and full of grace, and you never saw such beautiful timing. He went round the seven jumps twice, and at the fourteenth jump which was the triple bar he got a refusal and then brought the top bar down and got four more faults.

You should have heard the crowd yell. The Captain rode off laughing and making despairing faces.

Ann said she felt comforted to think that even the Great Could Fail, and Mummy said perhaps he had done it on purpose, and I said, 'Not likely. It's just one of those things.'

Near us Mrs Cholly-Sawcutt was standing with the three girls, and we heard May say, 'Hurrah, Daddy's made a mucker of it.'

April said, 'We'll never let him hear the last of this,' and June said, 'He hasn't got anything on us now, he's as bad as we are.'

Meanwhile, all the competitors had come in to inspect the jumps, and it was fun recognising the people we knew and admiring all the famous riders. You must have seen hundreds of open jumping competitions, so I need not describe this one. It was marvellous to watch, and there was always the excitement of not knowing quite what was going to happen when people who were expected to do well did badly, and people you didn't think were so good cleared four-foot-six jumps with inches to spare.

Six people got clear rounds, and among them were Mrs Darcy on Blue Smoke and James Bush on a new jumper of his father's, a long-backed grey hunter who had a wonderful sense of takeoff.

When it came to the jump-off we could hardly

watch for excitement. Two well-known riders went out, and Mrs Darcy and James both got clear rounds again and were in the last four. Finally Mrs Darcy was second and James got the Reserve. Diana rushed off to the paddock to congratulate her brilliant brother, and we went too because we couldn't keep away from the horses. Captain Cholly-Sawcutt was talking to Mrs Darcy and admiring Blue Smoke, and we didn't want to intrude so we were just oozing past when she caught sight of us and the Captain called out, 'Hello, Jill. You made a very good job of showing that hack. I never saw neater work.'

I could feel myself going all the colours of the rainbow, and I mumbled something about Sandy Two being so good that a child could have shown him.

Mrs Darcy said, 'Yes, I don't know anybody in the junior classes who has a better knack of showing than Jill.'

She so rarely praised anybody that I nearly fell flat on my back, and Wendy Mead who had just come up to lead Blue Smoke away and rub her down gave me a grin and a wink.

'When do you leave school?' said the Captain to me.

I looked a bit blank, as anybody would, at having that sort of question fired at one in such a horsy moment, and then I managed to mutter something about 'it might be two years because of course I had to get my GCSEs but I would be doing them next summer.' I couldn't imagine why he wanted to know.

He just said calmly, 'Well, if you're wanting a job after that I could use a person like you.'

I stood with all the breath knocked out of me,

trying to take this in. He gave a little wave of his hand, and said, 'Don't forget!' and walked off to join some friends who were waiting for him.

'Well!' said Mrs Darcy. 'That's a stunner for you, Jill. You're a very lucky girl.'

'D – did he mean it?' I stuttered, sagging at the knees.

'Of course he meant it. He's offering you a job when you leave school, and if you really want to make horsemanship your career it's the sort of chance you'll never get again. I'd have given my eyes for such a chance when I was your age, but nobody gave me one.'

'But how on earth would I ever get round Mummy?' I said.

She laughed and said, 'That's your worry, not mine. I've never known you to be very backward in devising ways of getting round anybody.' She looked round, and cried, 'Help! Everybody's getting ready for the winners' parade. Hurry up!'

I dashed off to get my ponies, feeling as if fireworks were going off all round me.

We all lined up and Mrs Whirtley came out to give the prizes. I got a pair of string gloves for showing Black Boy and a set of grooming tools for showing Sandy Two. They were just what I wanted, and I decided to hang them up in my tack room to give tone to the place, and go on using my old and rather scruffy ones. Mummy and Mrs Lowe came up to admire my prizes, and Mrs Lowe had saved some fruit cake as a special prize for Rapide and Black Boy, now that their day's work was over. I knew they didn't like fruit cake much, but they were too polite

to spit it out so they swallowed it down and made
faces at Mrs Lowe, and she said, 'Look, aren't they
enjoying it?' and I thought, That's what you think.

Then who should appear but my cousin Cecilia,
clutching her prizes, the riding stick and the hoof-
pick, and she said that having won these very
attractive things she was wondering whether to
turn her attention to serious horsemanship, and
what did I advise her to do? I said that if she
was serious the best thing she could do would
be to go to a good riding school and start from
the beginning, and she said she thought it sounded
awful, and I said, 'Well, it's that or nothing.' Per-
sonally I thought she would do better to stick to
her own line of embroidery and decorating dinner tables, as she was so good at it. She seemed
quite humbled and very kindly petted my ponies
and said she thought they were marvellous, and
I said I thought she had been pretty marvellous
too in her handicrafts tent, and we became terribly
friendly.

Then Mrs Whirtley got up on the platform, and
the band sounded a sort of fanfare and hundreds of
people gathered around.

Mrs Whirtley said that the day had been the wildest
success, a far greater success than anybody had ever
dreamed it could be. Everybody clapped and cheered.
Mrs Whirtley said that her committee had worked
terribly hard and been marvellous and everybody
clapped and cheered again, except the committee,
who blushed and looked smug in their white satin
rosettes – that is, those who hadn't lost them. I had
lost mine ages ago.

Mrs Whirtley said that of course they hadn't had time to count the money yet, but they were sure that it was going to be over three thousand pounds and it would all go to charities for the protection of horses. Everybody cheered like mad, and several people round me said, 'Gosh, three thousand pounds!'

Mrs Whirtley said that was the end of the proceedings, and now everybody could go home happy and contented, and just as she finished saying this there was a sort of disturbance on the edge of the crowd.

We all looked round to see what was happening. Everybody was looking the same way, and the crowd was beginning to give way and leave an open space. Mrs Whirtley and all the distinguished people on the platform looked a bit bothered. We couldn't imagine what was going to happen, but we soon knew.

The first thing I saw was a horse's head, and then my mouth came open and stayed that way. I nearly passed out. Into the open space walked three horses, and in the middle was a big percheron, and on its back was Dinah Dean, leading a pony on each side of her. She came calmly on amid the silent, staring crowd, who made way for her, wondering what on earth this was all in aid of. Dinah looked very determined. She came right on until she faced the platform. Then in a hush in which you could have heard a pin drop, she said in a very clear voice, 'If you really want to do something for the protection of horses, you can begin with these three!'

I have noticed in novels that when you come to a very dramatic bit, instead of putting Words Fail

Me, or some other phrase, the author just puts row of dots.

So here they are.

. . . .

18 Dinah wins

'And you mean to say you knew all about it and kept it dark?' said Ann. 'You old Bluebeard!'

We were sitting in our orchard under the cool boughs, eating a peaceful apple or two.

'I knew she was in the woods with the horses,' I said, 'but I didn't know what she was going to spring on everybody today. It takes Dinah to think up something like that. She paralyses me, but she certainly does have ideas.'

Ann said, 'You could have knocked everybody for six when she rode up like that and started addressing the crowd. And gosh, what a speech she made! It was like a film.'

'And there we were in Mrs Whirtley's drawing-room when it was all over,' I went on, 'and Mrs Whirtley with her loving arms round Dinah, and Dinah putting away an enormous tea and being the heroine of the occasion, and answering the reporters' questions as cool as an ice cream soda! She's a wow.'

'And to think that that Towtle beast nearly bought Seraphine!' said Ann, looking pale blue. 'It was only your presence of mind that saved her, Jill. You must have been psycho-what's-it.'

I said that I didn't know about being psycho, it

was Mr Towtle's hair that put me off, and Ann said that Seraphine was now awfully happy with William Arden, and that Pam had got friendly with William and went over to the Ardens' to see Seraphine sometimes, and that Mrs Derry was relenting and talking about buying Pam another pony if one could be found that was quiet and aged enough.

I said, 'Good show,' but my mind still kept turning over and over the remarkable events of the afternoon and the dramatic ending to Mrs Whirtley's fête, staged and carried out by the fearless Dinah. I was sure it would be talked about in Chatton for years. In spite of my trying to keep my part in it dark, Dinah had insisted on grabbing my arm and saying to everybody, 'I couldn't have done anything if Jill hadn't been my friend, the only one I had,' and Mummy had laughed and said, 'If you'd told me where the loaves were going to I'd have found some jam to go with them,' and Mrs Darcy said, 'We all know that Jill can get away with anything,' and thumped me on the back. (At that moment a press photographer came up to take a photograph of Blue Smoke, who had won second place in the open jumping, and next morning there we all were in the local paper, Blue Smoke and Mrs Darcy looking marvellous, and me with my tie under my ear being thumped on the back as if I'd swallowed a fly.)

Things moved rapidly during the next few days. Captain Cholly-Sawcutt said that the Beastly Towtle would be forced to clear out of the neighbourhood after all that publicity, and never show his face again, and that the R.S.P.C.A. would keep an eye on him and his practices in future.

Mrs Whirtley kept Dinah and the three horses at Blossom Hall, and got so fond of the four of them that she couldn't bear the idea of being parted from them. In the end, to make everything law-abiding and above-board, she paid the Towtle creature strictly what the three horses were worth and gave them a permanent home with her, and what was more she said the riding pony was to be Dinah's very own, and Dinah was to have riding lessons and the pony would be looked after for her. Everybody went on making a fuss of Dinah and talking about Dinah until Dinah began to wish that she was an oyster with a shell, and that they would shut up and stop Doing Her Good, because it was altogether too much for a person who had never been accustomed to Being Done Good To.

Dinah's mysterious father then appeared on the scene. He looked very pale and worried and was quite a nice person really, though a bit absent-minded and thoughtless. He had been so wrapped up in his work that he just hadn't bothered about Dinah and didn't realise that she was being neglected. He was so glad to get her back that he nearly wept, and he came round to our house and asked Mummy what he could do to make things nicer for Dinah in future.

Mummy and Mrs Whirtley went into a huddle about what Mr Dean could do for Dinah. It turned out that he wasn't really very poor at all, but just never thought about money.

The end of it was that Mr Dean got a housekeeper, and Dinah was to go to boarding school – which thrilled her very much – and Mummy and Mrs Whirtley made a list of all the clothes she would need, and went shopping and bought them, and Mr Dean paid for them without turning a hair.

Dinah came round to see me. She had on nice clothes and had got her hair cut and looked quite human, in fact very decent. She had been to the library and got out a lot of books called *The Girls of St Agatha's*, *The Fourth Form at St Faith's*, *The Secret of the School*, and similar ghastly titles.

She said, 'I simply love these, and now I'll know what to do when I get to school, and in the holidays I shall have my pony and my lessons, and would you mind frightfully if I do a frieze of ponies round my room, like yours? If you think I'm a copy-cat, say so.'

I said I didn't mind a bit, but if I were Dinah I wouldn't be too sure that boarding school was going to be exactly like it sounded in library books, and Dinah said she was sure it would be, so I left it at that. I could see Dinah turning out to be The Blot of St Bertha's if she wasn't careful.

So all that died down, and I would be back at school again myself next week. And there was the winter to come, the lovely autumn rides through the crisp lanes, and November mornings on which to follow the Hunt.

I said to Mummy, 'It's been the best summer holiday ever.'

'Yes, darling,' said Mummy absently. She was having a tussle with *Basil the Bird-Song Boy*, who had stuck in the fifth chapter. She then became conscious and added, 'I hope you're going to work hard next term.'

I said, 'I certainly am – ' and was going to add all

about wanting to leave school next July, but when it came to the point I daren't and thought I had better wait for a more suitable occasion when Basil had got himself going again and Mummy was in a really mellow mood.

I wandered out to the orchard and saddled up Rapide and went for a ride. I couldn't think of anything but a future of horsemanship, beginning with grooming the Cholly-Sawcutt horses in chilly dawns and finishing up in the show ring at Wembley. It seemed like a beautiful golden dream, but it could come true.

I cantered along the grass verges of summery lanes, and when we came to Neshbury Common I let Rapide gallop to his heart's content and felt the cool wind blowing through my hair. I felt so happy that I let out a few hunting cries, and the rabbits, thinking I was mad, scuttered away in all directions.

ANIMAL ARK SERIES
LUCY DANIELS

JACKIE PONY SERIES
JUDITH M. BERRISFORD

JILL PONY SERIES
RUBY FERGUSON

All Hodder Children's books are available at your local bookshop or newsagent, or can be ordered direct from the publisher. Just tick the titles you want and fill in the form below. Prices and availability subject to change without notice.

Hodder Children's Books, Cash Sales Department, Bookpoint, 39 Milton Park, Abingdon, OXON, OX14 4TD, UK. If you have a credit card you may order by telephone – 0235 831700.

Please enclose a cheque or postal order made payable to Bookpoint Ltd to the value of the cover price and allow the following for postage and packing:
UK & BFPO: £1.00 for the first book, 50p for the second book and 30p for each additional book ordered up to a maximum charge of £3.00.
OVERSEAS & EIRE: £2.00 for the first book, £1.00 for the second book and 50p for each additional book ordered.

Name ....

Address ....

....

....

If you would prefer to pay by credit card, please complete:
Please debit my Visa/Access/Diner's Card/American Express (delete as applicable) card No:

Signature ....

Expiry Date...